FAKER

Recent Titles by Katy Gardner

FAKER

Katy Gardner

This first world edition published 2009
in Great Britain and in the USA by
SEVERN HOUSE PUBLISHERS LTD of
9–15 High Street, Sutton, Surrey, England, SM1 1DF.

British Library Cataloguing in Publication Data

Gardner, Katy, 1964-
    Faker
    1. British - Bangladesh - Fiction 2. Man-woman
    relationships - Fiction 3. Missing persons - Bangladesh -
    Fiction 4. Bangladesh - Fiction 5. Suspense fiction
    I. Title
    823.9'2 [F]

ISBN-13: 978-0-7278-6718-6   (cased)

Except wher[ ]al historical event[ ] are be[ ]
described fo[ ] [ ]orpline of [ ]ovel, all character[ ] in th[ ]
publication a[ ]ictitious and any re[ ] to living pers[ ]s
is purely coi[ ]idental.

All Severn House titles are printed on acid-free paper.

Typeset by Palimpsest Book Production Ltd.,
Grangemouth, Stirlingshire, Scotland.
Printed and bound in Great Britain by
MPG Books Ltd., Bodmin, Cornwall.

Many thanks to Clare Conville, Kate Sebag, Anne-Marie Goetz, Nina Beachcroft and Graham Alborough for their invaluable comments on early drafts of this novel.

This is the voice of your conscience: a blast from the past that you prefer to forget. I gather you've moved on since our last encounter? You've remodelled yourself, turned into a good person, all bright-eyed and squeaky clean. It must have been quite a trip, no?

But before you disappear completely up your own saintly arse, remember this:

I know who you really are.

ONE

Sarah
Bangladesh, May 6th 2003

I t keeps coming back to me, like waves crashing down: the day I lost Ed. There are colours and there is noise. The sea's a weird translucent green; the sky, mauve at first, then blackening, like rot. Light has been sucked from the day, yet I am bathed in red, the colour of terror. I can hear water smashing onto the shore and the creak and splintering of the betel nut trees. The wind blasts into me, twisting my petticoat at my ankles; my hair whips my face. I am screaming Ed's name, yelling at him to come back, but my words are lost to the roar. Behind me, a sheet of corrugated iron slices from the skies.

What I see is this: Ed is on the beach, jogging towards the sea. I have come running down the path, in search of him, and the sight of his departing figure fills me with dread. His back is getting smaller, his shirt billowing around his shoulders like he might take off. Emerald water; black sky, like a hole; white cotton shirt that I'd mended the day before: Ed disappearing into the maelstrom. What was he doing? He should have been running towards the shelter, like everyone else, but he was moving in the opposite direction. I tried to follow him, was screaming myself hoarse that the sea was lethal, but it was too late.

We could have escaped the storm: only last night Dan Jameson had offered to drive us to Chittagong. Whatever the difficulties we'd encountered in the village, we'd be safe there, he said, flattening the remains of his rice with his fork; we could stay at his place. I glanced at Ed's face, expecting to see an expression of relief or gratitude, but to my surprise he was frowning and shaking his head. We'd make our own arrangements, he replied, almost curtly; it was true we'd been having a rough time, but we couldn't simply cut and run. I nodded cautiously, not sure what to think.

By the next morning I'd forgotten about Dan's offer. As usual, it had been too hot to sleep; we'd had weeks of suffocating humidity, and that night was worse than ever. I drowsed intermittently, waking at dawn to the crackling broadcast of the azan, then a little while later, Abdullah's broom, swishing at the bugs. For an hour, as the sun came up, the temperature was bearable. We ate pineapple and drank tea on the veranda. Despite his drawn face, Ed was more animated than he'd been for weeks, whistling jauntily as he prepared to leave. He was going to the bazaar, he said, packing his passport and wallet into his money belt. As we'd agreed, he'd call Biman Airlines and book our tickets to Dhaka. Gulping down his tea, he said he'd be back soon. Then he kissed me briskly on the cheek and was gone.

By then the sun had made its way over the coconut trees and sweat was trickling down my back. The day had established itself, chasing away the lingering traces of dawn. The dew that moistened the rubbery grass had evaporated, the moon fading from view. In the trees the magpie robins and mynahs were uproarious; across the fields the village hubbub drifted towards me like smoke from the morning fires: women scolding as they drained the rice, old men muttering holy words as they knelt to pray, the lads down at the tea stall, texting each other and revving their bikes. From the beach I could hear the screech of kids as they jumped in the waves. I had another headache coming. It fingered my temples, baiting me. Already it was too hot. I withdrew into the building, pretending that I was going to do something constructive but able only to slump by the window. The electricity had been off since the night before.

The truth was there was nothing to do. No real 'paperwork', just a wad of papers Ed had downloaded from the web and a pile of unused literacy textbooks. If I had the energy and things were normal I might have wandered into the village, the usual flock of children chirping behind. There'd be cups of tea, and stale biscuits, brought specially from the bazaar. I'd perch on the edge of wooden beds and rickety stools and the women would circle their hands around my wrists and say how thin I'd got, or insist on tying back my hair. How I'd loved those mornings, my broken Bangla turning me into someone new: village joker, adoring and adored. If there were visitors from outside they'd repeat the same predictable questions: was I able to eat rice? Was I married? How many children did I have? My friends would recite the answers, with a sorrowful shake of their heads. Rice only in the evenings; number of children: nil. But married to a good man, they'd conclude. Engleesh, Mr Edward, parents-in-law dead. Later I'd make them hoot with laughter, pulling the ends of my sari over my head and casting my eyes to the ground: my decidedly non-PC impersonation of a newly married bride.

But things were far from normal. So I lay brooding on the cramped wicker settee. It sounds ludicrous now, but I had no idea of the impending storm. Yesterday there had been a Red Cross man on a bicycle who'd yelled officiously through a loud hailer of a Grade One alert, but he had appeared once or twice the week before and all that had transpired was a grumble of thunder and a brief splatter of rain. They'd put out flags on the beach, too. I could see them from the bungalow, flopping limply in the breeze. We hadn't listened to the radio, and our computer had never worked. If we had checked the forecast, perhaps we'd have taken notice. Perhaps Ed would have stayed with me and we would have gone together to the shelter. Perhaps, rather than spending those precious hours dozing in the front room, I could have intercepted him on the path and wrested him from the sea.

Or perhaps not. Perhaps Ed knew exactly what he was doing.

I must have fallen asleep. The first thing I noticed when I opened my eyes was that the shutters were banging against the wall. The air had cooled, too, and the quality of the light changed, its usual brazen shine seeming somehow tarnished. In the background I could hear Abdullah pushing something heavy across the floor. For a while, as I gradually regained consciousness, I lay on my back, concentrating on the squeeze of pain in my forehead. I was grateful for the cooling breeze. I let it swirl around me, fanning my face. In a few months it would be the monsoon, and once more the world would turn to mud.

The wind was picking up; the papers that lay at my feet lifting off the ground in excitable flurries. Outside, I noticed, the birds had stopped singing. In the bedroom, a door slammed against the wall. Now Abdullah was hurrying into the room and fastening the windows.

'Mrs Sarah, a big storm coming . . .'

I gazed at him blearily. Since breakfast he had pulled a thin football shirt over his vest with Arsenal emblazoned on the back.

'Nice shirt!'

He glanced at me with incomprehension: this foolish foreign woman, lounging around when all hell was about to break loose.

'Typhoon!' he repeated. 'Very bad.'

Even then I didn't quite believe him. Frowning, I hauled myself on to my feet and paced towards the terrace. He had pinned the screen doors shut: through the netting I could see mountainous tropical clouds stacking up. On the beach the coconut trees were tossing feverishly, their elegant stems bending impossibly in the wind. The shore was unusually empty, the children and fishermen who had been there earlier disappeared, the boats and netting that were normally scattered under the trees cleared away. The sky was growing increasingly dark.

'I'm going outside,' I said. Abdullah shrugged, turning up his hands in the gesture that I had learnt meant anything from 'So what?' to 'It's the will of God'. Unfastening the doors, I stepped on to the veranda.

The wind crashed into me, sucking away my breath. The grass beyond the steps was already strewn with broken branches and a rickshaw that someone had left on the dirt track had tipped over, its wheels spinning helplessly. Besides me, Abdullah was muttering in Arabic, the language of Allah.

'*Bacha*,' he suddenly said, jerking his head in the direction of the village. 'Need to get *bacha*.'

My mind had turned to mush. For a second I stared at him, then I understood. On the other side of the road, marooned in an acre of paddy, was his small bamboo house. I had been there once; his wife had made me pitta cakes from rice flour that she rolled between her competent hands then roasted over the chula. There were too many small children for me to remember their names.

'God, yes, your children . . . You must go.'

He wasn't listening and nor did he need my permission. Not giving me a second glance, he rolled his lunghi up over his bony knees and leapt down the steps. The sight of him scurrying across the lawn and past the by now hysterically pitching trees caused my first stirring of alarm. He was normally so calm. When the other storms had come, he'd just chuckled and said, 'Bangladesh weather too much raining!' But just now his face had been grey.

Where was Ed? If there really was a cyclone approaching, surely he would have heard about it in the village and come back to find me? Shaking off my languor I hurried down the steps, across the grass and down the path in the direction of Syeda's house, the headache forgotten.

Yesterday the fields had been filled with men, their lungis hitched between their legs as they laboriously planted paddy seedlings in the steaming heat, but now they were empty. There was no one on the path: no rickshaws bumping over the potholes, no black-burquaed women, veils drawn across their faces, and no unruly kids bounding out to greet me. The only people I saw were a man with a toddler in his arms who was running in the direction of the shelter, and on the distant road, a jeep, bumping over the potholes.

All sunlight had been vacuumed from the sky. As I gazed across the paddy my attention was drawn to the large compound on the other side of the road where the chairman lived, with its fancy boundary walls and betel nut trees. In the time that it took for me to yelp with shock, the tin roof of his house popped from its moorings like a champagne cork. For a few seconds it floated soundlessly above the road. Then, slicing through space, it crashed to the ground.

I had to find Ed. Turning into Syeda's homestead, I started calling for her, peering desperately around the empty communal yard. I was hoping she would have spotted him, but it was too late: the wooden doors of the wattle buildings were bolted. All that remained were two cows tied to a post in the cattle shed, hay eddying around them. The tin roof was making an unhappy groaning sound. For a moment I took in the panic in the creatures' brown eyes. Then I turned away.

I ran out of the yard and into the fields, the clouds above me mushrooming. By now objects were flying through the air: palm fronds, coconut husks, a stretch of pink sari.

The garment shimmered briefly above me, then took off in
the direction of the road. I was convinced that Ed was no
longer in the village; that he might have gone to the shelter
without first coming to find me was inconceivable. Perhaps
he'd returned to the bungalow on the other path? Placing my
arms over my head to protect it from the debris, I started to
plough towards the bungalow, eyes smarting. The roar was
overwhelming.

In the five minutes since I'd been gone, the garden was
wrecked. Pots lay upturned in the dirt and the crimson
bougainvillea was dismembered, its ravaged branches flung
across the grass. On the terrace, the table where we had had
our breakfast was upturned, the screen door ripped off its
hinges.

'Ed!'

I bounded up the steps and into the building, surveying the
wreckage. The feeble windows hadn't stood a chance: shattered glass speckled the cushions where I'd been lying; books
and papers were strewn around the room. The walls shud-
dered at the wind, flimsier than we'd ever imagined.

'Are you here?'

He couldn't possibly be. And nor could I stay inside the
building, for the place was about to implode. Loping back
onto the veranda and down the steps I stood for a moment by
the broken bougainvillea, trying to control my rising panic.
This wasn't your run-of-the-mill, put-up-your-brolly spring
storm, it was just as the man on the bicycle had warned the
day before: a no-holds-barred cyclone, about to pummel us
to bits. I *had* to get to the shelter, it was the only safe place.
And yet, as I stood, panting, on the path, all I could think of
was Ed.

Perhaps he was on the beach. Turning left, I stumbled
towards the sea. In the wind, my sari was unravelling, the thin
cotton twisting between my legs and tripping me over. Losing
patience, I yanked it off, standing in my petticoat and blouse.
Kicking my flip-flops away, I started to run towards the shore,
desperately surveying the long stretch of white sand. The sea
was terrifying: an eerie emerald, with huge, rolling waves. On
the horizon a black funnel of cloud twirled ominously.

And there, as I had suspected, was Ed. He was about a
hundred metres away, running towards the area where the

fishing boats were normally beached. Next to them a cluster of stalls sold tea in clay cups to the fishermen and trinkets to the few intrepid tourists who made it this far. Very little remained. The stalls had been pulverized into broken planks that were strewn across the beach and the boats tipped onto their sides. In one case a large dhow had been deposited upside down in the mangrove trees that fringed the beach. By now it had started to hail, monstrous rocks of ice that ricocheted off the sand, turning the sea blurry and pelting my face.

'Ed! Come back!'

He couldn't hear. He was almost out of view, disappearing into the haze. As the twister approached, the sea had turned vicious, the waves towering up in great crests of surf that crashed on to the sand.

'Ed!'

I nearly followed him. If I had arrived a minute or so earlier there would have been time. I would have raced along the sand and perhaps he would have heard my voice. If I hadn't gone inside the bungalow, or wasted so much time in Syeda's yard, I might have stopped him. But I was too late. As the hail clogged my hair and I watched him disappear I was reduced to an animal shriek, no longer calling out anything comprehensible, reduced to the sum of my terror.

'*Abfa,* come.'

I spun around. A fisherman was standing beside me, his calloused hand at my elbow.

'I can't . . . I have to get Ed . . .' I gestured hopelessly at the beach.

He shook his head angrily. I knew him, I realized; he had shown me the catch just a day ago, squatting proficiently in the sand as he sorted the fish into piles. When I had tried to buy a large eelish fish, he had laughed good-naturedly at my half-formed Bengali.

'Come.'

He wasn't asking, but telling. Gripping my arm, he started to pull me away but my legs had gone weak.

'I can't . . .'

He was smaller than me but much stronger. Propelling my slack body up the path, he dragged me through the trees and into the fields. By now the hail had turned to rain; it sloshed against us in great wet sweeps, running down his muscled torso in torrents and soaking through my petticoat. We staggered on, leaning into the wind with our arms over our faces. I was numb, giving in to the fisherman's guiding hands. He moved swiftly along the path, dodging the collapsing trees and flying debris with accomplishment as I slipped through the churned-up dirt. On the road ahead I could see the shelter, a hefty concrete block, resting on its concrete stilts. Dragging ourselves up the ramp, we battered the doors with our fists.

I don't remember the rest that well. I followed the fisherman inside the shelter, squeezing through the crowd to where Amina's Ma, one of Syeda's many cousins, was huddled in the corner. Gesturing at me to sit beside her, she placed her strong arm around my shoulder, the first sign of friendship I had been shown for weeks. The differences that had recently divided the village and turned Ed and me into outcasts were temporarily suspended; the village united by the storm. The place smelt of damp and the *beedis* the men were smoking. Normally the building was used for panchayat meetings or what were earnestly described in donors' reports as 'participatory community development': gatherings in which NGO workers requested that villagers draw diagrams of their livelihood strategies on flip charts. Some were still pinned to the walls, along with government posters imploring the population not to smoke or to have their kids immunized.

There must have been about four or five hundred of us crammed inside the main hall, but it was deathly quiet. An hour earlier people were shouting at each other above the wind. Shutters were being fastened, cattle rounded up. But now homes and animals were abandoned. All I could hear was a baby crying and a low murmur of Arabic, prayer beads fingered in incantation. No one was laughing or talking or shouting. As the fury approached, the village cowered.

Bits come back in fragments. Like Amina's Ma, clutching at my hand. I could smell the paan she was chewing and the juice of the onions she'd been chopping for breakfast on her hands. The old man squatting beside her had brought his chickens; they hung upside down from his wrist, gently flapping. For a long time I had my face buried in my hands. There were constant crashes as trees and bits of houses flew against the walls. The hellishly shrieking wind went on, and on, and on, until it seemed to have become a part of me: my headache externalized. Next to me, a little boy was whimpering. I watched as his mother collected the tears with her fingers, whispering something that made him quiet. When he noticed me peeking he started to wail.

I keep picturing that coconut tree, hurtling through the air. Also, the Chairman's tin roof, spinning like a Frisbee across the fields. That must have been when I was still outside, still believing that I might find Ed and pull him back. The hail bounced off the sand, pelting into my forehead. Later the downpour would turn the sandy paths to rivers and wash the newly planted paddy away. It was relentless, the howling wind and battering rain. For about an hour it was so dark that we could hardly see. The building rocked to and fro and I thought we would die.

Yet it stood firm. After three or four hours the shriek of the wind became slightly less piercing. A little while later, a shaft of silver light appeared through the shutters. People started to rouse themselves, standing and stretching and clicking their fingers. Some were praying, some whispering Allah's name.

Outside, the world as we knew it was destroyed.

A day and then a week pass. Six or seven hours of the storm have collapsed into these fleeting scenes: the horrific yowl of the wind and the pop of that tin roof bursting from the Chairman's house; my raw hands, held by Amina's Ma, the huddle of people hiding in the shelter and in the middle of them, those upside down chickens, passive in defeat.

But the image I can't delete is of Ed's back as he raced across the beach. He had got so thin, that's one of the things that sticks in my mind; perhaps that's why his shirt had escaped from his trouser belt and was ballooning up. I never saw his face. He hadn't come to find me, as I'd assumed, but instead was running over the sand, past the crazy coconut trees, their tousled tops whipping to and fro like head bangers on speed, and towards the wrecked fishing boats. Dried seaweed and netting and bits of branch were rolling across the shore, the sand sucked up into whirling dervishes that danced in his path.

Ed ran through them, past the boats, and into the maelstrom. He did not look back.

TWO

We spilled out of the shelter, disorientated and blinking at the light. The landscape was unrecognizable, like a loved one who's been savagely attacked. All the familiar sights were gone: the graceful betel nut trees torn from the ground like weeds, the village houses demolished. I started to walk along the road that led towards the small bazaar. Rickshaws and mopeds were scattered around like discarded toys, the ruined fields filled with wreckage. People trailed beside me, none of them speaking; some simply sat by the ditch, weeping. That morning they had woken in their beds to their yards and fruit trees and cattle and crops, but now nothing remained. I could not see Syeda or Abdullah or anyone I knew.

I walked along the path that led to the beach. A family had set up home here a month or so earlier, building themselves a small hut with an ingenious mixture of bamboo, banana leaves and plastic sheets. The moneylender had snatched their land they told me; they had nothing left. Now a large doll was perched in the banyan tree next to where the hut once stood. For a few dumb seconds I stared up, not understanding: an oddly naked doll, with tangled hair and kohl around its eyes, hanging from the top branches like the fairy on a Christmas tree. With a sickening lurch I remembered the small girl who only a few days earlier had squealed with delight as I tickled her under the arms. I turned quickly away. I felt as if my insides had been sucked from my body.

Passing the remains of Syeda's house, I stumbled along the path that led to the bungalow. After seeing the child in the tree I had thought I would puke. Now I didn't feel anything. Above me, white clouds raced mockingly across the sky. The ruined fields were swamped with water, the puddles that pooled the paths glinting in the sun.

Our bungalow had stood on the other side of a cluster of betel and coconut trees. Disorientated, I scrambled over their broken trunks. All that remained of the building were the foundations and a couple of walls: a gaping mouth with its teeth punched out. Papers, rags and bits of broken wood covered the soaking floors. Glass lay everywhere. Surreally, the toilet squatted victoriously amongst the wreckage, a throne for the king of disorder. The metal sink and the shower unit had been flung a hundred metres into the trees. I gazed around, taking in the wreckage: the smashed plates and disembowelled pillows, the ripped curtains and shredded books. In a strange way I no longer cared. Ignoring the carnage, I moved towards the beach.

When I reached the shore, I paused for a while, looking around. The sand was smoothed out, blemished only by flotsam. Having done its worst, the sea had turned from green to grey. Bits of the village bobbed playfully on the waves: someone's roof, a fragment of bamboo fence, a rickshaw seat, fluorescent pink. There were bodies, too, splayed and naked like an obscene joke. What the hell had happened to their clothes? I counted five corpses then looked away. A few metres from where I was standing a waterlogged cow lay in a pool of water, hooves pointing heavenwards.

I don't know how long I stood there, staring out to sea. Ed was my future, my reason for living. Yet he had neither returned to the bungalow to find me nor sought refuge in the shelter. Instead, as I screamed his name, he had plunged towards the wild waves. What had happened in those terrible moments after the fisherman dragged me away?

Someone was calling my name.

'Sarah!'

The voice was growing louder, but it was taking me a while to respond.

'Hey, Sarah!'

I glanced round. Approaching through what was once the coconut grove was a man. Tall, European, with a flop of blond hair; I recognized him, but couldn't recall his name.

'Thank God you're OK!'

Now he was standing before me, his large hands on my shoulders.

'You're bleeding,' he said. 'Let me wipe your face.'

Pulling a hanky from his pocket, he started to dab at my chin. It had been stinging for a while I realized, the blood spattered down my pale-blue blouse. Frowning, I stepped away. I sensed that I should be responding to his administrations, but had no idea what to say.

'The road was blocked,' he went on excitedly. 'We got a few miles past Noton Bazaar and there was a bloody great tree over the road. It was complete chaos. The driver said to wait until it had passed, so we went to this school and hung out with all these kids. I was just praying that the roof wasn't going to blow off . . . It looks as if you got it worse. I can't believe the state the place is in . . .'

He stopped, glancing around voyeuristically.

'Where's Eddy?' he said, looking around as if Ed might suddenly jump out of the banana plants shouting, 'Surprise!' His name was Dan Jameson, I remembered. He worked for the Department for International Development and yesterday had paid us a surprise visit.

'I don't know.'

'But he's alright?'

I shook my head, unable to speak.

Up until now his expression had been animated by the thrill of a tropical drama. Now his face dropped, the handsome Teutonic forehead disturbed by a tremor of uncertainty.

'What do you mean?'

'I saw him running towards the sea,' I said flatly. 'I don't know what he was doing. It was just before the tornado hit.'

'But why would he run towards the sea?'

'I don't bloody know . . .'

Surrendering to the surge of tears, I put my hands over my face, tasting blood. I could hear Dan mutter, 'Christ.'

'I called at him to come back . . .'

'Look at you,' Dan was saying. Stepping towards me he put his muscled arms around my shoulders. 'Let's sit you down and get you warm.'

For a moment or so I stood passively in his sweaty embrace. It felt all wrong: his body was too bulky and padded, his hands, which gripped me awkwardly around the waist, too heavy. Pulling away, I allowed him to place his jacket tenderly over my shoulders.

'He'll be OK,' he said soothingly. 'Maybe he got to the road and is in Noton Bazaar or somewhere . . .'

We perched uncomfortably on a fallen tree.

'He'd never have gone into the sea,' Dan was muttering.

'He wouldn't be so stupid.' In the minutes since I'd told him about Ed his face had sagged, his eyes protruding from their sockets and normally bonny cheeks pale and sunken. Groping around the knapsack, he pulled out his mobile.

'We've got to get help . . .'

He started to jab at the phone. 'No bloody signal!'

Cursing, he flung the thing down. Further down the beach a group of men were wading into the water and pulling the corpses out. Dan was right about the trembling: I was shivering uncontrollably.

'They'll send the army or something,' he mumbled. He was doing his best to help, I know, but despite his man-of-the-world bluster he was an innocent: a public-school boy, raised to expect that everything would turn out his way.

'Sarah? Are you listening?'

I stared at him. He had been saying something more, but I was distracted by the line of corpses that was forming on the shore. There were at least six bodies, maybe more.

'We can't stay here . . .'

Ignoring him, I rose unsteadily to my feet. 'I'm going to look for Ed.'

I was focussing on two men who were hauling a body from the surf, the waves splashing around their legs in a preposterous parody of the daily catch.

'No, you mustn't,' Dan said gently. 'Let me.'

For a moment, his hand rested on my elbow. I peered uncertainly into his face. Like Ed, he had the classic good looks of the English upper classes: grey-blue eyes, the clear-cut features and height that resulted from centuries of good breeding. Unlike my rows of fillings, his teeth were white and even. His posture was erect, military even. But Dan wasn't Ed. His hair was blonder and he was thicker set. Unlike Ed's expressive face, which was once lit with impish good humour but recently had become gloomy and drawn, Dan's was blandly benign. He was like a more conventionally handsome version of Ed, a distant cousin perhaps, who was less bright and less troubled. Looking abruptly away from his face, I sank on to the sand. He was right. How could I make my way across the beach and inspect the line of sodden corpses as if browsing in a fish market?

Rising, Dan paced purposefully towards the men. When he

reached the corpses he stopped, pausing solemnly in front of each one. I watched the scene in terror, my heart knocking. Something about his stance – the air of detachment conveyed by the crossing of his arms, perhaps, or the way his chin was tipped slightly backwards – told me Ed wasn't there. After what felt like an eternity, he strolled on, rummaging in the rubbish before eventually moving behind the carcasses of the fishing boats.

When he finally reappeared, he was holding something in his hands, cradling his dripping find as lovingly as if it were a baby. Jumping up, I stumbled towards him.

'What is it?'

He held the sopping object out. It was a man's sandal, I saw with horror. Not one of the flip-flops or moulded plastic shoes that the local people wore, but a high tech affair in orange and black. A clump of seaweed was attached.

'Oh shit . . .'

My knees sagged, pulling me down. Ed's Nike sandals, sent from London by his sister. There could not possibly have been another pair of shoes like these in the village.

'It was washed up with that crap over there.'

If I were Syeda, or one of my other friends in Lalalpur, I would have prostrated myself on the ground, howling and pounding the sand with my fists. But I was English, so I remained standing, my arms clenched around my waist as if to stop my emotions from spilling out.

'I don't think we should make assumptions,' Dan was saying. 'Just because we've found his shoe doesn't necessarily mean he's drowned . . .'

I peered into his anguished face, searching for a sign that he really believed this to be true.

'Doesn't it?'

'It could have fallen off when he was running . . .'

I stared at the rubbery seaweed, wound so decoratively around the straps. 'Do you think so?'

He nodded uncertainly. 'Why don't I go and see if I can find anything more?'

Placing the shoe gently on the sand beside me he strode towards the flotsam that the retreating sea had abandoned. Leaving the sandal on the beach, I limped back to the bungalow.

*   *   *

All that remained of Ed was the waterlogged shoe. Dan brought it to me, laying it apologetically on the rubbery grass. If he spoke, I wasn't listening. Eventually he abandoned his attempts at communication; giving me a sorrowful, backwards glance, he stumbled over the fallen trees, making for the village. I sat on the upturned wicker sofa, trying to absorb what had happened. Everything was destroyed, but still, the sun melted into the distant fields. The village had been flattened by the force of the wind, but now, amongst the ruins, the cicadas were making their usual din.

When Dan reappeared, the sky had turned lilac, the air filled with the chanting of toads. Crouching in front of me, he peered anxiously into my face.

'You need to drink.'

He was offering me a bottle of water. 'We have to leave,' he was saying. 'As soon as it starts getting light.'

'I'm not going anywhere . . .'

'Please, Sarah. It's my responsibility to make sure you're safe and I can't leave you here. The place is a complete mess. There's no food, no electricity, all the tube wells are broken . . .'

'I have to look for Ed.'

He sighed, running his hand through his hair, which by now was standing up in dirty tufts. He had a cut on his hand, I noticed, and his face was smeared with mud.

'I know you want to stay and look for him, that's only natural,' he said quietly. 'But right now there's nothing more we can do. I've got my driver to ask around and no one in the village has seen him . . .' He paused, choosing his words carefully. 'He hasn't appeared on the beach, so he could be anywhere. If we stay we'll just be another drain on what little resources they have.'

'I can't just walk away . . .'

He shook his head regretfully, as if it were no longer up to him what we did. 'I managed to get through to the office,' he said heavily. 'They said to bring you back immediately. There might be cholera. I'm going to have to do what they say.'

'But what about Ed?'

I started to snivel.

'He would want you to be safe,' Dan said quietly. 'You can come back in a couple of days.'

'I have to stay here and look for him!'

'Sarah, please listen.' He sat on the sofa beside me, taking my hand. 'You're in shock. Whatever's happened to Ed, it isn't going to do any good staying here. Look, this is difficult to say, but in the worst-case scenario . . . I mean, if he's drowned, which he probably hasn't, but we have to consider it as a possibility . . . his body could be washed up anywhere along the coast. Or it might never be found. They're already burying the dead. It's thirty-six degrees . . . They're not going to hang around for identification . . .'

'He's not dead. I know he isn't.'

He took a breath, as if mustering his energy. 'I'm not saying he is. Just because we're getting you to safety doesn't mean you're giving up.'

I pulled my hand away, my fingers twisting Ed's ring. I was finding it hard to concentrate. 'I saw him on the beach . . .'

Dan nodded, still stroking my hand. When he arrived yesterday I'd noticed his jolt of surprise at my presence, a reaction he quickly concealed with his wide smile and easy, public-school manners. Last night Ed had called him a 'tosser'. He should have tried to help us weeks ago, he'd said; now all he was doing was wasting our time.

'Do *you* think Ed's dead?'

He frowned, examining his dirt encrusted fingernails. 'I really don't know, Sarah. I'm praying he isn't.'

'Do you think he was trying to rescue someone who was in the water? I keep thinking that would be the only reason why he'd have been running towards the sea . . .'

'It's a possibility.'

'He was like that, always trying to help people . . .' I stopped, my voice wobbling.

'He was certainly very well intentioned . . .'

'Maybe there were some children who'd got into trouble. He'd have done anything for those kids.'

I recalled the children I'd seen frolicking on the beach after breakfast. After the harvest Ed used to play cricket with them in the fields, fashioning a bat out of an old plank that had come loose on the veranda.

'It *has* to be something like that,' I murmured. 'Otherwise it doesn't make sense.'

Dan nodded. 'Or perhaps he didn't go into the sea at all,' he said slowly. 'Perhaps he's got confused after the trauma of the storm and is safe and well further down the coast. Anything may have happened. That's why there isn't much point in hanging around.'

He stopped, staring in the direction of the sea. Yesterday I had dismissed him as a civil-service flunky, a type commonly found in the expatriate enclave in Dhaka. They came on civil-service postings, working in immigration, or, if they were of a more liberal disposition, overseeing the aid budget. Most rarely ventured from the comfort zone of the city's diplomatic quarters, where they whiled away their time with drinks parties, film nights and exercising in the High Commission gym. Others enjoyed their jaunts 'up country', their swanky air-conditioned jeeps careering over the unsurfaced roads whilst the locals gawped. All assumed themselves inherently super-ior to the inhabitants of the countries where they were posted. They were here to impart important lessons: democracy, modernization, the need for borders to be controlled. Few stayed longer than a year or so.

'Is there anyone you could stay with in Dhaka, just for a few days while this place gets back on its feet?' he said, turning back to me.

'Not really. There were these friends of Ed's – Lydia and Mike Simmonds . . .'

'Do you have their number?'

'Ed would have had it . . . it's probably in his bag . . .'

I gestured vaguely at Ed's briefcase, which was lying by the shattered computer. Shuffling through the papers that were strewn over the grass, Dan picked the case up and started to rifle through it, eventually pulling out Ed's address book. It was surprisingly dry.

'Will it be in here?'

'It should be. He keeps everything there . . .'

He slipped the book in his back pocket. 'Will you be alright if I leave you here for a short while? I'm going to go into the village and see if I can get the phone working again. Stay here, won't you? I'm coming back.'

The light faded, dimming at the edges. I sat on the ruins of our home, my head resting in my hands. Ed wasn't drowned, I told myself, repeating the words over and over. He wasn't dead. It couldn't be true. If I stayed here long enough perhaps he would come and get me. I'd sit quietly and eventually I'd hear his footsteps, crunching over the sand. He was almost here, I was sure, pushing past the fallen trees and shuffling up the path. It wasn't the breeze rustling the palms, but his body, brushing past. I could feel his arm around me, his rough chin tickling my cheek. How could he be drowned, when he was here, with me?

Another hour must have passed, for by now it was completely dark. Mosquitoes droned around my face. I didn't bother to slap them away.

THREE

It was dawn. The birds were singing, the sun starting its fierce ascent. But whilst yesterday Ed and I had sat on the terrace eating pineapple and drinking tea, this morning I was alone. I hunched amongst the rubble, still breathing, but barely alive.

'Abfa!'

I peered around to see Syeda emerging from the bushes, her sari draped over her head as she stepped neatly through the undergrowth. She was carrying a bowl of rice with a cloth spread over it, which she placed on the ground.

'Eat,' she said, jerking her head at the bowl.

Rising, I put out my arms and pulled her thin body into my arms. She felt so fragile, like a bird. For a while we stood together, weeping. Eventually she pulled away, dabbing her eyes with the edge of her sari.

'Are your kids OK?'

'Allah be Praised, they're safe.'

'Did you go to the shelter? I didn't see you there.'

'Everyone went.'

'I can't find Ed . . .' I wanted to explain how I'd tried to stop him from running into the sea, but my Bengali wasn't good enough. 'This is his shoe,' I said instead, pointing at the sandal.

She nodded, her lean face mournful. 'May Allah protect his soul.'

It was what people said when someone died. I swallowed, not able to respond.

'You should go to your family,' she eventually said.

'I want to stay here . . . You're my family . . .'

She shook her head at my foolishness. She wasn't being unkind, just pointing out the truth, which was that without Ed and the school there was little point in staying.

'Eat your rice,' she ordered. 'Your English friend is waiting to take you away.' She glanced quickly away, shuddering as she pulled her sari over her head. There was something else that she wasn't articulating, but I was too fazed to nail the thought down. Squatting by the bowl I took some of the rice in my hands and tried to eat it, but the stuff clogged my mouth.

'Have more . . .'

'I can't.'

'I cooked it for you.'

'Forgive me . . .'

'Don't cry, Sister.'

Her arms were around me again, her rough hands wiping away my tears.

'Look,' she said. 'Your English man is coming.'

She nodded towards the beach. Through the ruined trees I noticed Dan's jeep, sweeping across the hardened sand. Syeda was standing now, fiddling with the loose end of her sari, where she tied cash, or her keys.

'Take this,' she said, handing me a scrap of paper that she had tucked inside the knotted material. 'It's my mobile.'

I nodded, glancing down at the pencilled numbers. Most people in the village relied on cheap mobiles. Folding the paper, I slipped it inside my bra. Pushing her face towards me, Syeda brushed her nose against mine.

'I'll pray for you,' she whispered. Pressing my hand one final time, she hurried back along the path.

I had a minute or so before Dan appeared. Jumping up, I grabbed Ed's briefcase. My fingers slipping on the wet metal, I pulled open the buckles. It had been his father's, he'd said, made in the days when things were supposed to last. Now, as I placed the scuffed leather on my lap, I pictured him returning from the bazaar, the briefcase clutched in his hands as he picked his way across the muddy tracks. Usually it was only the notebooks that he carried inside, but sometimes there were presents to be pulled from its compartments, like tricks from a magician's hat: a carved box that he'd found in Noton Bazaar, my golden bangles. When was it that the presents stopped? Before I could block it out, I pictured something else: the crumpled thing that had been dumped on our path only a week earlier. This was a different kind of present entirely, something for the flies, which covered the dark stains in a greedy mass. Pushing the image away, my hands reached inside the bag.

They were still there: four notebooks, neatly arranged. Despite everything that had happened, Ed remained almost obsessively orderly. For a moment I allowed my fingers to trace the crumbling cardboard covers, the dated labels faded in the humidity. He was so private; even now I felt like I was trespassing. Stashed behind the books was something else: a plastic folder filled with faded email printouts. I started to shuffle through them, my breath catching.

F.Carswell@Oxan, co.uk
Frank Carswell
Director, Corporate Social Responsibility Unit
Oxan

Dear Mr Salisbury
Thank you for your letter concerning recent events in the Noton Bazaar area. As you are no doubt aware, Oxan has been investing in the energy sector in Bangladesh since 1995. Our programme involves the exploration of gas and oil reserves, alongside drilling in established fields. In the last five years, our presence has allowed Bangladesh to double its production of natural gas, with a further predicted trebling of oil in the next decade. Whilst the loss of homes and land involved in some areas is regrettable, we are confident that the government compensation scheme is fair. In addition, our investment in the resource base is matched by significant programmes of infra structure and social development, which are administered by our sister company, the Bangladesh Natural Resource Company. You may not be aware, for example, that a budget of $1 million has been approved . . .

Blah, blah, blah: the usual corporate spin. I skim read to the end of the letter, flicking through a sheaf of similar responses produced by various contacts Ed had managed to establish in Dhaka and London. Underneath was one of the many reports Ed had downloaded: 'Investing in People: Towards sustainable energy development'. Pushing it aside, I thumbed to the back of the papers, finding the emails from Dan. Out of everyone that Ed had contacted, only his response had been positive.

> March 15th
> Dear Ed
> Thanks for your letter describing the problems that you've been experiencing with the Bangladesh Natural Resource Company. Here at Dfid we've been working with our corporate partners for a number of years in the development of corporate social responsibility programmes, so have an obvious interest in the local outcomes. If you would like to come to Dhaka to discuss the matter further I would be happy to meet with you. Please note however that I will be in Bangkok until the beginning of May so will not be able to make any appointments until after that time.
> Dan Jameson
> South Asia Advisor, Department for International Development

'What you got there?'

I turned to find Dan standing behind me.

'Nothing really. Just looking at all these emails . . .'

'He printed everything out, did he?'

'He had to. We don't have an Internet connection so he had to go to Noton Bazaar to get a connection . . . Look, this one's from you.'

Glancing down, Dan lifted the papers gently from my knee.

'Do you want me to look after them?'

'No, it's OK. I'll put them back in the briefcase.'

He handed the wodge of emails back, eyeing me with concern. 'He was in deep, wasn't he?'

I swallowed hard.

'It just spun out of control . . .'

Shaking his head, Dan placed a hand on my arm. 'I tried to help,' he said quietly. 'That's why I came all the way here.'

'I know. It was really good of you . . .'

For a moment our eyes met. 'I just wish we'd agreed to go with you last night,' I murmured. 'Before . . . all this . . .'

I couldn't finish the sentence. Putting his arm around my shoulder, Dan started to steer me across the wreckage of the garden. 'Are you ready to go?'

'I suppose so.'

'I've asked my driver to stay behind to see if Ed turns up. He's a good chap. He'll do everything he can to find out what's happened. In the meantime I'm afraid it's me driving. Speak any Bengali?'

'Yeah, sort of.'

'Good. I'm pretty sure I know the route.'

I attempted a smile. He was trying to be kind, yet my reactions felt muffled, like being trapped behind a thick pane of glass.

'Dan?'

'Yup?'

'Thanks for everything.'

He grimaced.

Once we'd passed the potholes and ruts of the small country roads, Dan drove fast. The typhoon had battered the coastal strip south of Cox's Bazaar, but had not moved far inland. A few miles from the sea, people were going about their business as if all that had taken place was a heavy rain storm. At Noton Bazaar the small lanes were filled with rickshaws, tempos and trucks painted with pictures of tigers and plump Bollywood stars. I slouched in the jeep's front seat, staring listlessly from the window. We were passing through the central market, where piles of stubby bananas and jackfruit were heaped by the road. People weaved through the gridlocked traffic: beggar women carrying pot-bellied babies in their arms, little girls selling popcorn, broken old men, their hands pushing through the windows of the cars. Rubbish lay everywhere. The smell of rotting fruit and frantic hooting made me nauseous.

The road was becoming increasingly narrow, the traffic ahead knotting hopelessly as a bamboo-laden truck backed out of a side road into the heaving throng. As we slowed, the cacophony of horns, bicycle bells and cat calls rose a pitch, as if the force of the noise might untangle the traffic. Dan drummed his fingers on the steering wheel.

'How are you feeling?' he said, glancing at me with concern.

'I don't really know . . . Kind of numb, I suppose.' I gazed out of the window, trying to jump-start my thoughts. 'Everything feels so surreal . . . I just can't take it all in.'

He nodded, his face solemn as he carefully edged the jeep past a calf that was dozing in the middle of the road. 'Me neither.'

'I'm *sure* Ed's not dead,' I said. 'He just can't be!'

'That's pretty much what I feel too.'

Finally pulling clear of the juddering rickshaws that crammed the narrow road, he accelerated past rickshaw workshops and a petrol station and into the open countryside.

'I'm going to do everything I can to find him,' he eventually said, pushing the jeep into top gear. 'Whatever's happened.'

FOUR

2002

Almost exactly eighteen months earlier I was waiting in the Departures Lounge in Heathrow. I was doing something I had always dreamt of: exchanging the comforts and suffocations of Britain for something meaningful, a voluntary job with a charity in Bangladesh. I had extracted myself from my life with surprising ease. No one seemed particularly surprised at my departure: teachers at the Brighton Language College came and went almost as regularly as the students, whilst over the last year my relationship with my boyfriend Nick had been deflating as rapidly as a collapsed soufflé. Yet if I was taking my life by the scruff of the neck and shaking it alive, the hugeness of the airport was making me unexpectedly panicky. I'd never noticed before how many people rushed around the place or the endless rows of place names that flickered on the Departures screens. I watched them nervously, waiting for my flight to board. I'd been to

Morocco on a student field trip and InterRailing in Europe
with Nick, but suddenly the world seemed vast and unfathomable. When my flight was finally called and I joined a long
line of passengers at gate thirty-two, I was breathless with
anticipation.

I had a window seat. As the plane taxied down the runway
and I watched the airport buildings jerk past I had the bizarre
sense that the officious stewardess who had pointed out my
seat was about to declare me a fake and chuck me off the
flight. Here she was now, clacking down the aisle in her black
court shoes. 'This woman's an impostor,' she'd bark, halting
by my side. 'She shouldn't be here!' At her command the
passengers would turn, straining their necks to peek at me,
an aimless young woman attempting to escape from her aimless
life. It was true that I had a degree in Development Studies,
but beyond some half-mangled economic theory and various
homilies concerning local participation I could barely
remember a word, despite having beefed it up on my appli-
cation form to Bringing The World Together. I should obviously be back in Brighton, teaching grammar to Japanese
students and saving up for a three-week holiday in Goa –
wasn't that what people like me settled for?

'*Fine*,' Nick had muttered when I'd told him my plans. For
a moment his face had turned scarlet and his bottom lip
drooped, then he had quickly recovered his composure.
'Personally I can't see you lasting long in a place like that.'

I clicked on my seat belt, staring at the acrylic headrest in
front. Not even glancing at me, the stewardess stomped past.

Ten hours later, I peered from my lozenge-like window at a
flat landscape of paddy fields and silver, snaking rivers; a
hundred shades of green, interspersed by sudden flashes of
water. As the crew prepared for landing, bamboo houses, with
hayricks and cattle in the yards, came into view. The plane
turned, gliding over an unexpected section of city: ramshackle
roofs, a railway line over which hordes of tiny people spilled,
makeshift shacks crammed into every space. Now I could see
the burnt grass of the landing strip; we passed the corpse of
an ancient aircraft and with a bump, the wheels touched down.

Whilst the cosmopolitan bustle of Heathrow had made me
feel small and provincial, Dhaka's Zia International Airport was

something else. I wandered into Luggage Retrieval, wide-eyed at the scrum of shouting men who surrounded the single, creaking carousel. The hangar-like building smelt of hot plastic and dust and echoed with the guttural rasp of the men's hawking. The heat was incredible: a smothering blanket that soaked me instantly in sweat. An hour or so passed as I waited for the carousel to yield my rucksack. When it finally juddered into view, looking pathetically small and battered amongst the vast blanket-covered cases, I pulled it from the merry-go-round and staggered towards Immigration. Here I stood in line for another hour watching the business and aid people ahead step forwards for a long-winded interrogation that was eventually concluded by the approving thwack of the immigration officer's stamp.

Finally disgorged, I dragged my bags through Customs and towards the Exit sign, feeling as if I might explode. Bringing The World Together had placed me with Mohila Shadinota Shamittee, a small NGO that worked in the city's slums. They'd meet me at the airport, I was told. Now, as I appeared on the other side of the doors, a small man with a moustache and glistening bald patch stepped forwards, bearing a card with 'Miss Sarah Flight BA 108' printed over it in block capitals. Beside him was a young woman dressed in a bright pink and turquoise sari: a parakeet, brilliant feathers splayed. A fleshy white lily was pushed into her raven hair.

'Greetings!' the man cried, proffering a few limp fingers for me to shake, before hastily snatching them away. 'I am Abrar, Director of MSS.'

'And I am Baby . . .'

Smiling regally, Baby stepped forwards and placed a garland of jasmine around my shoulders. 'Welcome to Bangladesh.'

As Baby fussed with my garland, delicately arranging it over my shoulders, Abrar beamed widely, wiping his face with a large white handkerchief. I gazed around the hangar, taking in the empty shops filled with gifts for non-existent tourists: straw dolls sporting stiff saris, miniature bicycle rickshaws, fashioned from brass. The building echoed with unintelligible shouts – whether orders or greetings, I couldn't tell – and the thwack and bump of battered suitcases being loaded on to the security machines.

Abrar picked up my bags with a flourish and started to proceed towards the Exit sign. I stumbled alongside him, dazed. Passing through the airport doors, we entered the melee that was pressed up against the smeared glass like prisoners, desperate for escape. Men dressed in lungis and tattered shirts shouted at me to take their taxis, children grabbed my shirt, an emaciated man waved the stump of an amputated arm in my face. '*Taka dei!*'

I brushed past them, not knowing what to do. A woman was pushing her malformed child at me, its head swollen like an egg, blank eyes oozing horribly.

'*Chup!*'

Raising his arm, Abrar chased the woman away. I trotted beside him, almost too excited to breathe. The air smelt sweet and heavy, like dusty fruit, that had been left too long in the bowl.

We drove into the city in a battered saloon, Abrar in the front next to the portly, heavily perspiring driver, and Baby and I in the back. It was still early morning, but already so hot that my skin seemed to have melted into the seat; when I shifted my bottom, my thighs made a grotesque squelching sound. The air-conditioning didn't work, Abrar joked as he wound the window down, just like the whole damn country!

I stared, agog, at the traffic that swirled around us. Buzzing by the side of the road were what Abrar informed me were 'baby-taxis': scooters with garishly decorated canvas hoods, fluorescent tassels and passenger seats in the back. As we turned into a larger road, we joined shoals of boneshaker bikes, puttering motorbikes, often bearing not just a father, but also a sari-clad mother sitting side saddle, and several children squashed in between, trucks painted with pictures of tigers and Himalayan mountains, and wreckages of buses that exploded with passengers, like burst pomegranates. More people paced the side of the road: emaciated women holding children on their hips; half-naked men, with jack fruits balanced on their heads; a group of workers who trotted in a line, a twenty-foot pole resting on their shoulders. The city sprawled into view: half-finished concrete buildings, interspersed with shacks. People were everywhere; every scrap of land covered by habitation. In places the land gave way to ponds in which people were bathing or scrubbing their pans amongst the trash as their ragged children played in the road. In patches of the scummy surface, lilies broke through.

As we drove closer to the centre, the buildings became more dense and less ramshackle. High-rise shopping malls appeared; a huge, half-finished construction that Abrar proclaimed was to be a hospital; the shimmering, modernist dream of the parliament buildings. The traffic concertinaed into frequent overheated stops. We crawled past shops displaying saris or mounds of exotic-looking sweets, dentists' surgeries, advertised by alarming depictions of chomping gnashers and a huge, blue-slated mosque: an oasis of calm amongst the chaos. A short while later we were stationary once more, black fumes pouring around us as the horns blared. Despite the traffic police, who were blowing ineffectually on their whistles, the tangle was tightening into an intractable knot.

'Jam!' Baby announced cheerfully.

'In London there aren't any such commotions,' Abrar added, turning and nodding at me. 'Ysh! Look at that fellow!' As the traffic jerked forwards a policeman was thwacking a passing rickshaw driver with his baton.

Mahila Shadinota Shamittee was situated on a busy arterial road close to the stadium, the steel rods of the unfinished fourth floor sticking from its flat roof like a cockroach's antennae. As she squeezed my hand, Baby explained that I was to stay in a small flat above the office, with herself and her husband, Mannan. Dragging my rucksack from the car, we climbed a flight of stone steps until we came to their front door, domesticated by a rubber mat and the flip-flops parked outside. Understanding that I should take off my shoes I grappled with my trainers, embarrassed by my sweaty feet.

'Come, Sarah. This will be your room.'

She showed me into a small bedroom, with just enough space for a wooden clothes rack, a dresser, and a large mahogany bed, covered with an embroidered counterpane. A window opened onto a tiny balcony, from which I could gaze on to the narrow alley beneath.

'It's lovely!'

'Do you need to rest, or will you take some refreshments now?'

She peered into my eyes, plump lips twitching. On taking my dimpled hand at the airport she had pressed it with such affection that I wondered if she had mistaken me for someone

else: a bona fide professional, perhaps, with something to
offer. I stared into her pretty face, a wave of euphoria sloshing
over me.

'I'm fine,' I said. 'No worries. All I want is to be useful.'
She burst out laughing, clapping her hands.

'Thank you!' she trilled. 'Thank you for saying that!'

'What exactly do you think I'm going to be *doing*?' I
glanced around the spotless flat as if this might give me a
clue. From the lane below I could hear the tring of bicycle
bells and the low, whinnying call of a pedlar. 'They said I'd
be helping to write proposals or something . . .'

'Later, Sarah,' Baby said, leading me to the dining area,
where a table was heaped with boxes of basmati rice, sweetmeats, and slices of mango. 'We have so much time together.
We can discuss all this later.'

Later never came. Over the next weeks I was plied with
umpteen gifts, visits and meals, but never given any actual
work. At first it didn't matter. I was busy attending Bengali
lessons with Baby's sister-in-law, and doing the rounds of her
relatives' houses. Sometimes we were unable to go anywhere.
The Opposition has called another General Strike, Baby would
say, sighing heavily. There might be trouble in the city, riots
or even bombs; it wasn't safe to move around. During the
strikes no one came to the office and we stayed in the flat,
the streets beneath our windows eerily quiet. On those days
Baby would lounge on my bed and ask me about my life.
When I told her about Nick she shrugged.

'Here in the city educated people like us often marry for
love. In the villages, the families decide.'

'But isn't that really hard for the women? Supposing the
families chose someone horrible?'

'Sarah, if your parents care about you, then they'll choose
someone good, won't they?'

Later that afternoon she oiled and plaited my hair, Bengali
style, and folded a sari around me. 'Marry a nice Bengali
man,' she whispered as she tucked the stiff material into a
pleat. 'Then you can stay here forever.'

On other days I visited the 'field', travelling pillion through
hours of 'jam' on the back of Mannan's motorbike to the shanty
where the project was based. The settlement was close to the

main railway station, the huts spreading around the criss-crossing lines like impetigo. It was hard to believe that people could survive in such a place, yet here, inside tents made from rags and plastic bags, families were being raised. I peered inside the huts, glancing guiltily away when I noticed a man's face, staring enquiringly out. Mannan's job involved picking his way through the rubbish-strewn lanes searching for the members of his credit group. Once located, the women would hand him a couple of worn taka notes, wound carefully into the end of their thread-bare saris, and he'd tick their name off on his chart. Meanwhile I would hover beside him, smiling daftly.

Back at the office long hours were filled with reading old reports. The weeks were sliding past, but still I had no proper work. I had left Britain with a misplaced optimism about what I might contribute, imagining that my degree might equip me for something meaningful. Yet increasingly my uselessness was morphing into new, unseemly proportions. If only I was *doing* something, I thought with increasing desperation. Perhaps I should take the place of the emaciated women and children breaking stones in the building site across the road, at least I'd be giving them a break. Instead I was trapped at my empty desk, sipping tea and twiddling my thumbs.

By the end of that first month I was wondering if I should stay. It was not the slimy heat, the fact that the stinky toilet was the only place where I could be alone, my griping belly or the way in which people stared at me in amazement every time I stepped from the door. The streets around Mahila Shadinota Shamittee were a tip, it was true, with rubbish rotting on the steaming streets and everyone's dirt sluiced away in the open drains. But the place was *alive*; it pulsated with energy. From dawn until one or two in the morning I could hear people in the alleys below talking and laughing and shouting at each other. Pedlars called from every crowded corner, dogs barked, the haunting cries of the azan marked out the days. Yet despite my excitement at being in Dhaka, I had nothing to offer. I had told everyone at home that I was going to be an 'aid worker' but the reality was that with my rudimentary grasp of Bengali, and general ignorance of Bangladesh, there was little I could really do.

'Wait,' Mr Abrar had replied, smiling uncertainly when I'd finally confronted him. 'Be at ease and relax.'

By week six I was beginning to despair. I leafed listlessly through my pile of reports, their pages fluttering under the fan. Whatever happened, I was thinking, I couldn't go back to Brighton; I would simply have to find another job. On the other side of my desk, Baby was fiddling with her mobile.

'Can I ask you something, Baby?'

'Most certainly!'

She glanced up, an inquisitive smile fixed to her face. Today her sari was canary yellow and she was wearing tiny gold rings in her ears.

'Why do you think Mr Abrar asked BTWT for my internship? I mean, there isn't actually any work for me, is there?'

She blinked. 'It's all about our standing, Sarah!' she said with a little laugh. 'All the other big NGOs have foreigners working for them, so I suppose we have to have one too!'

It was the last full day I spent in the office. I needed to practice my Bengali, I announced; I was going to explore. Over the next few days I took a baby-taxi to the Old City, paid a rickshaw driver to peddle me around the space-age Parliament Building, and visited the women's section of the Binat Bibi Mosque, where, covered in the burqua that I'd been handed at the entrance, I sat cross-legged on the cool floor, gazing up at the domed mosaic ceiling. The place filled me with serenity. Unlike the streets outside, no one was gawping at me or shouting out 'foreigner!'. In the unexpected quiet I could feel my pent up frustration and anxiety collapse into the simple juxtaposition of the golden light dancing on the floor and the stillness of the air. I stayed there all afternoon, not wanting to return.

The next morning I planned to return to the mosque. I stood on the broken pavement outside the office building, breathing in the heady, hot aroma of petrol fumes and drains. After sitting for a while in the quiet of the mosque, I had no further plans.

'Where do you want to go, Sister?'

Like a wasp whizzing towards fallen fruit, a rickshaw was already at my side. I eyed the driver. He was older than most, with a short grey beard and deep creases running across his thin face.

'Binat Bibi.'

Nodding, the man started to manoeuvre the ramshackle vehicle around. I climbed onto the plastic covered ledge that constituted a seat, the springs groaning. Straining against my weight, the driver pushed down hard on the wheels; pulling my scarf over my head, as Baby had taught me to, I braced myself for the blast of the traffic.

It was fun, speeding along like this, my scarf flapping in the wind. Gripping the wooden sides of the seat, I closed my eyes. Back home it would be early morning. Nick would be on his way to work, slouched on the 7.35 Brighton to Victoria train with his Ipod on. When we first met we had talked of travelling the world together, but over time our plans had shrivelled and died. When he took a job on the lower rungs of the civil service he'd suggested that we use our pooled saving for a deposit on a flat. He would, after all, only have three weeks' leave a year; the round the world trip wasn't exactly feasible. Without noticing it happening, our life had become dull. We'd had fun at first: we used to go out dancing, or would spend the weekend biking on the Downs. Yet things had curdled, like something sweet that had been left out too long.

For a second, just before I heard the rickshaw driver's shout, I pictured the classroom at the English college where I had worked for nearly four years without the slightest interest: the white board and rows of bored Polish au pairs. I should have worked harder at university, then I might have made something of my life.

I opened my eyes just in time to see the front of a battered taxi bearing down. With a screech of brakes, it smashed into the side of the rickshaw, catapulting me out of my narrow seat. The world turned upside down, concrete rushing towards my face. I tasted blood and dust; from somewhere above my head I could hear oaths and the frantic peep of horns. Now I lay stunned in the road, staring at the skanky drain. I'd put my hands out to break my fall, and my palms stung. Above me, the rickshaw driver was clutching his mangled vehicle and shouting a stream of abuse at the car that had bashed into us and was now disappearing into the petrol haze.

'Are you alright?'

'Hmmf . . .'

I gazed up in surprise. A young western guy was squatting in the dirt, peering down.

'Anything broken?'

He was British. A posh voice, but nice smiley eyes, and fingers that reassuringly kneaded my arm.

'I'm fine . . .' I hauled myself up. 'Went somewhat arse over tit . . .'

He regarded me thoughtfully through his frameless specs. His lips were slightly pursed, as if he wanted to laugh; perhaps it was the sight of such an ungainly lump, rolling in the drain. He had a nice face, though.

'You're lucky. That could have been nasty. What about your hand?'

My palm was bleeding where the skin had been scraped off. Hauling myself out of the dust, I started to wrap my scarf around it. The palm of my hand was sore and my hip ached, but I was otherwise unhurt. A few feet away the rickshaw driver was standing in the road, yelling in the direction of the long-departed car. Despite the streaming traffic, a gawping crowd had gathered around him.

'Hold on, I'm going to sort this out.'

Pulling a wallet from the money belt that hung around his slim waist, the man jogged towards the rickshaw driver, saying something in Bengali and handing over what looked like a large wad of notes. With his frayed jeans and loose Punjabi he didn't look smart enough to be one of the development experts that whizzed around the place in their four-wheel drives. When he spotted the money, the rickshaw driver's face changed. Receiving the roll of cash in his hands he put it first to his lips and then to his forehead. As he tucked it into the top of his lungi and dragged the wrecked rickshaw across the road, he was grinning.

'They don't exactly have accident insurance here,' my new friend was saying. 'That poor guy would have had to pay the owner of the rickshaw for the damage . . .' He stopped, frowning at the stump of my hand, now swaddled in yellow cotton. 'You should get that looked at. It could get infected.'

'I'll be fine . . .'

'No, come on. You have to take open wounds seriously in the tropics. I'm going to take you to a doctor's.'

Despite my feeble protests, he had already flagged down a baby-taxi and was ushering me inside. The truth was, I was only pretending to object. As the baby-taxi pulled, puttering, into the fracas, I could not think of a single reason why I shouldn't go with him.

'I'm Ed, by the way.'

He shot out his hand. We were squashed so closely into the back of the vehicle that manoeuvring my other hand from where it was wedged under my thigh would have been impossible. I waved my stump in reply.

'Sarah,' I yelled over the roar of trucks and tempos. The fumes rose from the road in grey smudges.

'Are you working here?'

'I'm meant to be helping with fund-raising at this NGO . . .'

I wasn't sure if he'd heard. He nodded, clutching the rusty handrail as we swerved around a corner. We were so close that I could feel his body through his thin shirt, our thighs pressing together. By now we had turned off the main thoroughfare and were careering along a less-populated boulevard, where large white houses with imposing gates were set back from the pavement.

'My place is just along here,' Ed shouted. 'You can have a drink and a sit down. I'll get someone out to look at you.'

We stopped outside one of the gates.

'This is nice . . .'

'Dhaka's very own Millionaires' Row!'

I gazed down the wide avenue. I had never been in this part of the city before, where generous gardens were surrounded by tidy walls and large jeeps rested in the drives. Some of them were guarded by armed soldiers: embassies and the residences of foreign dignitaries. The security seemed unnecessary, for there was hardly anyone around. Under a plane tree a man was sleeping in his rickshaw; a little further away, a scrawny cow munched at a pile of rubbish.

'Let me help you . . .'

Hooking his hand under my elbow Ed levered me from the baby-taxi. I could have easily managed without him, but I liked the sensation of his fingers clasping my arm so allowed them to stay.

'OK?'

Pushing open the gate, he led me up the drive and through the front door. Following him, I stepped inside, glancing around the large unfurnished room. A stack of packing boxes rested against the wall.

'I'm only renting it for a month or so,' he was saying as he strode across the room. 'Then I'm heading down south.'

He led me to a veranda which overlooked a square of rubbery

grass surrounded by jasmine and bougainvillea. Sweeping away the books and papers scattered over the wicker seats, he cleared a place for us to sit. He seemed nervous. 'Make yourself comfortable. I'm going to get you a drink . . . then I'll call Dr Malek. Are you in the sun?'

He scurried away. My hand had begun to throb, and my thigh was unnaturally stiff, but I was enjoying myself. Books were everywhere, I realized as I gazed around. Picking up a dog-eared edition of *North and South*, I skim read the first page.

'That's a fantastic book. Do you know it?'

Setting down a tray of drinks, he smiled at me expectantly.

'Not really, to be honest.'

There was a short pause. Closing the book, I dropped it on to the bamboo coffee table.

'I've become obsessed by Victorian novels,' Ed continued after a beat. 'They have so much resonance with this place . . . I know, different history, different culture, blah blah blah, but many of the struggles that go on in people's lives are remarkably similar to what was happening during the Industrial Revolution.'

There were so many potential answers that I simply gawped at him, my cheeks glowing.

'I was going to do English at uni,' I heard myself say. 'But in the end I chose Development Studies.' I bit down on my lip.

'How come?'

'I don't know . . . I suppose I had teenage fantasies about saving the world.'

For a moment he looked perplexed. Then he laughed. 'And does this degree in development studies help?'

'With what, saving the world?'

'Yeah.' He folded his arms, regarding me humorously.

'Not so far. In fact, not at all.'

'That's a shame. It could have come in handy here.'

'Yeah, I guess it could.'

He blinked, then sat down. 'How are you doing? Should I ring Dr Malek?'

'I don't know . . .' I started to peel the scarf away from my hand, wincing. I'd only excavated the first layer and already the material was a bloodied mess.

'Hang on, I've got a first aid kit.'

A moment later my hand was resting on his lap and he

was gently dabbing at my palm with an antiseptic wipe. For some reason I didn't want Dr Malek barging in. It was nothing, I kept telling him: a superficial graze, no need for medical attention. As Ed tended to me, I gave him an edited version of my seven weeks with Mahila Shadinota Shamittee. This included my desire for meaningful work but excluded my ignorance of the subcontinent and general uselessness. I wanted him to think that I was just like he presumably was: an educated and experienced type, on a mission to make the world a better place. He nodded sagely as I told him about Baby and Mannan. I'd started off with the official version of my post at Mahila Shadinota Shamittee, in which I was a 'senior fund raiser', but something in his eyes made me tell him the truth: my actual role was as an amusing office mascot, to be wheeled out for visiting dignitaries and on other special occasions.

'That's why I'm not here with an organization,' he said thoughtfully as he squinted at his handiwork. 'I'd rather be in control.' Having finished with the antiseptic, he started to wind a bandage around my hand. 'Sorry, did that hurt?'

'No, don't mind me . . .'

'Basically, I've got my own project in the coastal zone.'

'Uh-huh . . .'

'Have you been down there?'

'Not yet.' It was embarrassing, but I was only vaguely aware that there *was* a coastal zone. My only experience of the country-side had been the rivers and electric-green paddy fields I'd glimpsed from the plane.

'I'll have to take you, then. It's incredibly beautiful. You'll get the wrong impression of Bangladesh if you stay here. You can come and see one of my schools.'

He glanced up. He had a way of staring directly into my face that I found disconcerting. Blinking, he dangled the bandage above my palm as if he'd forgotten what he was doing.

'You've got a school?' I was picturing him standing in a classroom, a group of enraptured children gazing up.

'I run this organization, Schools For Change? We're basic-ally working with the Freire idea of empowerment through education. You've heard of Action Education?'

I nodded untruthfully. I really should have paid more attention at university.

'That's our method. We're aiming at the adults as much as the kids, especially women. Unfortunately that means a bit of resistance locally, but I've got some great people involved, so I'm optimistic that the communities we're working with will eventually come round to it. I mean, Grameen and BRAC are so well accepted now that in a way the doors are already open.'

I had no idea what he was talking about. 'Cool . . .'

'We also run a couple of schools here in Dhaka. At the moment our work in the coastal zone is at the planning stages but I'm really hopeful that this time next year we'll have a functioning building. Recruitment's a bit of a challenge, too. It's actually bloody hard trying to persuade people to go somewhere so far off the beaten path.'

I nodded, pretending it was an issue with which I was familiar. 'The problem is, the aid community here are so cynical,' he went on. 'It's not a can-do mentality, it's a "let's work within the parameters" kind of defeatism. I simply don't believe in that sort of attitude. Things *can* change, but only if we have the highest of expectations. I mean, the people here are amongst the poorest in the world, *fuck* the bloody rules and regulations!'

'You sound like Bob Geldof.'

He grimaced. Like a burp, the comment had popped, unconsidered, from my mouth.

'Do I? Oh, bloody hell.'

'You don't look like him, though,' I added.

'Well that's a relief.'

He grinned sheepishly. There was something jagged about his manner that I liked, as if he didn't much care how he appeared. He was tying the bandage neatly around my palm now, frowning in concentration.

'There you go, all done.'

He carefully rested my hand on one of the silk cushions that were scattered over the sofa.

'That's brilliant. I bet your doctor wouldn't have done it any better.'

'Is that right?' he said, looking at me in a way that made my tummy lurch. 'We'll have to make sure you look after it, won't we?'

FIVE

May 7th, 2003

By the time Dan and I reached the airport, the sun had gone down. There was an evening flight, he said. He'd been on to Lydia Simmonds; she was going to meet my plane. Meanwhile he had to stay in the south, awaiting instructions from London; in the days to come there would be emergency aid to administrate. They needed, as he put it, 'a man on the ground'.

He stayed by my side until my flight was called, even accompanying me to the departure gate. 'Are you *sure* you're OK?' he kept asking. 'I wish there was something more I could do.'

Earlier we had stopped at a market where I'd bought a *shalwar kameez* to replace my tattered clothes. Yet even after changing and washing my face, a cursory glance at my reflection in the burnished mirror of the airport Ladies revealed how dishevelled I was. The bump on my chin had scabbed over and looked like a boil; my hair was wild. In Lalalpur I had not had a mirror. Now I saw how thin I had become, my head too large for my bony shoulders, my cheeks hollow.

I waited with Dan on the plastic airport seats, barely able to respond to his attempts at conversation. He was trying to be kind, but I couldn't wait for him to leave, for his stolid presence reminded me only of Ed's absence. What was I doing, boarding a flight to the capital, when Ed had disappeared?

'It's best this way,' Dan said as he finally relinquished me to the Biman crew, who were beckoning at me to progress through the gate. 'There's going to be chaos down there for weeks. As soon as I hear anything I'll let you know.'

I nodded, glancing at his unshaven face. 'Ed said there was some really heavy stuff going on with Oxan,' I blurted. 'Far more than just local politics. Do you know what he meant?'

Dan looked at me sadly. 'It's probably best I don't go into the details now.'

'Why not?'

'Because . . . well, because of what's happened. Look, go

back to Dhaka, and try and get some sleep. At least you'll be safe there.'

I only had a few seconds left before I was forced to pass through the gate. 'What do you mean, I'll be *safe*?'

But rather than replying, Dan was propelling me gently towards the white gloved Biman stewardesses. 'We'll talk about it later,' he said. 'I'll call you as soon as I have some news.'

He kissed me with tender formality on either cheek. Perhaps it was because he was my last link to Ed, but for a moment, as I leant towards him, I did not want him to go.

Dan may have had the impression that Lydia Simmons and her husband Mike were my friends, but the truth was I had only met them once before. Now, as promised, she was waiting for me at Zia International Airport. As I pushed through the jostling throng in the Arrivals Hall, I instantly spotted her blonde head above the mass of darker hair on the other side of the barrier. She looked disgruntled and slightly repulsed, as if being forced to eat something she neither liked nor approved of. As soon as she noticed me her expression changed to one of naked relief quickly masked by compassion and, perhaps, a dash of prurient fascination.

'Sarah!' Her hands were doing little fluttery things, a mixture of waving and wafting herself. It was certainly very hot. The fans that lazily stirred in the rafters of the building had no impact at ground level. The dusty smell reminded me of my first arrival here, another lifetime ago. Mosquitoes were everywhere.

'Oh goodness, you poor, poor thing!'

She smelt of expensive perfume. I stood stiffly in her embrace, aware of people turning to watch.

'How are you *feeling*?' She peered at me, sympathy oozing. I wished she would let go of my arm.

'I'm OK.'

'We're all *devastated* about what's happened.'

I blinked at her. She was trying to be kind, but I didn't have the energy to respond in the way she wanted. Colouring slightly, she finally freed my elbow, smoothing down her shirt.

'Is this all you've got?' She tried to yank Ed's briefcase away, but I held on tight. 'Come on, we've got the car outside.'

She led me out of the airport and through the mob of touts that pressed up against the doors. Out here the night air was only marginally cooler; maddened by the dull yellow lights, kamikaze moths blundered into our faces. Swishing them away, Lydia steered me across the muddle of waiting cars and into a smart jeep, with smoked-glass windows and shiny bull bars, presumably to shove bothersome beggars out of its path. The driver, who had been lounging on the front seats jumped to attention as we appeared, making a show of opening the back doors and helping us inside.

'Alrighty!' Lydia said briskly. 'Let's go home, shall we?'

Like most British expats, they lived in Banani, the smartest suburb of the city. Ed had taken me to meet them a few weeks before we'd finally moved to Lalalpur. Mike had been so helpful when he'd first arrived, he'd explained, his eyes twinkling at how he knew I was going to respond. We should treat the dinner as ethnographic research, an investigation into the exotica of expat society. He was right; after six months in Bangladesh, I found the experience extraordinary. We sat in Mike and Lydia's palatial dining room as their staff had served us course after course of delicacies and Lydia had recounted the hardships they faced in Dhaka. They were hoping for Delhi next year, she'd concluded, where at least things were a bit more 'advanced'. I could tell they found Ed and I perplexing. They kept referring to our plans as 'courageous'. Mike had been to Chittagong once on business, but Lydia had never been 'down country' as she put it. 'I'm not into adventure travel,' she'd said, smirking ruefully. 'Being here's bad enough, let alone being stuck somewhere with squatty lavs!' Once or twice during the meal I had caught her looking at me, a discreet frown of bemusement denting her forehead.

Today the house seemed even grander. After so long in Lalalpur, the heavy mahogany furniture, enormous widescreen TV and thick rugs seemed ridiculously indulgent. With the full force of the air-conditioning it was also bracingly cold. Lydia guided me through the reception hall into another large room, with a black leather suite that they must have had shipped from the UK. A vase filled with artificial flowers rested on the glass coffee table, the walls covered with arty photographs of the country that neither Lydia nor Mike had actually seen: fishing nets in the morning mist, wooden dhows, gliding down the Brahmaputra. The room smelt of insecticide.

'You must be exhausted,' Lydia was saying. 'Do you want

to go straight to bed? Or shall I get Shalini to make you something to eat?'

I sat on the stiff settee. Goose bumps had appeared on my
bare arms, I noticed, prodding my flesh distractedly. Since the
cyclone I registered physical sensations but felt oddly detached
from them, as if they were taking place in someone else's body.

'I shouldn't be here,' I murmured. 'I should be looking
for Ed.'

'Gosh yes. I do so understand . . .'

'Do you?'

She flinched. I stared back at her carefully made up face,
the neatly cut hair and pearl necklace. I knew I was being
rude, but I was unable to respond in the way she wanted.

'It's best that you try and get your strength back,' she said
slowly. 'You've been through a terrible trauma . . . maybe we
should get someone check you over? The High Commission
has a very good chap. He was marvellous for Jenny Mitchell
when poor Bruce had his stroke. He gave her some wonderful
pills to help her sleep.'

'Ed's not dead,' I said sharply.

She swallowed. I knew I was behaving badly, but I couldn't
help it. 'You're all acting like he's dead, but he can't be . . .'

'Sarah, dear, I know this is all absolutely frightful. You
must be feeling so terrible.'

'Don't tell me how I feel!'

I burst into tears.

I was given tea and toast and put to bed. Since the deluge of
snotty tears, when I'd sobbed until my ribs ached, Lydia had
assumed a high, sing-song voice, as if I was a little girl. She'd
run me a bath, she said, it would be nice to have a good soak.
Then I should try and have a little rest. She'd give me one of
those pills, she was sure it would help. And I could borrow a
nightie, too. I did as I was told, sorry that I'd misbehaved.

Later, when she had tiptoed out of the guest room and I
was lying on top of the soft bed, I could hear her voice floating
up the stairs.

'I know, it's absolutely *dreadful* . . . Well, of course she's
had quite a shock, poor girl . . .'

She was on the phone. Rolling off the bed, I gently opened
the door.

'Of course, yes . . . terribly lucky, given the circumstances . . . No, I don't know either. He was such an odd young man . . . Exactly, no one did . . .'

I stepped quietly on to the landing. For long seconds, all I could hear was the whirr of the air-conditioner. Then suddenly Lydia said, 'I don't think she knows the half of it. I mean, if she *had* . . . Well, yes, exactly, but that's not exactly the kind of thing one can say, is it?'

Her voice dropped to a whisper. I couldn't make out the words, only their scandalized tone. Then suddenly she said brightly, 'Anyway, we all do what we can!' She laughed loudly. 'Alrighty . . . I'll leave it to you to book the court . . . No, Shirley can't do it then, maybe on the twenty-third?'

I crept back to my room, where I crawled under the covers. I couldn't stop shaking.

SIX

2003

After bandaging my grazed hand, Ed delivered me back to Mahila Shadinota Shamittee with a gentlemanly concern that, I decided, was solely the result of his good manners. When we reached the crumbling building, I clambered on to the pavement, expecting never to see him again. He was just a nice bloke, helping a stranger. Why would he be interested in me?

But the next day he arrived in the office. I heard his voice before seeing him, so had a moment or so to prepare myself, smoothing my hair, and pressing my hands against my flaming cheeks. He was speaking Bengali and a small crowd had gathered around him, exclaiming at how brilliant he must be, as if expats had some vital chink missing in their brains which prevented them from acquiring a foreign language.

'I'm actually here for Sarah,' he said in English, turning and looking at me in a way that made my face even hotter. 'That is, if you can spare her?'

He had a taxi waiting outside.

'Thought you might want a break from rickshaws,' he muttered as we climbed into the back. 'How's your hand?'

I waved my bandaged palm at him. 'Much better.'

The car pulled into the gridlocked traffic, fierce spears of sunshine pinioning us to the sticky seats.

'How come the magical mystery tour?'

Ed laughed. 'You know what I was telling you about the schools? I'm taking you to this project I've been running. I thought it might interest you.'

'Okey-dokey.'

He glanced at me, one eyebrow raised. 'Are you sure? I mean, I don't want to butt in, if you've got other fish to fry . . .'

'I don't have any fish to fry. *Nunca*. I was just reading through these old reports. There wasn't anything else to do.'

He nodded, apparently pleased.

'How long have you been out here?' I asked as the car pulled into the traffic.

'Me? Quite a time. It's taken ages just to get things up and running.'

'What did you do before?'

'Oh you know, this and that. Some work in India. Before that I was based in London, doing consultancies and stuff.' He laughed elusively. 'I've always had a thing about poverty. You know, even as a kid when we used to go to exotic places it would do my head in, seeing the terrible conditions that people lived in . . .' He trailed off. 'But look, tell me about you. What brought you here?'

'All the usual reasons . . .'

I glanced out of the window. We had joined a ring road, in which the snarled traffic flowed a little more easily. Unlike the dense buildings of the city centre, fields lay beyond the thin layer of shacks and mechanics' yards that stretched beside the highway. Large billboards advertising Biman Airlines and Breezy Soap Powder straddled the dusty roadside. Beneath them, a long line of people straggled alongside the bicycles and rickshaws that jostled for position in the slow lane: barefooted women carrying pots of water on their heads, gaggles of schoolgirls in blue pinafores, traders pushing carts loaded with bananas or plastic jewellery, boys with trays of paan.

'I guess I'm trying to find something to do with my life,'

I finally said. 'I've never really worked out what I want to do. You know, I had an OK job and a nice relationship and everything but I was just drifting. In the end I couldn't believe that this was all there was. It was like I was suffocating.' I turned, squinting at him in the bright light. 'So I decided to turn into someone different.'

Picking up my uninjured left hand and grasping it, Ed grinned. 'Me too.'

Twenty minutes later we were passing through an area of brick factories: large yards, filled with stacks of bricks and huge chimneys, striped red and white like seaside rock. Labourers trudged through the fumes, the bricks piled into baskets that they balanced on their heads. On one side a group of women and children squatted around a mound of rubble, bashing the stones into tiny pieces with primitive mallets.

'Welcome to the inferno.'

Swerving from the main road, the car turned into one of the yards, pulling up outside a row of low breeze-block buildings which faced each other like barracks. At the end of the row was a tube well where a group of women had gathered, their battered metal urns balanced on their hips. A little further away some boys were rolling marbles in the dirt. When they spotted us they jumped to their feet.

'Mister Edward! *Taka!*'

'*Taka nai.*' Pulling a clownish face, Ed held out his hands. 'Oh go on, don't be a meanie.'

Already I was reaching into the fabric bag that I had taken to hanging from a cord around my neck. Proffering the boys a ten-*taka* note, I flashed them a grin. It was so easy making people happy! Glancing back, Ed raised his eyebrows.

'Now they'll *never* leave us alone.'

Hurrying past the barracks, he led me towards a makeshift shelter.

'Come and meet Tasneem.'

It was a school, constructed with bamboo walls and a gappy tin roof that revealed patches of sky. There were no desks, just the earth floor, where a group of children sat cross-legged in front of a young woman who was standing in front of a board covered in Bengali letters. As we appeared, they rose, chanting, 'Good morning, Mister Edward,' in English. Waving at them to sit down, Ed stepped aside to allow me to take the teacher's outstretched hand.

'Tasneem, this is my friend Sarah. Tasneem's been running the school for the past year,' he added. 'All these kids were working in the brick field before the school was set up. Now we've got the yard owners to agree that they only have to work in the afternoons. In the mornings they have their lessons.'

Tasneem smiled demurely. She was about my age, dressed in a simple cotton *shalwar kameez*, her hair tied in a loose plait.

'We do our best. We're doing our sums today.'

'Did you get the books?'

She nodded. 'We had a flood last year, and everything was ruined, so until Edward arranged things, we only had three arithmetic workbooks. He's our great patron.' From the arch of her pretty eyebrows I understood that she was teasing him.

'What rubbish!' Ed retorted happily.

'Has he told you about the coastal zone projects?' Tasneem went on. 'Schools for Change Bangladesh have got these *grand* plans. They keep trying to entice me to go there, but I absolutely refuse. It's very naughty of them to try and steal me when there's so much to do here.'

'We'd find you a replacement . . .'

She laughed, waggling her finger at him. 'I won't hear any more about it.'

'OK. I'm not going to mention it again. We'll let you get on, Tasneem. Come on, Sarah, let's go and annoy someone else.'

Taking my arm, he steered me out of the school and back into the barracks. Within seconds we were joined by the women who had been gossiping by the tube well. Dragging me away from Ed, they propelled me towards the barracks, where I was seated on a stool. Pressing around, they laughingly started to examine me. Thin hands encompassed my own thick wrists, as if sizing me up, my straw-coloured hair was fingered in amazement. To my surprise, I found that I could understand a little of what they were saying.

'Are you married?'

The woman who had asked this glanced slyly towards Ed. Perhaps she had only recently finished her shift, for her thin hair was covered in red dust. When she grinned, she revealed a single front tooth. Her eyes sparkled.

'No.'

'How old are you?'

'Twenty-eight.'

'She's *twenty-eight*,' the others murmured, apparently astonished.

'Is he your brother, then?'

'No . . . I mean, *jie, amar biye . . .' Yes, he's my brother.* Their eyes widening, the women nodded. They had actually understood me!

Putting her fingers to my face, the woman with the dusty hair stroked my cheek.

'You're beautiful. So *pale.*'

I stared at her, shaking my head. 'No,' I said, wrinkling my nose. '*Shondur nai. Apni shondur!' Not beautiful at all. It's you who's beautiful.* For a second there was silence, then the women guffawed loudly, showing their broken teeth. Suddenly they were all talking at once; probably about my chances of attracting a groom. I gazed at them, trying to follow what was being said. On the other side of the buildings Ed was in deep conversation with a man in chinos and reflector shades. They laughed, then the man patted Ed on the back, as if congratulating him.

'Put these on.'

One of the women had produced a handful of plastic bangles. Gripping my left hand, she crushed it in her strong fingers in an attempt to ease the bangles over my knuckles.

'They'll never go on!'

'They will.'

'No, Sister!' I would never have said such a thing in English, but now the phrase tripped merrily from my lips. Hooting, the women repeated the phrase. 'She called me Big Sister! She's always making jokes!' Squeezing my hand so forcefully that I thought the bones would crack, the bangles were pushed on to my wrists. I jangled them on my arms, enjoying myself.

'Do it like this.'

My *orna*, which I had been wearing over my chest, was taken and pulled over my head, then wrapped tightly around my neck and shoulders.

'Now you're a bride!'

'Don't you look lovely?'

Ed had appeared behind me. Screaming with laughter, the women covered their heads, nudging me in the ribs.

'I see they've taken you in hand,' he said quietly.

'That's one way of putting it.'

They were gabbling at him, speaking too fast for me to understand.

'What are they saying?'

He pulled the expression I remembered from my accident: a puzzled frown, suppressing laughter. 'They're telling me off for not marrying you.'

Jumping up, I pushed the *orna* off my head, cursing my pink cheeks for giving me away. 'I should get back. They might need me at work.'

'Come on then. Let me just say goodbye to Sadid.' He nodded at the man in the shades. 'He's one of our teachers.'

Much later, after I had been delivered back to the office by Ed and fobbed off Baby's questions by explaining that he was 'someone from BTWT', I locked myself in the bathroom. Pulling off my grimy *shalwar kameez,* I stepped under the trickling shower, peering down. In Britain I had been on a permanent diet, which never really worked. Nick called me 'cuddly', but I hated my plump tummy and chubby thighs. Now, as I examined my body, I was astounded: I could actually see my toes, I realized; I wasn't remotely fat, just a little curvy. Glancing in the cracked mirror, I noticed something else. The pale girl who normally stared nonplussed from the glass had gone. My hair was messy, I had a rash of spots on my forehead and my skin was untouched by make-up, but my eyes flashed with something new. Grinning at myself, I stuck out my tongue.

SEVEN

I spent the next day feeling ridiculously tense. I had not come all the way to Bangladesh to meet a man. I supposedly had no interest in 'a relationship'. But despite my attempts to concentrate on the funding form I was supposedly typing, my thoughts doggedly returned to Ed. He hadn't mentioned meeting again and I had no means of contacting him; I should put him from my thoughts. Yet try as I might I couldn't stop myself from peering for the thousandth time through the smeared office windows at the teeming road below. The day crawled past, and still he didn't come. Why should he? Nothing had *happened* between us: he'd probably found me boring. Yet as I lay in bed that night, I imagined his slim body stretched alongside mine, his fingers tracing my skin.

A whole week passed, and Ed did not appear. As each dreary day segued into the next, I grew increasingly despondent. For a few days I had imagined a future in Bangladesh, but now the weight of my situation hung ever more heavily around me. There was no point in anything, I decided as I scratched my name on the grimy window pane. I might as well go home.

'Miss Sarah.'

I turned to find the office peon offering me a note. A name and number was scrawled on it.

'Your friend called. He says he is coming to pick you up at seven.'

I sat in Ed's kitchen, watching him cook. He'd been unexpectedly called down south he explained; there was some business that needed sorting out. He bustled good-humouredly around, chatting and chopping and handing me vegetables to peel. He refused to have servants, he announced as the noodles boiled over; it was just another manifestation of post colonial domination. I tried not to look dismayed, this not being a problem I'd yet encountered. Now he was describing his attempts to set up the schools, recounting the tale of a lengthy meeting with a government official in which only after his third cup of tea did he realize that the man had nothing remotely to do with the education department, but simply wanted to practise his English.

I hooted with laughter. I could not remember when I had last enjoyed a conversation so much; it was like being tumbled, fast and furious, along a frothing river. He talked constantly and had a habit of suddenly interrupting himself. 'Am I droning on?' he said more than once. 'You need to tell me to shut up! It's just so long since I've had someone around who I can really talk to!' Then he would launch into a hilarious account of his attempts to get his visa extended, or a complex description of national politics, which was abruptly ended by him clapping his hand to his forehead. 'Fuck me, I'm doing it

again! I'm going to take a vow of silence and you're going
to tell me about *you*.'

I started to falteringly tell him about my 'job'.

'I just don't get why they've bothered to have me as an
intern if there isn't anything real to do,' I said. 'Every time I
ask them what I should be doing, they're like, "Oh, Sarah,
are you suffering very badly? It must be so hard coming from
England to a poverty-stricken country like ours. You must rest
if it's too hot for you." Yet all I want is to actually get on
with *doing* something!' I banged my drink down. It was such
a relief to be sharing my frustrations. 'I've basically decided
that the reason I'm here is to give them a laugh. It's doing
my head in – one minute I'm the local clown and the next
some lady laa-di-daa who can't stand being out of air-
conditioning for a second without swooning.'

He chuckled. He was wearing a long white shirt which
accentuated his blue eyes. 'They're probably trying to make
it work but are as much at a loss as you.'

I gazed into space, knowing he was right.

'It makes me wonder if I shouldn't forget it all. I mean, I
can't help thinking that I'm just wasting everyone's time. I don't
know what I thought I could achieve here, apart from just
wafting around being *white*. I keep seeing all these UN jeeps
zooming around and everything and I can't see how I fit in.'

Ed was silent, frowning as he chucked vegetables into a wok.
'I mean, take you,' I went on, 'you haven't just parachuted in
on a whim, have you? You've spent years building up to this.
You can speak the language, you know how things work, what
the possibilities are. I *really* admire that.'

He shrugged; he seemed oddly downcast. 'Maybe I'm not
the person you think I am,' he said quietly. 'Maybe you've
got me all wrong.'

I chuckled. 'What, you mean that you're not really a nice
guy running an NGO in Bangladesh but a Foreign Office
spy, sent here to rout out Islamic extremists? Or maybe
you're on the run, having committed a multimillion-pound
fraud, and this –' I gestured at the kitchen – 'is actually a
money-laundering operation.'

He smiled. 'OK, I admit it. I'm a serial killer.'

'A serial killer doing some voluntary work on the side.'

'Yeah, that just about covers it . . .'

We paused, the joke exhausted. Ed regarded me quietly, his face suddenly serious.

'Outward appearances can be deceptive, you know,' he finally said.

'What do you mean?'

He sucked at his cheeks then suddenly grinned. 'Just that we should spend more time getting to know each other, I guess. You know, uncover all the layers.'

He smiled at me enigmatically, making my belly do a little jump.

'It's like this place,' he continued, apparently oblivious to the effect he was having. 'You've had a particular experience of it in the months that you've been here, but underneath the surface it's much more complicated.' He started heaping the sizzling vegetables on top of the noodles. 'Just when you think you've got the measure of it, another layer falls away and there's something else in its place.'

'How do you mean?'

'Just that you can't trust first impressions. And at the moment with your NGO, that's all you've got. But there's probably lots of things going on under the surface that you don't see, just like everything else here. *Voila!*'

He put the plate of food in front of me. 'Eat up. There's somewhere I want to take you.'

It was after ten when we reached the winding alleys of Old Dhaka. The taxi bumped along the narrow lanes, stalling interminably behind the rickshaws and pedestrians that clogged the road. When progress became impossible, Ed paid the driver and we got out of the car. I did not ask where we were going.

We walked east, in the direction of a blue-tiled minaret that rose over the massed roofs. Lines of flags fluttered above us, relics of a bygone election. There was going to be another election next year, Ed said as we passed a row of campaigning posters. The opposition parties were already accusing the government of gerrymandering; that was why there had been so many strikes and marches. It was a volatile situation: only last week three people had been killed in a riot.

By now we had entered a bazaar, passing triangular mounds of spices, jars filled with indeterminate powders and sacks of gnarled roots. Plump traders sat cross-legged over their wares, yelling cheerfully at the passers by: men in lunghis and Punjabi shirts clutching shopping bags and umbrellas; youths with reflector shades and baggy jeans; safari jacketed office workers driving mopeds that meandered through the crowd. Darkness had perfumed the air with spices, incense and the heady stench of the open drains, the grey sludge trickling at our feet. I pulled my scarf over my head, uncomfortably aware of the glances I was attracting, for the evening streets were the reserve of the men who jostled around the stalls and the few women we passed were covered by black burquas. Finally we turned off the main thoroughfare into a dark alley, the buildings on either side closing in. There was no one around.

Stopping outside a small wooden door, set several feet from the ground, Ed bent down and pulled back the rusty grill. The building seemed ancient, its decrepit walls bulging alarmingly, as if collapse were imminent. After a short pause I heard a low voice on the other side. Ed said something in Bengali, and the door swung open.

'This is what I meant about the layers,' he whispered as we stepped over the door's high wooden lip. 'The way nothing's what it seems.'

We were standing in a courtyard, surrounded on all sides by the decaying storeys of an old-fashioned family house, its upper balconies screened from the gaze of strangers by metal grilles, over which rows of brightly coloured saris were hung. A large birdcage, filled with yellow canaries that hopped hopefully from bar to bar, was suspended from the lowest balcony.

I gazed around the courtyard, astonished. It was crammed with weird-looking men, who with their ashy dreadlocks and ragged beards, resembled the crusties that used to camp in the fields near Brighton, with their trucks and decommissioned ambulances. Half-naked, the revellers shook their heads in time to the tablas that two men in red dhotis were frantically beating on a raised platform in the centre. Others may have initially been more respectable, but now had torn off their shirts, beating their naked chests and chanting 'Allah Huh', their glistening faces turned towards the chink of night sky above.

Enthroned on a heavy wooden chair in the centre of the platform was the object of the crowd's devotion: an enormous man whose black beard reached his chest, his long white robe stretching tightly over a bountiful belly. He had his eyes closed, as if in a trance. The place reeked of ganja.

'It's Abdul Pir,' Ed whispered. 'Their guru?'

'You what?'

'A guru. Like, a kind of living saint? Tasneem's brother is a follower.'

I nodded, not sure that I had understood.

Steering me by my elbow he led me through the crumbling stone pillars to the other side of the courtyard where an area was separated off by bars.

'This is the women's section. I won't be far off.'

'Where are you going?'

'To have an audience with Abdul Pir. I'm going to ask his advice!'

He plunged into the crowd.

'Hey, Sister, be with us!'

Hands grabbed my arm, pulling me inside the cage, where twenty or so women were squashed up against the bars. I glanced nervously around, taking in the swaying bodies. Some of the women had untied their hair, allowing it to whip across their faces as they moved back and forth in ecstasy; others stood in their petticoats, their saris unravelled and thrown aside like sweet wrappings. These were not the plump ladies of the middle-class districts, but poor women in bare feet with gaunt bodies and pinched faces. Next to me, a young woman was working herself into a froth of passion. Her eyes rolling back in her head, her body jerked rhythmically to the drums. She was moaning something I had no hope of understanding.

The fug of dope was making me woozy; it was so hot that I could hardly breathe. Through the bars I noticed Ed by the stage, whispering into the robed man's ear. Then suddenly he disappeared, engulfed by the crowd. Now the Pir had risen from his throne and was reciting strange, magical prayers into his mike. The ululating words seemed to go on forever, pouring around me as my body pressed against the bars. I wanted to get away, but the woman was gripping my arm, her eyes wild. Leaning towards me, her body started to rock forwards, her eyes dilating as she muttered Allah's name, over and over again.

I stood transfixed, hopelessly caught in the pulse of the moment. I did not know where Ed was but no longer cared. We would find each other, I thought with gathering euphoria.

Finally giving in, I closed my eyes, reduced to the sum of the physical sensations: the chanting and drumbeat and over-powering reek of skunk. I had become joined with the massed devotees, my body moving in tangent with the other women, my hair trailing across my face. As I shook my head to the tabla I could feel my mind separating off. I was moving upwards, hovering above my limp body which tossed beneath, the silk *orna* that earlier I had draped over my head falling around my shoulders, my *kameez* scrunched up behind.

'Sarah!'

Opening my eyes I saw Ed on the other side of the bars; he was touching my fingers, pulling me back. Beneath me, the floor tipped queasily.

'Are you OK?'

I blinked at him dizzily. Sweat dripped from his face and his shirt stuck to his chest in damp patches. He seemed excited.

'Let's go, shall we?'

'*Eh, Beti, aychen . . .*'

Their hands levering me through the crowd, the women helped propel me from the cage into his outstretched arms. Finally reunited, we scurried to the back of the courtyard where people were slumped in various stages of blissful collapse. It was cooler here, under the stone pillars. We stood for a moment in silence, panting and giggling, like kids who'd gatecrashed a forbidden party.

'Whew!'

Ed nodded at me happily.

'Not quite what you'd expect, is it?'

'It reminds me of this heavy metal gig I went to when I was about fifteen.'

'Is that why you were doing that head banging?'

I glanced into his smiling eyes. With his wireless specs and slim frame, some people might have thought him a geek. His hair was thinning on top and he had a slight stoop, as if constantly trying to appear smaller. Yet to me he was so hand-some that it was an effort not to put out my hand and place it against his cheek.

'It was quite freaky, actually.'

'Was it, now?' His fingers touched mine.

'So what were you asking your guru?' I eventually said.

He chuckled. 'I was asking him what I should do.'

'About what?'

'About you, of course.'

Pushing me against the wall, he kissed me on the lips, so swiftly that it could almost have been an accident.

'That was very naughty,' he said. 'One really isn't supposed to do things like that in public.'

He had taken my hand, and was surreptitiously lacing his fingers through mine.

'Is *that* what he told you to do?'

'Nope. He said I should marry a nice Muslim girl.'

'And are you going to take his advice?'

Pulling off his glasses, he started to polish them on the side of his shirt. Without them he looked younger, more vulnerable.

'Doesn't look like it,' he said softly.

'Doesn't it?'

Pushing the glasses back over his nose, he reached out and pressed his forefinger to my lips.

'Not right at this moment, no.'

Much later, when we had returned to his quiet, dark house, it was I who Ed unravelled. Uncovering my layers with his gentle hands it did not take long to get to my core. Here, there was nothing hidden, no more to reveal; we were two halves, no longer apart.

Afterwards, we lay in the half light, listening to the cicadas.

EIGHT

Now that we had discovered each other Ed and I were rarely apart. Finally, pushing thirty, I discovered how it felt to fall in love. As I'd suspected with Nick, this wasn't so much the comfortable satisfaction of riding down a well-trodden road but the overwhelming thrill of arriving somewhere unexpected. It was a place where I was certain I wanted to stay. I loved everything about Ed: his shoulders, the fuzz of hair at his belly, the length and elegance of his slim hands; his ability to laugh at himself, his understanding of the world.

He was so energetic, filled with a purpose that swept me along. He had come to Bangladesh to 'make a difference' and that was what he was going to do. Whenever he uttered the phrase he pulled a goony face. Yet despite the surface irony, he was serious. Our roles were clear. Here was a place filled with need, and here we were, with so much to give. How could anything go wrong?

We didn't discuss the past, only the future. When I told him about Nick, he simply shrugged. I grew up in Hampshire, I added, my dad was an accountant, my mum a primary school teacher; it was hardly very scintillating. In turn, I knew the bare bones of his background, but not much more. His parents had died when he was small; he'd been brought up by his aunt and older sister. On the finer details he refused to be drawn. It didn't seem to matter. We were in Bangladesh, thousands of miles from our old lives. Why should either of us dwell on the people we used to be?

Eager to leave Mahila Shadinota Shamittee I quickly moved into Ed's house in Banani.

'I've decided to work for Schools for Change,' I told Mr Abrar, my face turning puce. 'I hope I haven't let you down.'

'Ah, Sarah, this is very sad. Can I not persuade you to stay?'

'The thing is, I mean, I'd love to, but at the moment there isn't really much for me to do, is there? Perhaps later, when I've got more experience, I can come back?'

Standing up from his desk, Abrar gave his head a tiny, almost imperceptible shake: a gesture that I had learnt signified agreement.

'That would be very fine. When will you be leaving us?'

'Er, today . . .'

His face fell. 'So soon!'

'It's just that I feel like I don't really have much to offer here.'

He didn't contradict me, just twitched his head again. 'But you will be visiting us?'

'Of course I will!'

By the time the afternoon azan called I had packed my few possessions, given Baby a hug, and hailed a baby-taxi to take me to Ed's place. As the puttering vehicle pulled into the traffic I felt light-headed with relief. I may no longer officially have a 'job' but finally I had a purpose.

*   *   *

That evening, Ed and I discussed the future.

'Come and help me in Lalalpur,' he begged. 'There's so much you could do.'

'Like what?'

'What do you mean "like what"? You're an experienced teacher. You've got masses to offer.'

I was lying in his arms. Bending over, he kissed my forehead.

'I don't want to be a kept woman,' I mumbled.

'Don't be idiotic! You'd be working for your keep. Come on, please say yes . . .'

I glanced at him. 'I don't know . . .'

He sighed in exasperation. 'Of course you know! What could be more simple?'

'I suppose it's just that we don't really know each other that well . . . I mean, supposing you find out what a horrible rat bag I really am?'

I pictured Nick's tight expression as he'd watched me pack my things. I should have put my arms around him, told him he'd find someone else, but I was so filled with guilt that I was unable to speak. We had been together for three years: he had stayed at my parents' place at Christmas and wanted us to buy a flat in the Marina; yet my feelings for him had dried up, like a dew pond in a drought.

'Don't be ridiculous,' said Ed. 'How could you ever be a rat bag?'

Sitting up, he stared at me ferociously, then suddenly whipped the sheet off my naked backside. 'I'm going to hold you hostage on this bed until you agree,' he hissed. 'And you'll be stark bollock naked!'

A week later, we were almost ready to leave. There was just one detail that we needed to arrange, Ed announced the evening before our departure. We were sitting in the garden, fireflies flitting around the lamps. He seemed nervous.

'We'll have to say we're married,' he said. 'The villagers will want to know.'

Placing a gold ring on my lap, he glanced shyly at me.

'Would you mind wearing it? It's just a cheap thing I got from New Market.'

I picked the ring up, weighing the imitation gold in the

palm of my hand. The request had made me feel oddly giddy, as if I had climbed too far up a cliff.

'Sure,' I said, feigning insouciance. 'Whatever.'

It was almost the monsoon. Ed had hired a minivan for the journey from Chittagong to the village, but a section of the road had been washed away, so we had to walk the final mile. It had been raining heavily all morning, thick sheets of water that reduced the world to a blur. As we approached our new home the sky was clearing, the clouds scattering towards the sea. On either side of the muddy road clusters of low bamboo buildings huddled in the waterlogged fields, islands of habitation in the swampy morass. On the road ahead was a small mosque, a cluster of stalls that sold chai and *chanchuri*, and the cyclone shelter. It was beside this that Ed was planning to build his school.

'The sea's over there,' he said, pointing left. 'Near our house.'

Already people were emerging from their homes. The children reached us first, yelling 'Mister Edward!' and trying to pull our bags from our hands. Glancing across the fields I noticed a group of women hovering like brightly coloured butterflies on the edges of their homestead.

'Not far now . . .' Ed winked at me. 'OK?'

'Never been better.'

We had reached the mosque. Beside this was a large stone house divided by the road by an ornate wall, then the chai stalls. Now, as I peered along the road, I noticed a young man, hurrying towards us.

'Ed! You have arrived!'

Grabbing Ed's hand, the man started to pump it up and down, chuckling with pleasure. He had hazel eyes and teeth that protruded a little, giving him a slightly startled expression. His check shirt was tucked into stone washed jeans and his neat brown feet encased in leather sandals: an educated guy, from the city. Turning to me, he took my hand enthusiastically.

'Sarah, meet Aunik,' Ed said. 'Aunik, meet Sarah, my wife.'

I sucked on my lips, trying to prevent myself from giggling. 'Hiya.'

'Aunik is our brilliant teacher,' said Ed. 'He's going to be working in Jhomgram, over there.' He indicated a clump of trees and buildings across the fields. 'In the meantime he's been getting us established in Lalalpur.'

Aunik grinned. 'As you will find, there's a lot to do!'

The cheering children in tow, we proceeded towards the tea stalls, where a small crowd had accumulated. I eyed the waiting figures nervously: despite Ed's assurances, it seemed audacious to be walking into their community with my broken Bangla and inexperience. It was, however, too late for doubt, for by now we were surrounded by people: young men in shirts and *lunghis*, barefooted children with amulets strung around their necks, labourers from the fields, their *lunghis* looped between their legs.

'This is our Chairman, Roul Syed,' Aunik announced, indicating a large, well padded man in a white Punjabi and *lunghi*, who was nodding at me genially.

'*Salaam-e-lekum*,' he murmured, bowing slightly. I had been about to offer him my hand, but now remembered that this was not expected of a woman.

'*Wha-lekum-salem*,' I repeated, smiling hopefully. The Chairman chuckled. Turning his head, he hawked up a stream of red, paan-stained spittle, which landed neatly on the grass beside the path.

'*Bangla janen!*' *She knows Bengali!*

'Well, kind of . . .'

We were being ushered towards the tea stalls, our heads shielded from the sun by the large black umbrellas that had mushroomed above us. As chairs were fetched everyone was talking at once: tea and sweetmeats called for, directions given concerning our bags, which had been seized from our hands. As I sat down, I caught a glimpse of my rucksack disappearing down the path on the back of one of the thinner, more ragged-looking men.

'Where's he going?'

'It's OK,' Ed said. 'He's taking it to our house.'

By now we were surrounded by so many people that it was hard to see beyond the wall of bodies. Catching the eye of a little girl who peeped from behind her father's legs, I winked. For a second she gawped at me with her large, kohl-painted eyes. Then, her face creasing with a giant grin, she winked back. Beside me, Ed had pushed back his chair. Seizing Aunik's arm, he stood up.

'My friends!' he said, in Bengali. 'Thank you for welcoming us into your beautiful village . . .'

There was an appreciative murmur from the crowd, followed

by a ripple of applause. I stared into Ed's glowing face, amazed both by his speech making ability and my own comprehension of what he was saying.

'We come with one mission,' Ed went on, his face suddenly grave. 'And that is to provide a school for the poorest children here. You have a school in Noton Bazaar, I know, but can everyone afford the uniforms and books? My friend Aunik has told me all about how few of the children in your village attend school at all because of the costs, and with him and my wife Sarah . . .' I blushed furiously, studying my muddy toes, '. . . we plan to create a school for the whole community.'

Standing, the Chairman cleared his throat. 'Allah be praised,' he said softly.

'*Eh, beti.*'

Someone was tugging on my sleeve. Glancing around, I saw an old woman standing behind me, her white hair tied into a tight bun, her plump body covered by a worn green sari. '*Aychen.*' Come.

Hooking her fingers assertively around my elbow, she pulled me up. 'It's not good to be sitting with all those men,' she muttered.

Gripping my arm firmly with her leathery hand, she led me along the road and into the compound next to the mosque. Unlike the small huts we had passed on the outskirts of the village or the straw-roofed buildings that were scattered across the fields, these buildings were made of brick. Surrounding a generous sandy forecourt, the low houses were divided from each other by bamboo screens, their wealth obvious from the TV aerials that protruded from their cement roofs and the huge, lily-covered pond on the far side of the court, with its fancily painted stone ghat.

'Roul Chairman's *bari!*' the old lady shouted as she pulled me inside the first building. 'My son!'

At first it was too dim to see anything, but as my eyes grew accustomed to the darkness I realized that the room was filled with women. I peered into their curious faces, smiling hopefully. Several were holding infants on their hips; one girl had the damp bundle of a newborn baby tucked into her sari. More giggling children pressed around the doors or squatted by my feet on the earth floor.

'Sit down, daughter!'

Indicating the huge wooden bed that dominated the room,

the old lady hoisted herself nimbly onto the hard wooden slats. As I sat down beside her, she took my hand, squinting at me through her thick, pebble glasses.

'What's your name?'

'Sarah.'

'No, you're wrong!'

'Am I?' I stared at her in surprise.

She peered back, straight faced. 'To me, your name is "daughter". And Mr Edward is my son-in-law, and we welcome you into our home!'

Hours later, after I had drunk many cups of tea, been served a large dish of biriani and been shown into every house in the compound, the women folded a stiff cotton sari around my waist and led me back to the chai stall, where, surrounded by a fug of cigarette smoke, Ed and Aunik were being entertained by the men. Across the fields, the sun was setting in a blaze of orange.

'Nice sari.' Ed murmured as I reached him. 'Had fun?'

'A blast.'

'Shall we go?'

Our hosts led us down the path that snaked across the fields towards the sea. It was dusk now: the sky turning lilac, the air scented with incense. As the azan started to wail, we filed in a long line through a grove of coconut trees, my hand tightly gripped by the Chairman's mother. Mosquitoes whined around my face.

'Here we are!'

Set back from the path in a thicket of mango and coconut, the decrepit building crumbled into the sandy soil. Thick boards covered the windows; the wooden steps that led to the front terrace had partly rotted away.

'We're going to fix it up,' Ed said hurriedly, glancing at my face. 'Make it really nice.'

It was growing too dark to see. Squatting, one of the men lit a hurricane lamp that he'd had hanging from his arm. Now that we had been safely delivered to our destinations, our hosts were turning back. Later, I would hear stories of ghosts that possessed anyone foolish enough to be wandering under the trees at dusk.

'Shall we go?' the Chairman asked, nodding at us.

'Yes, go.'

The exchange was a formality, another custom that Ed had effortlessly acquired.

'May God be with you.'

'*Kuda Hafis.*'

Finally alone, Ed and I climbed the rickety steps and pulled open the screen doors, spluttering at the dust.

'Are there going to be cockroaches?'

'Erm . . .'

We stepped inside, dead insects crunching under our feet as we swung the lantern around. Besides a large wooden bed and some pots and pans, the place was empty. A bare bulb hung from a flex in the centre of the cracked ceiling; Ed was fiddling with the switch, but as we soon discovered, the electricity only came on for an hour or so each day.

'What do you think?'

In the dim light I could just about make out his face. He squinted at me, frowning.

'I think . . .' I looked at his furrowed face and burst out laughing. 'I think it's bloody horrible!'

It was too hot to sleep and the thin mattress that accompanied the monstrous bed too hard. We escaped to the beach, where we sat in the cool sand, gazing up at the stars. The sea was calm that night, apparently benign. Behind us, palm trees shifted in the breeze; a few hundred yards away we could make out the shapes of fishing dhows, resting on the shore. Besides a barking dog, all we could hear was the suck and slap of the waves.

NINE

We awoke the next morning to the rain battering on the bungalow's tin roof.

'It's just a shower,' Ed muttered as he peered through the rusty window shutters. 'Look, it's already clearing up.'

Rolling out of bed, I padded across the dusty floor towards the terrace.

'Come back . . .'

'No, let's get up. It's a brand new day.'

I pulled open the veranda doors. Sunlight streamed in, trans-forming the puddles into dazzling pools. On the wooden slats before me, a large toad was flopping cumbersomely towards the steps. I gazed into the distance, taking in the luminescent fields and wide arching sky. The world seemed to be spread before me, sparkling and new.

'Good morning, Sarah!'

Aunik had suddenly appeared through the coconut grove, his umbrella hooked jauntily over his wrist.

'Are you and Edward ready? Your students are assembled.'

Thirty minutes later we were back at the Chairman's house; until the school building was completed classes were being held in an outhouse on the far side of his compound. As we pushed open the tin door, we could hear the excited hubbub of children's voices.

'Everyone is eager to meet you,' Aunik whispered.

Holding my breath, I followed him and Ed into the gloomy barn.

Before us, a group of twenty or so boys were sitting on jute mats that had been spread over the dirt floor. I scanned their faces, taking in their shining, expectant expressions. A couple were wearing *lunghis* and had fluff on their lips; others looked as young as five. As we appeared, they jumped to their feet, shouting '*Salam-e-lekum!*' Holding up his hand, Aunik signalled for them to sit down.

'These children are very poor,' he said in English. 'This chap here –' he signalled at a boy in shorts and bare feet who was grinning at us from the front – 'has to support his mother and four sisters.'

'What, you mean he *works*?' I asked, appalled. He did not look much older than ten or eleven. 'When?'

'After class. You'll see him later, labouring in the fields.'

'What about the rest?'

'They all work. It's normal.'

Clapping his hands, Aunik addressed the class. 'Today is very special, because we have our new teachers who have come all the way from England, Mr Edward and Mrs Sarah.'

The children stared at us gravely.

'Shall we show them our alphabet?'

Taking a stick that was leaning by the door, he pointed to a poster pinned to the mud wall. On it, the letters of the Bengali alphabet were depicted: a snake for the 'sh' of *shaf*, a cow for the 'gh' of guru. As Aunik pointed to each picture, the children droningly repeated the sounds.

'Bravo!' Ed cried as they reached the end. 'Now watch this.'

Producing three small balls from the pocket of his jeans, he started to juggle them in the air. The children watched, open mouthed. Suddenly he tossed one to the boy with the bum fluff.

'What's your name?' he called, still juggling.

'Jamil!'

'Throw it back then.'

Pirouetting, he threw the second ball just as he caught the first. This time, it landed in the lap of one of the smaller boys sitting in the front.

'What's *your* name?'

'Tufael Abdul Mohammed,' the boy mouthed, astonished.

'And mine's Ed!'

The children glanced at each other, unsure how to react. Then slowly, in a cresting wave, they started to laugh. As he threw a third ball, the boy who caught it called out his name, lobbing it high in the air for Ed to grab. A few minutes later, everyone was joining in, shouting out their names and waving for the ball to be thrown in their direction. After each boy had had a turn, Ed snatched the balls from the air and held them behind his back.

'OK. As I throw, Sarah's going to point to the letter, and the person who catches the ball has to shout out the sound.'

Taking the baton, I turned to the poster. Out of the corner of my eye I saw Aunik creeping out of the door.

'Good luck,' he whispered.

Grinning, Ed lobbed the ball at Jamil.

'*Go!*'

An hour later, we emerged from the barn, exhausted and exhilarated. The children swarmed happily around us, grabbing at our hands.

'I didn't know juggling was part of Friere's methodology,' I muttered.

'Didn't you?'

'No, and nor did I know I was having a relationship with Coco the Clown.'

'Well, as you can see, I have many and varied skills.'

'You can say that again.'

In the compound the Chairman was sitting astride a wooden chair in the centre of the yard, watching as a labourer herded his cows into their barn. The animals plodded nonchalantly across our path, ignoring the young man's attempt to hurry them along with the stick that he swished at their scraggy behinds. As he noticed us approach, the Chairman rose, snapping on the large silver watch that was hanging from his hairy wrist.

'Please,' he said, taking Ed's hand. 'You are my guests. My wife has prepared your lunch. You must eat it with me.'

From the doorway, I could see the women from yesterday peeking out. Ed smiled widely, placing his hand on his chest.

'It would be an honour,' he said, nodding politely.

We followed the Chairman inside his house. From the cattle shed we could hear soft bovine munching and a sudden snatch of music: his work completed, the labourer was playing a bamboo flute.

TEN

We developed a routine. Whilst I dozed in the warm hollow where he had lain, Ed rolled out of bed at dawn. After ten minutes of pacing he'd sit at his rickety desk and fill his exercise books with his small, precise writing. Despite his manic energy he had an orderly side to his character; he liked to keep notes, to record meetings and appointments, compiling long inventories of 'things to be done'. Mainly these lists were practical. There was work to be done on the bungalow, provisions to be acquired, plans for the establishment of the school. In other books he would jot down ideas, fragments of conversations, or even passages from the books he'd brought from Dhaka: histories of Bengal, treatises concerning the nature of rural empowerment or the state of the Indian peasantry. 'Power is the currency of the Bengali village,' he had scribbled on the one page I glanced at before he'd indignantly grabbed the book back, 'and hierarchy its rate of exchange.' Underneath this he had recorded the entire citation, as if preparing for a dissertation.

By the time I usually awoke, he had embarked on his yoga, shooing the toads off the veranda as he lay down his mat. Watching him contort his lanky legs gave me the giggles. 'Quit snickering!' he'd hiss, if he noticed me peeking. 'Come and join in!'

After breakfast we'd walk across the fields for our classes: Ed taught the boys whilst I held an English class for a small group of women who gathered in a room in the Chairman's compound. Much of what I attempted was wildly inappropriate: amidst much hilarity I tried to make them participate in role-play exercises, or learn the English for their body parts. At this, they had pulled their saris over their heads, hooting with laughter. Clearly, it was I, not them, who had most to learn. No matter: my long-term plan was teach literacy to the poorer girls and women. First, I had to improve my Bengali.

In the afternoons, as Ed attended his meetings or fetched provisions from Noton Bazaar, I would wander across the fields and visit my new neighbours. I had only to walk down the path and someone would come running through the trees to pull me into their yard. There, I was seated on a stool and quickly surrounded by women and children. Their arms around my waist, the women would stroke my hair or arms, exclaiming at my beautiful white skin. Ed and I were such good people, they'd say. We'd come all the way from our rich country, to help them. They should thank Allah for their luck. I'd smile and nod, then say something to make them laugh. It was me who was lucky to be with *them,* I'd quip, and they'd fall about. Please, please, I'd respond when, on cue, one of the women offered me her baby to take to London, couldn't I just stay here? My coarse Bangla, ever littered with mistakes, turned me into the local comedian. Despite my inability to hold a decent conversation, to tie my sari neatly, or to cover my head when the azan called, I had never felt so adored

There was one woman in particular whose face I sought out: Syeda. She must have been around my age for her thin face was unlined, but like most people in the village she had little idea of when she was born. She and her children lived with her mother in a rundown homestead a few hundred metres across the fields. When I clumsily enquired about her husband she shrugged in a way that indicated disgust. 'Gone,' she said, jerking her chin in the direction of the road. I never found out why.

Something drew me to her – her ready laughter, perhaps, or the unspoken rebellion hinted at in her stance: hand on her hip, she'd plant herself before me, her head cocked back as she quizzed me about my life. She was less likely than other women to hurry away when unrelated men appeared; so long as she was neatly buttoned into her black burqua she seemed unfazed by visiting the bazaar, an area of the village to which women rarely ventured. She and her elderly mother managed their affairs alone, she declared when I'd asked about her family. They didn't need a man.

Syeda was not only my closest friend in the village, she was also my teacher. Most of the phrases I had learnt in Dhaka made her giggle, some she didn't understand. 'That's big people's talk,' she'd say. 'I can't get the hang of it.'

In its place she taught me the village lingo. She was a patient teacher, taking care to enunciate carefully and keeping a straight face at my mistakes. 'Say it again Sarah,' she'd mouth. '*Khet* not *Kat*.' Her training programme had its limits: despite my pleas she never allowed me to help her peel the small heap of gnarled vegetables she was preparing.

'It's too sharp for you,' she said, indicating her *dag*: a lethal curving blade that rested in a block of wood on the ground. To cut with the blade, one had to sit astride the wood, and swipe downwards. 'You're not used to it.'

'Teach me then!'

She regarded me steadily. 'Sister, you're too soft.'

She was right. My pampered British upbringing had left me unprepared for the realities of life without electricity or running water. If one wanted to wash, it was with a bucket or in the pond; if one wanted to cook, a fire had to be lit. Back home we knew nothing about real work, I concluded, and nor did we know how to be content. With nothing to do and no God, we'd settled for stuffing our faces on processed pap and worshipping celebrities. I didn't believe in Syeda's Allah, but I had nothing to offer in his place.

I did not linger over thoughts of home. I sent the odd letter to my parents, but rarely thought of them or of Nick, my memories of my old life dwindling to a small section of my mind that I rarely probed. Here, in the present, there was so much to do. We held our classes in the morning and in the afternoons visited the poorest homes in the village in an effort to recruit more pupils. In the evenings Ed taught fishermen and agricultural labourers by the light of their hurricane lamps. The bungalow was swept, swabbed and filled with wicker furniture that we brought from Noton Bazaar. Then there were the endless visits to people's homes, where rice and fish were piled on our plates and even after the third or fourth helping we were berated for not eating enough. When Ed and I were alone we would discuss the school and the village, not Britain or the past. It seemed irrelevant.

I made a garden. With Syeda's help I dug the land in front of the bungalow, where we planted tomato plants, peas and a trailing jasmine for the veranda railings. Every day there were visitors to entertain: locals who came out of curiosity or to pay their respects. Despite Ed's attempts to explain that all he was doing was establishing a school, most treated us as if we were living saints, donators of limitless charity, sent from the bountiful West to distribute medicines, loans, and hand-outs. One old woman who had staggered to the bungalow to ask for alms, fell to the floor, pressing her forehead to Ed's feet. Another man presented a boy, his arm bent at a sickening angle, requesting money to get it fixed. If someone was ill, a representative from their family would be sent to solicit medicine. The supply of plasters, bandages and painkillers that we'd brought from Dhaka was quickly depleted.

'Are you sure about this?' Ed muttered, after I'd handed over another dose of oral rehydration salts. 'Aren't we just creating more dependency?'

I glanced at him. In my third year at university I had written an essay on the power relations created by Northern charities in the South. Yet now that I was here, the difference between the essay and reality were like that between a cartoon and a real person.

'We can't not give them anything, can we?'

'I dunno. It bothers me . . .'

'Come on, don't make everything so bloody complicated.' Leaning over, I kissed him on the tip of his nose.

Yet whilst I was revelling in my role as Mother Theresa, our attempts at cookery were disastrous. The kitchen consisted of a tin shed at the back, with an earthen fire. Neither Ed or I could ever get the sticks to light properly, we burnt the rice and were hopeless at producing the strong, sweet tea that the locals drank. Eventually a man appeared before the bungalow, smiling meekly. He was one of Chairman Roul's many cousins, he said. The Chairman had sent him.

'He's called Abdullah,' Ed whispered as he showed him to the kitchen. 'The Chairman says he really needs the work . . . I promised we'd take him on.'

I poked my finger in his ribs, grinning. 'I thought you said that having servants was a sign of colonial domination.'

'Hmm, well I guess "local conditions call for local strategies" . . .'

'You what?'

'It's in this book I've been reading. It's the latest development catchphrase.'

I eyed him sardonically. 'That's OK then.'

The rains set in, pounding the countryside and turning the sea into a blur. It seemed as if the whole village would slip into the muddy morass. Everything we owned was damp; our books mouldy, the mosquito net that hung around our bed rotting. It even got inside my skin. The strange red marks that had appeared on my hands were ringworm, Aunik proclaimed, a tropical menace.

As the deluge became more insistent it was increasingly difficult to move around. To get to the road we had to wade, knee deep through deep gullies filled with mire, picking off the leeches when we reached dry ground. The rain could last for days, so classes were out of the question. Ed and I would lie on the bed, listening as the water pounded the tin roof. I loved the sense of being marooned; curled against his body I imagined that we were castaways, floating forever on warm seas.

By October the clouds finally pulled back and the sun regained control of the sky. Gradually the bogs that for weeks had surrounded the bungalow dried and shrank into passable paths and earth boundaries and tracks appeared from the water-logged fields. Suddenly everyone was busy. People pulled their bedding into the yards to dry, *chulas* were rebuilt from the claggy mud, roofs repaired. The building season had arrived.

The school's foundations were laid. On Chairman Roul's suggestion a small ceremony was held in what one day would be the school courtyard. As with most religious rituals, women were not allowed to attend, so the Chairman's mother and I observed from the road as the village imam led the men in prayers. Ed stood amongst the worshippers, head bowed and hands cupped in supplication. As I watched him kneel, his face furrowed in concentration as he tried to remember what to do, I adored him more than ever.

That night, Quranic verses were broadcast to the village over an antiquated sound system. Ed and I lay on our lumpy bed, listening to the strange, wavering notes of the imam's Arabic, drifting over the fields. On the horizon, the sky flickered with distant lightning.

ELEVEN

May 8th, 2003

The first thing I think when I wake is that Ed is on the terrace, doing his yoga. For four or five seconds I lie in a state of innocence. Then I open my eyes, see the Laura Ashley chintz that surrounds me, and remember everything: I am in Dhaka and Ed is *gone*. Gasping, I stuff my hand into my mouth.

It's amazing that my body can produce so many tears. Stuffing the pillow over my face I lie on my back for a while, shuddering. After a while I stop crying. Ed is *with* me, I'm sure; I can feel the warmth of his body, pressed against mine. If I keep my eyes screwed shut, I can even hear his voice.

'Ed?'

'Hiya, sexy.'

He's stroking my hair. 'What are we going to do with you today?'

In a minute he will kiss me. If I stretch out my fingers I will feel his face, the weight of his damp body, rolling against my back.

'Ed?' I whisper. 'Are you here?'

'Of course I am. I'm not going to leave you behind, am I?'

'Do you promise?'

But I can't hear his answer, for someone is rapping briskly on the door. I sit up, wiping my slimy cheeks with the backs of my hands. Morning must be well advanced, for bright slabs of light fall through the curtains.

'Sarah, dear, are you awake? There's a call.'

It's Lydia, bearing the phone. Clambering out of bed, I grab it from her soft hands. My heart is hammering.

'Hello?'

'Sarah?'

It's Dan.

'Have you found Ed?' I gasp. 'What's happened?'

It probably lasts for only a few seconds, but his silence seems to extend forever. Eventually he says: 'There's still no sign of him I'm afraid. But you need to leave.'

'*What?*'

'You need to get on the next plane to London, if not today then tomorrow at the latest. I've checked and there's an Emirates flight that has seats. If you like I'll arrange your ticket. It isn't safe for you here.'

I can't breathe. Exhaling, I fix my eyes on Lydia, who is hovering by the bed, gazing at me with concern.

'But why?' I whisper. 'What's happened?'

'I can't talk about it over the phone,' Dan says quietly. 'But I've unearthed some rather unpleasant things about this mess Ed was in . . . I may be overreacting, but there's a chance it could affect you . . .'

'What sort of things?'

'I really can't go into details,' he murmurs. 'Suffice to say, he's got himself into far worse trouble than we thought.'

'Has he?' I want to scream that he should explain what he means, but my voice is pitching too high and hysterical to continue.

'I'm still trying to get to the bottom of it . . . At this stage I can't tell you anything definite. If you go back to the UK, I'll be in touch in a couple of days.'

'But what about *Ed*?'

Frowning, Lydia steps across the room and fiddles with the hairbrushes arranged on the dresser. Perhaps she regrets allowing me into her home. It can't be very pleasant, having a screeching stranger installed in her guest suite.

'I still don't know exactly what's happened,' Dan continues soothingly. 'Given my position here I have to be really careful, but as soon as there's any news I'll be in contact. You'll leave a phone number in the UK with Lydia and Mike?'

'OK . . .'

'And you still have his briefcase, with all those emails? You say he always printed everything out?'

'Yes.'

'Good. Whatever you do, don't give them to anyone else. They might be important. Oh, and Sarah?'

'What?'

'Don't say anything about this to anyone here, OK?'

'Why not?'

It's too late. The phone goes dead.

For a moment I stare at the receiver, blood pounding at my temples. The call has left me breathless and queasy, like being winded.

'Are you alright dear?'

I glance into Lydia's smooth face. This morning she has tied her hair back with an alice band and is wearing a blouse covered in large red poppies. She must be about my mother's age, maybe a couple of years younger. I know next to nothing about her or Mike, I think, as she peers at me. Downstairs is a framed photo of a young man on their coffee table who may be their son, but beside that their spotless home reveals nothing.

'Not really . . .'

'What did he say?'

'That Ed was in some kind of trouble.'

She blinks, her forehead twitching.

'Oh dear.'

'He says I should go back to Britain . . .'

She refuses to meet my eyes. Turning away, she swipes her finger along the dresser, removing an imaginary covering of dust.

'Maybe that *would* be sensible,' she says slowly. 'I mean, until there's some definite news . . .'

'But supposing Ed *needs* me?' I can't stop myself. Placing my hand over my mouth, I start to weep. Lydia turns, gazing at me with such pity that I can feel another onslaught of sobbing gathering in my chest.

'Poor, poor Sarah,' she says gently. 'You must be desperate

to find out what's happened. But it doesn't sound as if it's a good idea to go back to the coastal zone at the moment. There are often awful diseases after these cyclones – cholera, and heaven knows what else . . .'

'But what if he's hurt, or lost or something?'

'Sarah, dear, I know it's terribly hard to face, but I really do think there's only the slimmest of chances that . . .' She stops.

'The slimmest of chances that what?'

'That he's survived,' she says softly.

I clamp my hand over my mouth, trying to reign myself in. *Of course* he's survived!

'He isn't dead!' I wail.

I roll into a ball, weeping. Grief extinguishes all rational thought: my mind keeps straying along strange, meandering byways. I picture Syeda, with the bowl of rice in her hands, and then, like a blow from behind, Ed walking across the fields with his umbrella hooked over his wrist, an unintentional parody of a city gent. In the rainy season, when the paths turned to mud, he'd pad around in bare feet. 'You're turning into a real Bengali,' people would laugh, shaking their heads at him in amazement, as if they expected him to be dressed in a safari suit and galoshes. Forty-eight hours ago I was drinking tea with him on the terrace; the night before, he'd said everything was going to change. What happened?

When I open my eyes I realize that I'm lying in Lydia's arms, her soft hands clasping mine. 'If you decide to go to Britain we'll arrange the flight,' she's saying. 'If not, you're more than welcome to stay here.'

I nod, not really listening. 'I need to call Ed's sister,' I say. 'She doesn't know.'

I perch on the edge of the bed, trying to summon the courage to dial the number that Lydia has retrieved from the British High Commission, where details of expatriates' next of kin are held. It is after two in the afternoon; in London, Ed's big sister should be waking up. I clutch the handset, forcing myself to punch her number onto the keys. There is a short, static-filled pause and then thousands of miles away I can hear her phone ringing. When she answers I'm not sure what I'm going to say.

'Hello?' An upper class female voice, slurring with sleep.

'Is that Alexandria?' There's a slight echo on the line. My voice bounces back, young and querulous.

'Yup. Who's calling?'

'It's Sarah . . . Ed's friend in Bangladesh?'

The line crackles. My heart has started to thud.

'*Sarah* . . . yes of course . . .' She sounds suddenly breathless as if suspecting what might come. 'Is everything OK?'

'No . . .' I gulp down the rising sobs. 'It's Ed . . . there was this terrible storm . . .' I can hear my blundering words echoing distantly down the line. 'He's disappeared . . .'

'I don't understand . . . what do you mean?'

'There was this tornado. It hit the place where we live. God, look, I'm so sorry to be ringing you up to tell you this. I mean, he's your brother and everything. I tried to stop him, but he was running towards the sea . . . We found his shoe . . .'

A long, agonizing silence. When Alexandria next speaks her voice is very faint.

'You mean you found his shoe in the sea?'

'It was on the beach . . .'

'But you didn't find his body?'

'No. I don't know what's happened to him . . . I mean there were all these horrible things happening in our village, people threatening us and everything, and now this British guy Dan, who's helping me look for him, is saying I might be in some kind of danger too . . .'

'What do you mean, you might be in danger?' Her voice is so quiet I can hardly hear.

'Ed upset all these people. You know, with this campaign of his? About the oil—'

'Yes,' she interrupts. 'I know all about it.'

'I think he's got involved in something really bad. Dan says I should get out of Bangladesh . . . I don't know what to do . . .'

'I'm going to come out to help you look for him,' she says falteringly. 'You'll have to tell me how to get there. Oh Christ, what am I going to do with Joseph?'

I think she may have started to cry. There is another long pause. I had forgotten that she had a little boy. He was a toddler when Ed had left for Bangladesh; he'd shown me his photo.

'I'm sorry,' she eventually says. 'I can't take this all in . . .'

'I know.'

'Can you come to London?'

'I think I'm going to have to.'

'You can stay with me.'

She has to take Joseph to his nursery, she says; she'll call back in an hour. I am about to put down the phone when she adds something else.

'There's something I have to ask you.'

'Go on . . .'

'Was Edward OK?'

'How do you mean?'

'In himself . . . was he behaving normally? Or was he, you know, kind of . . . *manic*?'

My throat contracts. I can feel the air being squeezed from my diaphragm, like a fist pushing down.

'Of course not,' I say tightly. 'He was absolutely fine.'

TWELVE

Mike is home. He has been in Delhi and is delivered from the airport in the sleek black car that his office keeps specifically for his use. Ed told me that he was an economic adviser to the World Bank, something involving trade and budget control, and this afternoon, in his cream linen suit, he looks every bit the international consultant. He's a small chappie, with a close-cropped grey beard and peppery hair, whose faintly aggressive air of entitlement reminds me of a Jack Russell. Dropping his luggage by the door for the servants to retrieve, he struts around the house, calling for Lydia. He must have forgotten that I'm here, for when he notices me sitting on the sofa, something passes over his face that I doubt I'm meant to see. Partly it's surprise at the sight of an outsider in his house. Yet something darker flashes in his eyes too: a fleeting disquiet, quickly concealed.

'Sarah, my goodness, there you are!'

Given the circumstances, it's unclear how to greet him. In contrast to Lydia's overbearing hug, Mike settles on a faint imprint of dry lips on my check but I pull away too soon, wrecking his attempt to kiss my other cheek and forcing his lips to collide with my nose. We step hastily away from each other.

'Well!' Mike says. 'How *are* you?'

'Not great, actually.'

I was probably supposed to say that I was fine. Then Mike could have replied: 'Well done, old girl', or something similar, thus reducing Ed's disappearance to a minor trial, to be endured. He grimaces, nodding his head at me in a show of empathy.

'Terrible business, absolutely terrible.'

My brain has frozen over. Temporarily stalled, I'm unable to think of an appropriate reply.

'Lydia's been looking after you, has she?'

'She's been great.'

'Terrific. And your plans?'

'I'm going back to the UK for a few days. I'm going to stay with Ed's sister.'

Mike grimaces. 'Good plan.'

He sinks on to the sofa, unbuttoning his shirt to reveal a frizz of grey chest hair. He looks tired. I stare at my hands, not wanting to make eye contact. If I pinch at the flesh between my thumb and forefinger, perhaps I'll stop these thoughts. I dig deep, trying to focus on the bare necessities: Mike is home; chat politely, escape. Yet despite my efforts, the words come crashing through. Dan said Ed was in terrible trouble. There was a tornado; he ran into the sea. Everyone thinks he's dead.

'You were OK, of course?' Mike is saying. 'You went to one of these new shelters they've been putting in?'

If I bite down on my lip, I might prevent myself from screaming.

'Yeah.'

'Nice to know they work.'

'Mmm.'

Is this what you are meant to do when disaster strikes? In Lalalpur people prostrate themselves on the floor, wailing. No one is afraid of grief. It's part of life, as natural as laughter or blowing one's nose. But here in Mike and Lydia's sani-tized mansion, what has happened feels like an embarrassing unpleasantness, to be carefully steered around, like a dog turd on the lawn.

'I don't get what he was doing,' I whisper. 'It was like he

was running away from something. I mean, I saw him on the beach, heading for the sea . . .'

'Ah . . .' Mike shifts his buttocks on the black leather. He's looking increasingly uncomfortable.

I pause. 'What exactly were Oxan so worried about, anyway?'

He stares at me, the muscles in his face tightening. 'What do you mean?'

I breathe in, trying to steady myself. I knew he wouldn't like the question, but I had to ask it. 'I mean, why did they get so upset about Ed's campaign? No one important was taking any notice and apart from Dan Jameson, none of the aid people were interested. So why were they bothered?'

There is an icy silence. '*Were* they bothered?' Mike asks faintly.

I take another breath. I don't like the way that he is looking at me, yet now that I have started, there's no going back. 'You must know about what was going on . . .'

His mouth puckers, as if he's bitten into something unpleasant. 'It was a local dispute,' he says sharply. 'You were blundering around in something you didn't understand. Edward would have been well advised to keep out of it.'

'But you heard about our friend Aunik? It was horrible. We were completely freaking out . . . And now Dan Jameson says I might be in danger too.'

He pulls a face.

'He rang me, just now. He says Ed was involved in something really heavy . . .'

Mike doesn't reply, just sighs, stretching his hands above his head and not making eye contact. I swallow hard, trying to calm down. I was half hoping that he'd retort that Dan was overreacting, but from his nonplussed expression it's obvious he isn't remotely shocked.

'Edward's behaviour was inappropriate, to say the least,' he suddenly says. I stare at him with surprise. Straightening his back, he places his hands on his knees, about to push himself up. 'If you must know, the last time I saw him was at the Hilton, last week. He blanked me.'

My face has gone rigid. 'You *what*?'

He turns and gazes at me, a faint line of displeasure ruffling his brow. Does he have any idea how I'm feeling? Perhaps he thinks I was just some casual fling, who Ed was using to ward off the boredom and isolation of life in the sticks.

'Oh, come on, don't look so shocked. Where else can you go in this bloody place to get a decent drink?'

'But he wasn't in Dhaka last week! I would have known!'

'Well I definitely saw him last Tuesday. Unless he's got a doppelgänger . . .'

'Even if he was, he would never in a million years go to the Hilton. He hated the people who stayed there. He said it was grotesque, all that luxury when there were people starving on the streets outside . . .'

I am about to burst into tears. My eyes are hot, the tip of my nose numb. Mike glances at me with undisguised disdain.

'I obviously can't describe the machinations of your boyfriend's psyche to you,' he says curtly. 'The fact of the matter is that he was involved in all sorts of things he shouldn't have been.'

'Like what?'

'Like ignoring everyone's advice and running this *campaign* of his. This isn't toy town, you know. The politics can be vicious. What he was doing was naive, to say the very least.'

'So what *was* he doing?'

He exhales heavily, then takes a large handkerchief from his pocket and blows his nose. 'If he didn't share it with you, then there probably isn't much point in going into it.'

'He shared *everything* with me.'

Liar! I gulp down a wave of misery, but it's too late; my sight blurs with tears. I wipe them furiously away. 'He always used to . . .'

It must be because I am weeping, for Mike's face softens. 'Listen,' he says. 'You're doing the right thing in going back to the UK. I presume you have family there?'

I start to reply but he turns towards the stairs that lead to the first floor, not waiting for my answer.

Back in my room, I grab Ed's briefcase from the floor. Tugging at the buckles, I yank it open and pull out the notebooks. Ed always wrote everything down. There *has* to be something in here.

The first books are just as I expected: tidy lists of things to be done; an inventory of hope. One is marked 'UK:

Accounts, addresses etc.' In others, he's jotted down notes of meetings or builders' prices. I've seen these pages before, I know what they contain. I toss them aside, grabbing the most recent book, the one which he never shared. On the cover of the others he had written: 'Things to be done', but on this one there is nothing. The book has an oddly collapsed appearance, like a cocoon from which the moth has emerged. Pulling open the cardboard covers, I realize that the book is empty. Traces of writing remain on the stubs of paper caught in the binding, but the pages have been torn out. For a moment or two I gaze dully at the stubs then stuff the book back in the briefcase, scrabbling through the front pockets until I locate what I've been searching for: Ed's moleskin diary. Flicking quickly through the pages, I turn to the last few weeks, my hands trembling. In contrast to earlier pages which are filled with notes and appointments, most of the recent days are blank. I'm sure Mike has made a mistake. Ed definitely wasn't in Dhaka last week, the only place he went was Chittagong.

I turn the page, swallowing hard. On May 4th, exactly a week ago, Ed has scrawled a name: SADID.

Informing Lydia that I'm going to visit a friend, I hail a baby-taxi outside the house. I think I know the way.

The journey takes longer than I recall. As the baby-taxi careers over the uneven roads I clutch the handrail, my head bumping the tarpaulin roof. I don't remember the smog being as thick as this, or the heat so oppressive. I peer apprehensively out at the streaming traffic. It's almost a year since I was in this part of the city. I had imagined it as full of colour but today everything seems dull, the beggars that linger on the dusty roadsides more emaciated, the stench of rotting garbage and drains so repulsive that like the other people sitting in the backs of cars, I cover my nose with my *orna*. I keep remembering Dan's warning. Each time the sludgy traffic halts and a beggar lurches towards me, my breath catches. When a shining Mercedes draws parallel with the baby-taxi and I notice a man in the back, staring accusingly at me, I have to force myself not to whimper with alarm.

After an hour of 'jam', we join the dual carriageway, with the billboards for airlines and soap. The Mercedes has disappeared, but I'm still rigid with tension. Glancing at the image of the Biman stewardess holding out her gloved hands in welcome, I see that her face has been blotted out. The baby-taxi whizzes past. As the road sweeps left the brick fields finally appear, their striped chimneys spread out against the horizon, the sky blotched with smoke. When we reach the largest factory, I tap the driver on the shoulder and ask him to wait.

The colony is just as I remember: lines of low, tin-roofed buildings, like a prison camp. I am expecting to see the women who gave me their bangles gathered around the tube-well, but there's no one around. Hurrying past the buildings, I try to get my bearings. Ed said that Sadid was one of the teachers, so hopefully I'll find him in the makeshift school, yet I'm feeling increasingly disorientated. It should have been at the end of the first barrack, but all I can see is a blackened wall and a pile of rubbish. As I approach the wall I stop. My mouth is hanging open, so I clamp my hand over it, crossing my other arm over my chest. A dead feeling is spreading over my body.

The school has been burnt down. What appeared to be garbage now appears as the wreckage of the classroom: burnt chair legs sticking from the carcass like some grotesquely roasted creature, a portion of the tin roof slumped by the side. By my feet are the remains of a school book, its singed pages fluttering in the breeze. Picking it up, I glance at the colourful pictures illustrating the Bengali alphabet: a little girl, skipping; a plate of rice; a monkey. Hurling it down, I lumber across the yard, back towards the colony.

As I reach the low buildings, I pause for a moment, staring around. Saris hang from the washing line that reaches across the yard and the *chulas* are still smoking, yet the place is deserted. When I hear the scrape of bolts being pulled back, I jump and turn around. A young girl has appeared by the door of one of the rooms. In the shadows behind her, more faces peek out. Dressed in a grimy frock, her matted hair is browned by malnutrition. I gurn at her, trying to look relaxed.

'*Salaam e-lekum.*'

She does not reply, just stands in the dirt, gazing at me.

'What happened to your school?' I ask, adding idiotically: 'Did it burn down?'

She stares at me accusingly. *'Oxan manoosh korechen,'* she says unsmilingly. *Oxan's people did it.*

Before I am able to formulate a coherent response she disappears into the building. With a blur of movement, the door slams shut. Turning slowly away, I start to walk across the yard towards the road, where the baby-taxi waits. I feel completely hollow.

The first stone hits me on the shoulder. As I spin around, a second ricochets off my forehead: a bolt of pain, between the eyes. Pressing my forefingers to my face, I can feel warm blood, trickling down.

Gasping, I stumble towards the road.

THIRTEEN

May 11th, 2003

The plane approaches Heathrow over a counterpane of green. I slump by the window, staring at the rolling green fields and the neat curve of the suburbs, each dinky house backed by a small strip of lawn. There do not seem to be any people beneath us, just traffic; when we descend, it is over acres of parked cars. The dawn skies are pale, washed clean by the retreating night.

It's seven in the morning. I wander through the airport, not sure where to go. The people here are so *large*: not merely tall, but padded and fleshy in a way I had forgotten. Nobody meets my eye, or smiles. When I pass what I assume to be a Bangladeshi family, the head-scarfed mum pushing a toddler in a buggy, the dad holding the hands of two little boys in matching blue anoraks, I am on the verge of *salaaming* them but they pass by as if I wasn't there.

I drift through airport shops selling plastic-wrapped fruit, bricks of chocolate, enormous bottles of 'high tech' water and thick magazines, each costing more than our friends in Lalalpur would earn in a week. The quantity of gleaming goods is incredible, as is the orderly queue of people who wait by the computerized till. How did life become so ruthlessly efficient?

The only people who speak are talking into their mobile phones.

The months that I have spent in Bangladesh have turned me into a stranger, unable to function in my own country. I hover by a call box, fumbling for the handful of change that I have just been given by a spotty girl in WH Smith's. 'Thanks,' I said, hoarsely, surprised at the sound of my voice. She flicked me an expression that I had forgotten, but now realize is peculiarly British: an on/off smile which resulted from a minuscule flexing of muscles around her mouth. Locating a one pound coin, I shove it into the phone machine, and dial the number that I have jotted down.

Alexandria answers immediately.

'Do you know how to get here?'

I scribble down her instructions. She says she will be waiting.

The cold has seeped into my bones and is running through my blood. I sway with the motion of the tube, trembling in the clothes that Lydia lent me in Dhaka. Back there, the cotton trousers and silk shirt clung to my skin in sweaty patches and the cardigan she insisted I carry in my bag seemed a ridiculous aberration. Now I have it buttoned to the top. I am even wearing Emirates socks under my sandals. I wrap my arms around my middle, trying to stop the shaking. When I look up, I notice a woman, staring. She looks a bit like me in the life I might once have had: neatly made-up and conventionally dressed, a copy of *Metro* under her arm: boredom personified. As our eyes meet she glances away.

The carriage becomes increasingly crowded. I am relearning the rules: not to look directly at anyone, but to gaze stonily ahead. As the train trundles towards central London I try to keep myself occupied by reading the headlines on people's papers: a sex scandal involving an MP, bombs in Iraq. I feel as if I have been transplanted in another reality, as distant from Lalalpur as the moon is from Mars. I keep picturing Syeda, sitting in her yard. She is rolling out chapattis on a small board, singing quietly. Her youngest son Mobed is sitting on my knee, his small head resting on my shoulder. I used to tickle him on the palm of his hand, making him squirm. I want to hold on to the memory, but it slides away. Now I am standing on the edge of the beach, palm fronds hurtling through the air. Further down the shore the wind is playing roly-poly with the boats. And there is Ed, running away.

When I reach the address that Alexandria recited over the phone, I worry that I've made a mistake. I got off the tube at Covent Garden, and have spent the last ten minutes gawping at the shops, with their haughty mannequins and impossibly expensive clothes. Now I have turned down a small lane, past a cafe selling latte and croissants on the corner and a trendy florist's that has bunches of flowers in tin buckets for twenty quid, and am standing outside what looks like a converted warehouse, with sheet-glass windows and a bright orange door. Yet when I ring the bell and announce my name to the intercom, the door swings open.

I climb the narrow stairs, taking in the marigold walls. On the floor above, a woman is leaning over the wooden railings. Peering up, I glimpse white dreadlocks coiled around her head. She's dressed in black; something heavy hangs from her neck.

'Come on up!' she calls.

As I reach the top of the stairs, Alexandria steps solemnly towards me, arms held out. After Bangladesh her appearance seems bizarre, although it's probably me who's out of place. My immediate impression is of Medusa, with her strange, snake-like hair and large green eyes. She has Ed's aristocratic nose, and the same curving cheekbones but her lips are fuller, her stance more determined. She is wearing a black woollen dress over skinny jeans, and fuchsia clogs. A heavy metallic necklace hangs around her neck, the kind of decoration a Masai might wear and she has a diamond in her elegant nose. For a moment, I see Ed in her slim features. Then her face crumples and he's gone.

'Oh, God . . .' she gasps, as she pulls me into her arms. 'Bloody hell, I can't believe it . . .'

It feels perfectly natural to stand with my arms clasped around this glamorous stranger as she weeps into my shoulder. I place a tentative hand on her back.

'I tried so hard to keep him safe . . .'

I'm not sure what she means or how to respond. Giving my shoulders a squeeze, she finally steps away. The tip of her nose has turned red, and her cheeks have assumed a sticky glaze. 'Sorry,' she says, sniffing. She has tried to dull it with London inflections, but her voice is unmistakably upper class.

I shrug. 'It's OK.'

I follow her into the apartment. From the street the building appeared narrow and cramped, but inside it has taken on industrial proportions. On one side of the open space a kitchenette is spread with the remnants of breakfast; in the middle, suede banquettes are arranged in an L-shape. The brick walls are decorated by large, confident canvasses: vivid blocks of colour, a giant, fluorescent daisy. Sunshine pours from the skylights. I stand awkwardly in the centre of the room, unsure how to proceed.

'Good God, look at the way you're shaking,' Alexandria cries. 'You must be freezing.'

She brings me a shawl and a mug of thick black coffee and sits beside me on the banquettes, curling her long legs underneath her lithe body. She was a model for a while, Ed told me. Then she turned to art: perhaps the canvasses on the walls are hers. For a moment she looks closely at me, her eyes sombre. Then she says something that makes my heart contract.

'I don't think Eddy's dead.'

Tears rush to my eyes. I shake my head, blinking them away. 'I feel the same! If he was, I'd *know* it, I'm sure I would. But he seems so close, all the time . . .'

'That's how I feel too . . .'

For a while neither of us can speak. We sit together on the suede cushions, clutching each other's arms and weeping. Eventually Alexandria composes herself and draws away. 'I want to know everything about what happened,' she says. 'If you can bear it.'

I can feel her eyes on my face. 'Do you think you can?' she adds gently.

I nod. 'I'm going to try.'

I tell her about the cyclone, and how I saw Ed running across the beach into the frenzied waves. We had been having problems, I say. People were threatening us; bad things had happened. Now that I have started, the disparate events of the last few months emerge as an almost coherent story, a dot to dot picture with the lines filled in. Alexandria has pulled her knees up to her chest and is gazing at her chunky silver rings. She does not interrupt.

FOURTEEN

Lalalpur, March 10th, 2003

E d was late. He normally returned from his afternoon class well before sunset, but it had been dark for several hours. I waited for him under the coconut trees, peering anxiously across the fields for the glow of his lamp. When it eventually appeared, it was not from the direction of the road, as I'd expected, but the bazaar. As I watched the swaying light grow closer I could make out the outline of his briefcase bumping at his thigh, and his long loping legs. Something was wrong, I realized as he grew closer. His gait was different, as if he was wounded, and rather than looking expectantly towards the bungalow, he was glaring at the ground.

'Hi, sweetie, what's up?'

He brushed past me, heading for the steps.

'It's *shit*.'

'What is?'

Grabbing his arm, I pulled him around, so that he was forced to stop.

'What's happened?'

'There's this huge band of *goondas* forcing people out of their homes in Jhomgram . . .'

'What's a *goonda*?'

He glanced at me impatiently. 'A thug. And if people refuse to leave, they're burning down their houses. Haven't you seen the smoke?'

I remembered the dark plumes I'd seen that afternoon, rising from the direction of Jhomgram, the small village a few miles to the east where Aunik was working. It had been too hot to go outside, so I had spent the afternoon dozing on the bed. I assumed that the distant shouts I'd heard from across the fields were from the herders, whose stunted cattle grazed the village paths.

'Why are they doing that?'

'Someone must want their land. If you've got the clout you can pretty much do what you like round here.' He glowered at me, his face clenched. 'There was this bloke lying by the road. It was horrible. He'd been beaten up . . .'

I put my hand on his arm, but he brushed it away. 'I wanted to help him, but the guys I was with said to keep out of it. They just walked off, leaving him lying there in this pool of blood . . .'

Removing his glasses, he rubbed his eyes vigorously with his knuckles. I wanted to put my arms around him but the rigidity of his shoulders made it impossible.

'The worst thing is the police. There's a group of them in the bazaar drinking tea, like they've spent the day helping little old ladies cross the road. Apparently they've been beating up anyone who refuses to leave. It's disgusting.'

'They can't do that!' My voice sounded shrill and silly.

'This isn't the UK, Sarah,' Ed said wearily. 'People don't have any rights. If you've got the money you can do pretty much what you like.'

He pushed past me, clumping up the steps and on to the terrace, where he collapsed into a chair. He looked exhausted.

By the next morning, a handful of hovels had appeared by the side of the road. Ed had been up for most of the night, writing a long treatise addressed to the head of the police in Chittagong; each time I had drifted into the room, asking him to come to bed, he had covered the paper with his hand and told me to go to sleep. Now he stood tensely under the trees, peering across the fields.

'I'm going to go and talk to them,' he announced. 'Find out what's been going on.'

I followed him. This morning the village seemed unusually quiet; I didn't recognize the boy who was herding the scraggy goats that roamed the path, or see anyone we knew. Perhaps it was the heat. All week it had been building in intensity, driving people inside their houses, where they lay on mats on the cool earth floors, or had their children wave fans over their heads. As I stepped over the stubble, a large lizard scuttled into the burnt grass. In the paddy, the crickets ticked and whirred.

When we reached the huts we saw that many more people had been sleeping on the open ground, the belongings that they had salvaged from Jhomgram spread over the bare earth: pots, a few battered suitcases, piles of clothes, secured with string.

Children pottered aimlessly. Now, as we approached, people started to gather around us. One old man, with a hennaed beard and a face like cracked earth, was jabbing at his forehead, yelling that the fate that had befallen his family was Allah's will. Another woman had collapsed on the ground, pawing at Ed's feet and wailing whilst a young man was pointing in the direction of Jhomgram, his face contorted. I glanced at Ed, trying to follow the stream of words – something about fields and something about 'Amerika', the latter followed by a glob of spittle.

'What's he saying?'

Ed gestured at me to be quiet. 'Hang on . . .'

Everyone was shouting again.

'They're saying that some company have discovered oil on their land . . . A man came a few months ago, offering to buy them out, but it wasn't enough so they refused to take it. It's hard to make head or tail of it.'

'What are they going to do?'

'I don't know. They want us to give them money. They say they've got nowhere to go, and the people here won't help them.'

'But won't this company that's got the land be offering compensation?'

He shrugged. 'I doubt they'll actually get it.'

I was already fumbling with my money belt. 'Let's give them as much as we can . . .'

I started to hand out one-hundred *taka* notes. It wasn't much, but at least it would keep them going. As they took the notes from my fingers, the people began to drift away. Ed regarded the scene in silence.

'Giving them hand outs isn't going to change a thing,' he muttered. 'All it does is make *us* feel better.'

'It's better than doing nothing . . .'

'I don't intend to do nothing.'

Turning on his heel, he stalked away.

By the time I returned to the bungalow, he was halfway down the steps, his briefcase tucked under his arm.

'Where are you going?'

I stood tentatively before him, trying to catch his hand, but he shook off my outstretched fingers.

'To find out what's going on.'

'Shall I come?'

He frowned. 'Probably not a good idea.'

'Why not?'

'Because people won't tell me anything if you're around. They'll say it's men's business.'

I raised my eyebrows. 'Is that what *you* think?'

'Of course not – for God's sake, what do you take me for?'

'I don't take you for anything. I'm just surprised that you're happy to support the patriarchal order that's all.'

I wasn't serious; it should have been obvious. Yet rather than slipping into our usual banter, Ed's face stiffened. 'For God's sake, Sarah, don't go all feminist on me,' he said coldly. 'It's boring beyond belief.'

For a moment I remained standing beside him, my hand hanging humiliatingly over his shoulder. Then I turned and walked back down the path.

I found Syeda squatting by the pond, pounding at her washing. Glancing at me, she grinned widely, showing her paan stained teeth.

'*Ki kobor?*' What's up?

'Haven't you heard what's happened at Jhomgram?'

Her face fell. 'I heard.'

'It's terrible, isn't it?'

'That's what life's like, Sister.' She gave a small, resigned sigh. 'The poor lose everything and the rich take what they like.'

'But we have to help them!'

She shrugged, tapping her forehead with her wet fingers. 'We can't change their fate. It's written on their foreheads.'

Perching on the slippery steps, I sat down beside her. It was a saying that people in the village repeated when things went wrong.

'I don't believe in fate,' I said. 'I think if we try hard, we can change things.'

She gave a hollow laugh. 'That's because in your country the government is good. Here, everything is rotten.'

Spitting into the undergrowth, she pummelled her washing with her strong arms. There was no disputing her analysis. Ever since arriving in Bangladesh, I had heard the same thing: despite the hard-working and entrepreneurial spirit of its population, the country was held to ransom by government corruption. Dipping my feet into the cool water, I gazed at the water lilies.

The scene was so peaceful; it was hard to believe that only yesterday the next door village had been burnt down.

'Can I help with your washing?' I eventually said.

Jerking around, Syeda shot me a furious look. '*Chup!* What a thing to ask! Don't make me ashamed!'

'But you've been working all day. I haven't been doing anything.'

Attacking the sopping pile with renewed vigour, she seemed genuinely annoyed. 'How can I allow you to come to my house and do my work, Sister? What would people say?'

'It could be our special secret,' I muttered, splashing at the water with my feet. On the step beside me, a white hen was pecking at the dirt. I stared glumly at its mean little beak. For the first time since moving to Lalalpur I could feel the familiar, dragging weight of my uselessness. I had imagined that Ed and I were working as equals on the school, but just now he had slapped me down like a tetchy parent with a bothersome child. I accepted that women were treated differently here, and that in general we should try to conform to local customs. But did that mean I had to be excluded?

Shooting me a sideways glance, Syeda straightened up and chucked her suds into the pond. The impact of water on water made a slapping sound, a sudden splattering that made the dragonflies lift lazily from the water, then pooling rings.

'If you want to do some work, why don't you go back to your husband's house and do *his* washing?'

Her words sounded harsh, but her face was lit with humour. 'If I had a good husband like yours, I'd spend every minute of my day cooking and caring for him. Isn't that what a wife is supposed to do, Sarah?'

I snorted. 'Yeah, right,' I said in English.

Rising from her haunches, she gave me a wry smile.

'Don't be angry, Sister. Mr Edward loves you.'

'I know . . .'

'Then go home and give him this with his rice.'

Leaning down, she grabbed the squawking hen and with an assured twist of her strong wrists, snapped its neck. For a second or so its scraggy body jerked in her hands, then it suddenly sagged. Brushing away a few loose feathers, she pushed it into my hands.

'Go on then.'

I stared at her, aghast. 'But that's your chicken!'

'It's yours now.'

Gingerly holding the bird by its greasy yellow legs, I stood up. I had no idea what I was going to do with it. 'Thank you.'

'Well go on, then! Go home and be a good wife!'

Back at the bungalow, Ed was lying under the mosquito net, staring up at the feeble fan. I paused in the doorway, the chicken still swinging from my fingers.

'What have you got there?' he said, rousing himself.

'One of Syeda's chickens. She wants me to cook it for your dinner.'

'Good grief.'

There was a long pause. 'Did you find anything out?' I eventually asked.

'Yup. I went to see Aunik.'

'And?'

Ed sighed. 'He says it's this multinational, Oxan, that's working through a local outfit, the BNRC—'

'The *what*?'

'The Bangladesh Natural Resources Company. Oxan provide the capital, then contract the local operations out to them. It means they don't have to get their hands dirty dealing with all the local politics. Apparently Oxan and the BNRC have been excavating for oil in the area for ages. Now they've found bloody tonnes of the stuff under the fields at Jhomgram, so it's pay time. According to Aunik the land's been in dispute for years. The BNRC offered nominal compensation but the locals refused to take it, so now they've torched the whole village.'

'But how can they get away with it? Aren't there rules against that kind of thing?'

He glanced up. He seemed crushed. 'Aunik says it's actually the government that's taking the land. It's all totally legal, there's some Land Acquisition Act or something. Then the government lease it back to the company . . . they obviously get a huge cut of the profits. And if anyone stands in their way, they call in the heavies. It's all about so called economic growth, isn't it? Everyone's going to get rich, apart, of course, from the poor sods that have lost their land. Meanwhile the fat cats in London and New York or wherever, get even fatter. It makes me *sick*.'

I couldn't stand hearing him so defeated. He was my saviour;

I thought he knew the answers. Placing the chicken on the ground I walked over to the bed and sat beside him, pressing my face into his tummy. I could feel his fingers in my hair, his arms around my shoulders, pulling me up.

'I'm sorry I snapped,' he whispered. 'I just can't stand seeing people get done over.'

'I know.'

I kissed his damp forehead. 'We'll fight it,' I said. 'We'll do whatever we can.'

FIFTEEN

'Sarah! Wake up!'

I opened my eyes to find Ed peering down at me. It was not yet dawn, the room dim and the toads still chanting, yet he was dressed. Pulling aside the mosquito net, he placed his hand tenderly on my cheek.

'You do want to come, don't you? Or should I just let you sleep?'

'Where are you going?'

'Jhomgram. I'm going to take some pictures.'

Pulling on my clothes, I hurried after him.

'Wait for me . . .'

Outside, the air was cool. We paused for a moment on the terrace steps, breathing in the sweet scent of jasmine and gazing up at the lavender sky. Only a few stars remained.

'Come on then.'

Leaping down the steps, we walked briskly through the coconut grove, emerging to a landscape of silver fields, hung with mist. By now the sky was emerald; through the betel trees that lined the horizon, a finger of sun suddenly poked through. On cue, the azan started to wail, calling the village to prayer over the mosque sound system with a crackle of static, followed by the imam's cry. Our feet squelching the mud, we cut through the fields, moving away from the mosque and tea stalls, towards Jhomgram. Ed walked swiftly, his face lit by the dawn sun. Jogging beside him, I caught his hand, my spirits soaring.

'It's so beautiful.'

Smiling, he swung me around and kissed me on the lips.
'Just like you.'

On the path ahead, a man wrapped in a shawl was hurrying
through the mist, a fishing net hanging over his shoulder. He
eyed us with amazement: perhaps he thought we were spirits,
come to possess him. Leaping apart, we hurried past with a nod.
All around us, the world was waking up: women emerging from
their homes to light their fires or fetch water from the wells,
dogs stretching and shaking in the sun, a lone rickshaw, rattling
slowly down the path. Across the fields, a cock was crowing.

By the time we reached Jhomgram the mist had evaporated and
the fields were filled with labourers. Bent double, they were
planting paddy seedlings in the waterlogged mud, their conical
bamboo hats shading their heads from the morning heat. Only
one man noticed us as we passed; straightening up, he gawped
at us in surprise, his mouth hanging slightly open.

'Are we near Jhomgram?' Ed shouted.

Nodding, he signalled a clump of trees about half a mile
ahead. 'After those trees.'

'Thank you, Brother!'

The man laughed. 'Where are you from?' he called as we
walked past. 'Can you take me back there with you?'

We strode on, taking in the debris that was appearing by the
path: a bit of roof, a sheet of corrugated iron, a heap of singed
clothes. The air was beginning to smell acrid and unpleasant.

'Hang on . . .'

Pulling his camera from his pocket, Ed started snapping.

'Look over there . . .'

I started to run towards the trees, stopping at the ruins of
a large homestead that stretched beside the path. Once, there
must have been about ten bamboo houses gathered around a
large yard, with cow sheds and a pond at the back. Now, with
the exception of the charred wood and jagged lumps of metal
roof that were strewn around, nothing remained. The fire had
left scorch marks over the sandy track; in its epicentre, where
the houses once stood, the ash still smouldered. Kneeling,
Ed clicked at his camera. Gazing around, I saw that this was
the first of many fires; through the broken trees, I glimpsed the
burnt remains of one house after the other. Smuts floated in
the air.

'Jesus Christ . . .'

Picking up a charred pot, Ed stared at it mournfully. 'I wonder if everyone got away . . .'

'I bet lots of children lived here . . .'

Throwing the pot down, he kicked it back into the ash. 'Bastards!'

'What's that?'

With a start, I turned and peered down the path. I could hear the sound of an engine. 'There's a car . . .'

The noise was coming from the direction of the Noton Bazaar road. Trotting back through the trees, I scrutinized the horizon. It was growing steadily louder.

'It's a jeep, Ed. It's coming this way.'

'So what?' he called. 'We're not doing anything wrong.'

As I drew level with the first homestead, I spotted the vehicle bumping over the potholes. Something about it made me uneasy: the speed at which it was approaching perhaps, or maybe just its presence: this far from the main road anything other than a bicycle or a rickshaw was unusual.

'Let's go . . .'

Ignoring me, Ed was crouching on the ground as he framed more shots. 'We're here to record what's happened,' he called. 'And that's what we're going to do.'

It was almost upon us: a Japanese four-wheel drive, with two men in the front. As they hurtled towards the trees I saw with a lurch that they were dressed in khakis: soldiers. As the jeep skidded to a halt by the side of the road they jumped out, their heavy boots scuffing the path.

'*Ki Koren?*' they shouted. *What are you doing?*

Bumping past me, they strode towards Ed. They had guns tucked into their belts, I noticed, my stomach contracting. Despite Ed's cheery wave, they did not return his greeting.

'*Salaam-e-lekum . . .*'

Ignoring this, the larger of the men grabbed the camera from Ed's hands.

'Photography is forbidden on government property!' he shouted. 'Do you understand?'

Squaring his shoulders, Ed glared back. 'This isn't government property. This is the property of the people of Jhomgram'

There was a long, terrible silence. I stood, frozen, remembering the man Ed had described two days earlier, who had

been beaten to death and dumped by the road. For a second
or so the soldier's hand twitched by his belt. He could arrest
us, I thought; we might be accused of spying.

'Give me my camera back,' Ed said calmly. 'I'm not doing
anything wrong.'

'You fucking foreign pig,' the soldier whispered in English.
Dropping the camera on the ground, he crushed it under his
heavy leather boot then kicked it into the dirt. 'Get out of
here.'

'Fuck you, too,' Ed replied with a smile. Turning his back
on the soldier, he marched down the path towards me. His
face was pale, but his eyes glinted.

'Come on, Sarah,' he said loudly, taking my arm. 'Let's go.'

We walked quickly away. Behind us the jeep's engine was
revving. I was dreading hearing it bump over the track behind
us but after a second or so it was clear that it was moving in
the opposite direction, back towards the road. I was trembling,
I realised as I hurried to keep up with Ed, my heart hammering.

'Arseholes,' Ed was muttering. 'Wait till I tell people in
Dhaka about this . . .'

'I'm not sure you should have talked back to them like that.'

'What do you mean? You weren't scared of them, were you?'

'They could have arrested us, or done anything.'

He snorted. 'I doubt it. They were just throwing their weight
about. For God's sake, Sarah, don't look like that! I know
what I'm doing, OK?'

I glanced at his thin face. We were back by the paddy fields
now, the labourers still progressing slowly along the rows of
seedlings.

'OK,' I mumbled.

The incident with the soldiers only made Ed more determined.
He wasn't going to be put off by a bunch of uniformed thugs,
he announced. In fact he was going to highlight their intimi-
dation of us at Jhomgram and the destruction of his camera
as an example of the government's disregard for human rights.
We'd start a campaign. Aimed at the donor community and
the international media, the aim would be twofold: to gain
compensation for the people who had lost their land at
Jhomgram and to prevent Oxan and BNRC from further developments within the area. Fired up by this prospect, he left

Abdullah's rice, dhal and eelish fish supper untouched and hurried off to Noton Bazaar, where for one hundred taka an hour – about eighty pence – he had access to the Internet in a dark back room separated into booths by bamboo partitions. He was going to email everyone he knew.

SIXTEEN

A few days later a meeting was held outside the school. Since the inauguration ceremony, when the village men had prayed by the foundations, the walls had been completed and the roof girders secured. All that remained to complete now was the concrete roof. The building was due to be finished in a month, the contractors promised. Already we had fifty wooden chairs and desks, stored in a small room at the back of the mosque; a week earlier Ed had travelled to Chittagong to pick up a consignment of books and pencils. Now we arranged the chairs on the sandy ground outside the main building, and strung a light bulb from the banyan tree that grew by the path. The meeting would take place at seven, after evening prayers.

'We need to make sure everyone knows what's happening in Jhomgram,' Ed was muttering as we hauled the chairs across the yard. 'If we don't, this village could be next.'

He hurried away, intent on finding a microphone with which to make his address; apparently someone's cousin had one. Like the light bulb, we could run it off the car battery which Habib, the owner of the tea stall, was providing and Aunik was currently attaching to a string of wire. Everyone would be coming, he said. There was a great deal of interest in Ed's campaign. He grimaced as he said this, and when he had turned back to his electrics, did not meet my eye.

I straightened the chairs, my anxiety mounting. We were surely right to protest at what had happened at Jhomgram. As foreigners with connections in Dhaka and Britain, we should fight for the locals' rights. So why did I feel so uneasy?

Dusk fell, bringing out the mosquitoes. They droned around our faces, inured to the insect repellent that we spread over our arms. Our work completed, Ed and I sat by the podium that the imam had lent, staring at the empty road.

'What if no one comes?'

'Don't be silly, of course they will.'

He was right. By the time the moon rose over the mosque's faded pink dome, the yard was filled with about twenty men: not the poorest labourers who worked in the fields, or the youths who raced along the paths on their Hondas, but the village elders, with their walking sticks and beards. Most I recognized; some I didn't. As they took their seats, smoking and chewing paan as they muttered amongst themselves, I eyed them apprehensively. We had eaten in their homes, even taught their children, but this evening something hung in the air that I had not expected: a vague antagonism that I found hard to define. Chairman Roul was not yet here, I noticed. Perhaps he had been delayed.

Approaching the podium, Ed tentatively tapped the microphone. Above him, the light bulb flickered and hissed. By now it was covered with bugs; every second or so, a singed corpse dropped to the ground.

'*Salam-e-lekum*,' Ed said with a smile. 'Thank you for attending.'

He paused. One of the men sitting in the front burped politely. 'As you know, the multinational Oxan have found a reserve of oil in the land at Jhomgram,' Ed continued. 'Many of the people of that village have lost their homes. My friends there tell me that despite the government being legally compelled to pay them compensation, none have received a paisa. The profits will go to the richest people, those in the government and the Bangladesh Natural Resource Company and Oxan, whilst the real owners of the land of Bangladesh, those who farm it like you, will get nothing . . .'

At the back, someone was muttering; in agreement, I assumed. I peered into the crowd, twisting my hands in my lap. I wished Ed was not doing this, I suddenly thought; it was a mistake. Blinking rapidly, I forced myself to concentrate on his speech.

'I have spent the week contacting important people in Dhaka, who may be able to prevent Oxan and their associates from further atrocities. But I need your support. We have to act together, in order to stop more land in the area from being stolen . . .'

From the back of the audience, the muttering was growing louder.

'If we don't take action now, it could be Lalalpur next. *Your* homes burnt down and *your* land lost—'

'These are lies!' somebody suddenly shouted. 'You are foreigners, how can you understand these matters?'

We stared, shocked, at the speaker. It was Abdul Marek, one of Syeda's cousins: a small, wiry man, with curly black hair that stood up from his scalp like a bush. Like some other men in the village he had worked in Saudi Arabia; perhaps this was why he had an air of self-importance and pomposity which took the form of long lectures on the inherent superiority of Islamic society. 'Allah good!' he'd yell at me. 'Your Christian religion no good!' After a few such run-ins at Syeda's compound I made a point of avoiding him. Now, pushing back his chair, he was pointing angrily at Ed.

'Why are you spreading the lies of our enemies?' he shouted. 'Our country needs oil for our development. If Oxan come here, we will all be rich!'

I swallowed hard. He was saying something about America and foreigners, but was speaking so fast and furiously, his beard covered with specks of spittle, that I could no longer follow. At the podium, Ed was standing very straight, a tight smile fixed to his face. Gesturing at Abdul Marek to sit down, other men in the audience had also started yelling.

'Why are you showing disrespect to our English visitors?' one of them cried. 'Sit down and be quiet, Beta.'

'It is indeed wrong to show disrespect to our visitors, but neither do we want missionaries here.'

The speaker was a man who I had never seen before. Dressed in Arab robes and with the hennaed beard of the pious, he spoke with the gravitas of a man of learning. Now he was motioning at us dismissively. 'These people tell us they are bringing schools for our children, but what else do they bring from the West? Are they bringing their immoral ways? This is a conservative area; we don't want such things here. We have the opportunity to develop the oil that lies under our ancestral fields. Why should we listen to Christians, who seek to deflect us from our own religion, when our countrymen are about to enrich us?'

As the man spoke, Ed's foot was jiggling so energetically

he almost kicked me. Now he jumped up, staring around beseechingly. 'We are *not* missionaries! All of you . . . our friends . . . who have experience of us and our work . . . you all know that! We're only here because we love Bangladesh and want to work with you to bring education to your children! This isn't to do with being Christians or Muslims. It's to do with criminals stealing land from our neighbours!'

After that there was mayhem. Everyone started shouting at once; one old man even raised his stick at his neighbour, his eyes popping with fury. I think he was defending us, but since I could no longer follow what was being said I wasn't sure. I watched the scene in dismay. Pulling a face, Ed stepped back from the podium. For a second, our eyes met. Then he glanced quickly away.

'Friends!' Aunik was shouting. 'Please, listen to what we have to say!'

'Why should we listen to you? You are a city person with city ways.'

Shoving past those sitting close to him, Abdul Marek turned and stomped past the rows of chairs and the banyan tree, towards the road. It was what everyone was waiting for: a signal that the brief meeting was at an end. Almost as one, the assembled men rose, turning away from the school with apparent relief.

'Wait!' Ed implored. 'Please, don't go!'

It was too late. The men streamed out of the school yard and down the road, some still gesticulating angrily. After a few minutes only Ed, Aunik and I remained.

Pulling my *orna* around my shoulders, I wandered past the emptied chairs and leant against the banyan tree, staring up at the sliver of yellowed moon. I was experiencing a mixture of emotions so unpleasant that I yearned to be alone: embarrassment at the hectoring tone of Ed's speech, hurt that our friends should not have defended us more vociferously, and, most of all, a deep unease at what would happen next.

'Well, that was good, wasn't it?' Ed said glumly. Sighing, he sat down heavily on one of the chairs. 'What a bloody disaster.'

I glanced at him. Hunched almost double, his head was in his hands, a posture of defeat which shocked me almost as much as the way in which the audience had responded at the meeting. His cotton trousers were grimy, I realized, and he hadn't shaved for days. I had not known he was going to make a speech like that. I thought he would ask for the village elders' views rather than tell them what to do.

'Why would they say we were missionaries?' I mumbled. 'I don't get it.'

'Progressive NGOs such as ours are often accused of such things by their enemies.'

I had forgotten he was still with us, but now, as Aunik spoke, I turned and saw that he was sitting quietly beside the podium.

'But who would think of us as enemies?' Ed cried. 'What harm could we possibly be doing?'

Aunik sighed. He was only in his mid twenties, a recent graduate, with an MA in Sociology, but already had deep creases in his forehead and a slight stoop to his shoulders. His father had died when he was a child, he had told me one evening over dhal and rice; since then he had acted as head of his family. Wiping his oily hands on a handkerchief that he was now neatly folding and replacing in the pocket of his jeans, he turned to face Ed. 'Edward, our country is very complicated. There may be some who want progress and modern ways in our villages, but others who are very conservative. These people seek to stop any development from coming.'

'What, like schools?'

Aunik shook his head sorrowfully. 'Especially schools. These people don't want women and the poor to be educated—'

'Yeah, we know all that,' Ed said abruptly. Jumping to his feet, he started to pace between the rows of chairs. 'What I don't get is how come, if these guys are so anti-development, they aren't trying to stop BNRC. I mean, it's obvious that Lalalpur is going to be next on their agenda. If there's oil a mile across the fields, there's probably oil here. So they're going to lose their land too, right?'

Looking down, Aunik scuffed the dirt with the toe of his sandal. His face was flushed, I noticed. Either he was hurt by Ed's rude interruption, or there was something else that he was not articulating.

'I think you should not say anything more about BNRC here, Edward,' he eventually said. 'It would be better if you just were concerned with the school. Then people will no longer say these things to you.'

Ed scowled. 'How can we be "just concerned about the school" when we know that if global capitalism gets its way, all this –' he gestured impatiently to the unfinished building, the mosque and the surrounding fields – 'will be an oil field in a year or so? Come on, you don't really mean we should ignore what's happening, do you? Isn't that against everything that we're meant to be achieving?'

'Or is there something you're not telling us?' I added quietly.

Aunik continued to stare at the ground. He seemed lost in thought; when a giant moth blundered into his face, he batted it distractedly away. Looking over to Ed, I realized that he was watching me. 'Alright?' he mouthed as our eyes met. I glanced away.

'It's like this,' Aunik suddenly said, folding his arms and looking straight at me. He'd been brought up in the city, he explained when I'd asked him to tell me more about his background. Yet despite this, he loved the villages of his country with all his heart. Many of his university friends had got jobs abroad, but he'd always believed it was his duty to assist his countrymen; what else should a good man do?

'What is happening is that some people, those in the most powerful positions, are going to make a big profit from BNRC. That is why they don't want you to activate the people against them.'

Ed frowned. 'You mean people outside the village?'

Very slowly, Aunik shook his head. 'No. I mean people inside it.'

'People inside?' Ed echoed.

Aunik shrugged. 'Those with the connections.'

For a while we were silent. Shivering, I wrapped my arms around my shoulders. It was just as Ed had pronounced during that first evening in Dhaka: nothing here was straightforward. At the time, the prospect of all those layers of meaning had left me breathless with excitement. Bangladesh was simply a place to explore, filled with unexpected corners and exotic crevices. Now, however, I appreciated the true meaning of Ed's statement. We thought we understood life in Lalalpur, but in reality we understood nothing. And if nothing was as we imagined it, then nothing was secure.

'And that's why you think we should stop the campaign against BNRC?' Ed said solemnly. 'Despite everything that Schools for Change stands for?'

'Ed, you must understand, things are not like in your country. These affairs can get very unpleasant. There is a great deal of money involved . . . sometimes lives are lost. You've seen for yourself what transpired at Jhomgram. If we proceed in this manner, I fear for all our endeavours in the area, as well as the future of Schools for Change. As you know, I am just a humble teacher—'

'Oh come on, Aunik, don't give me that crap! You're an activist not a teacher!'

Biting my lip, I glanced away. This belligerent bullying was not a side to Ed that I'd expected.

'What you've just described is exactly the kind of thing that we're supposed to be standing up to!' he cried in agitation. 'If anything, it justifies our work even more. The rich are getting richer whilst the poor lose everything. You *know* what we should be doing! What would your student friends say if they could hear you now? Wouldn't they say you were behaving like a coward?'

Aunik's face coloured. Swallowing heavily, he glared at the ground. He was going to resign, I thought in panic. Ed's bluntness had offended him. How on earth would we cope?

'Come on, Ed,' I muttered. 'Give the guy a break.'

Yet even as I said this, Aunik was pulling his mobile from his jeans pocket. 'You are right,' he said slowly. 'We should be fighting for the poor. That's what we came to the rural areas to achieve.'

'Yo!' Laughing, Ed punched his hand in the air. Smiling hesitantly, Aunik did the same.

'Down with multinationals!' Ed shouted, giving him a salute. 'Power to the People!'

I don't think Aunik got the joke. Peering at his phone, he started to fiddle with it.

'What are you doing?'

'I'm calling my friend,' he whispered with a smile. 'He has many contacts.'

We walked back to the bungalow, Ed enthusing about the plan that he and Aunik had hatched. Tomorrow they would travel to

Chittagong where they would meet with Aunik's activist friends; veterans of anti-government demonstrations, several were journalists, with contacts in the international media. Edward was right, Aunik had sheepishly concluded. It did not matter if we met with opposition within Lalalpur: the dispossession of the people of Jhomgram was a cause worth fighting for. I had nodded cautiously in agreement, surprised at his change of heart.

'It's a shame we can't present a united front, but maybe that's just the nature of village life,' Ed was saying as we passed Syeda's homestead. 'The key *has* to be organized resistance, people coming together against the corrupt nature of globalization. Like that campaign against logging in India, you know, where all those tribal people were hugging the trees . . .' He trailed off. 'Anyway, what's up?'

I shrugged.

'What's *that* meant to mean?'

We were almost at the coconut trees. I stopped, gazing up at their fronds, which were rattling gently in the night breeze. I should have been able to tell him how I felt. Yet try as I might, I was struggling to put my emotions into words. In principle, I believed that he was right. We should stand up against Oxan and BNRC. Yet if, in practice, we were alienating the very people on whose support we depended, what future was there for our school?

'I guess I'm just worried that we're doing the right thing . . .' I eventually muttered.

Wrinkling his nose, Ed grimaced. 'Of course we're doing the right thing! What else can we do, faced with what's happening? You saw what those guys did to Jhomgram.'

'Yeah, but maybe what Aunik said was right . . . maybe if we start up some huge campaign we'll end up pissing everyone off and losing the school.'

'So basically what you're saying is that you're scared of making a stand?'

'No, it's not that. It's just that I'm worried we're barking up the wrong tree. Maybe we should concentrate on what we came here to do – getting the school running, and everything. If we carry on like this, we're going to turn everyone against us.'

In the darkness I could sense Ed stiffen. 'You can't just stand by and watch these things happening,' he said quietly. 'If you do, you're as guilty as these bastards who think they can just shove people off their land because they want to make a fast buck.'

Sighing bitterly, he turned and paced through the trees.

At the bungalow, a letter was waiting for us. Someone had pinned it to the door: a sheet of lined writing paper, roughly folded and jammed onto a crooked nail. Tearing it free, Ed peered at the paper, his brow furrowed.

'What does it say?'

'It's about our friend Chairman Roul. Here, you can read it for yourself.'

Placing the letter in my hands, he moved to the terrace railing, where he absently plucked at the white jasmine, tearing off the petals and shredding them with his nails. He seemed to be deep in thought.

> Friends,
> You should know Chairman Roul is taking monies from Oxan plc for his own betterment and not the community development programme for which it is intended. Ask Mohammed Jaheed in BNRC how these monies are spent. Ask Roul and Jaheed who paid the dacoit who burnt Jhomgram and beat its people. Ask them who pays the police to stand and watch.

'What community development programme?' I muttered as I reached the end.

Ed sighed, scattering more petals on the floor. 'Oxan claims that it's providing benefits for the communities it works in. It makes them look more respectable. Then they write it up in their reports as part of their Corporate Social Policy.'

'And whoever's written this is saying that rather than the money going for that, BNRC are using it to keep the Chairman and the police on the right side?'

'Seems like it.'

'Which explains why the Chairman wasn't at the meeting . . .'

'And why his cronies are shouting that we're evil apostates.'

'Blimey . . .'

Sinking into a chair, I stared miserably into the darkness. I felt as if someone had shoved their fist into my belly.

'Aw, don't look like that. This is actually really *good.*'

Grinning, Ed plucked the letter from my hand. 'We can use this against BNRC. Perhaps Oxan will rethink their Bangladeshi operations once they realize what's been going on.'

I glanced up at him. He was gazing at the letter, nodding and muttering to himself. 'I wonder if Aunik knows about it . . . I can't wait to email Oxan London and tell them all the gory details.'

'I'm just scared that we're getting into things we don't understand,' I blurted. 'I mean, who would have sent this?'

For a moment Ed blinked at me without replying. I stared back at him, struck by how much he had changed in the last few weeks. It was not just how thin and drawn he had become, but more that the humour which normally lit his face had been replaced by a manic energy which turned his eyes beady and pulled his mouth into a tight grimace.

'For Christ's sake Sarah,' he retorted impatiently. 'Why can't you just *relax?*'

SEVENTEEN

A few days later we were summoned to the Chairman's home. We walked apprehensively across the steamy fields, the road ahead shimmering with heat. I did not want to arrive at his compound for ever since reading the anonymous letter I had dreaded the confrontation that must surely take place. As Ed strode ahead, I lingered and delayed, peering through the trees to see if Syeda was home, then petting a goat that was chained to a stake in the baking earth. In contrast, Ed walked fast, as if relishing what lay ahead.

At last we reached the boundary wall with its Arabic inscription and ornate turrets. We entered the yard, gazing around. Usually the Chairman received us in his house, where he liked sit on a large stool, overseeing his servants. But today the place was deserted. Wandering across the courtyard, we took in the rows of red chillies laid out to dry in the sun, the firewood heaped by the outhouse and fishing nets hanging on the washing line. With his herd of cows and acres of land, Roul was the wealthiest farmer in the neighbourhood.

'*Salaam e lekum*,' Ed called softly. 'Hallo?'

Stepping on to the long stone terrace, we moved hesitantly inside the building. I wiped my hands nervously on my hips; all week the temperatures had been rising and I was slimy with sweat. The absence of our hosts seemed ominous: a signal of the hostility to come.

For a moment, as we stepped into the cool room, we were plunged into darkness: like most village houses, there was only one small, barred window. Peering into the gloom, I gradually made out the familiar shape of a large wooden bed, hung around with a mosquito net, a dresser and, underneath a framed photograph of the Kaaba at Mecca, a table. This was the room where I'd been taken by the Chairman's mother during my first afternoon in Lalalpur. Today there was no sign of the children and women who had crowded inside that day. Where *was* everyone?

'Sit down, please.'

I started, staring around the room in surprise. The Chairman was sitting motionless on the bed, I realized: in the shadowy recesses I hadn't noticed his thick form.

'*Salaam e lekum*,' Ed was saying, moving towards the bed and extending his hand in greeting. In return he received a few limp fingers, quickly retracted. For a moment we stood awkwardly before the bed, smiling and nodding. Suddenly the Chairman clicked his fingers, shouting for his daughter.

'*Eh, Nasneen, chai!*'

We sat down. Staring into Ed's face, the Chairman smiled. 'How are you?' he said pleasantly.

'We're great!'

There was a long pause. 'Please,' the Chairman suddenly said. 'You must explain something to me. Why do you come into my village, ask for my help, which, as Allah's servant I have sincerely given, then make problems for me? I don't understand why someone would do this.'

Ed visibly gulped. I could see the ripple of his Adam's apple in his scrawny neck.

'We're not making problems for you,' I said quietly. 'We're simply trying to assist the poorest people in Lalalpur . . .'

The Chairman's lips stretched over his paan-stained teeth.

'You hold meetings to oppose our country's economic development. You tell the people to stop our government from enriching our nation through its oil. This village will become rich through oil. Why would you stop us from becoming rich, unless you were an enemy of our country?'

'All we're doing is trying to stop people from being evicted,' Ed said slowly. 'If everyone agrees to selling their land and they get a fair price for it, then that's up to them, but—'

'I hear that you have been meeting with criminal elements in Chittagong,' the Chairman interrupted. 'Enemies of our country, who seek to overthrow our government.'

Ed snorted. 'I don't know what you're on about. It's like I said, all we're trying to do is make sure that people in Jhomgram and Lalalpur don't get exploited. We're not against Islam. It isn't anything to do with that . . . It's the dacoits who burn down people's homes that we're against.'

'Ed . . .'

Touching his hand with the tips of my fingers, I twitched my head, trying to signal at him to stop. I was dreading him losing his temper and blurting something insulting. Now he was silent, scowling and glaring at the floor.

'We're so grateful for everything you have done for us—' I started, but Chairman Roul interrupted me.

'You are foreigners,' he said dismissively. 'There is so much you don't understand. I therefore urge you to stop these actions. Then everything can continue without problem.' Standing, he brushed a hand over the creases in his Punjabi. He seemed very calm. 'Tssh, it is so hot in here,' he said, motioning towards the door. 'And I have other business to attend to.'

'What do you mean?' Ed said. 'What kind of problems?'

Not replying, he brushed past.

This time no one urged us to stay and eat rice. If Nasneen made the tea, it was never served. Instead, within five minutes of our arrival, we were back on the path, walking hurriedly through the electric green fields.

'He's a Jamaat-i-Islam man,' Ed declared triumphantly. 'That's why he always turns it into a thing about being for or against Islam. And why that mullah in the robes was having a go at us at the meeting. You know they're linked to the government?'

I shrugged. So far I had only vaguely grasped the rudiments

of Bangladeshi politics. All I knew was that in the main they were vicious and violent.

'Well, fuck him! We can carry on with or without his support . . .'

'How are we going to do that?'

'Easy. We'll refuse to respond to his threats.'

'But what about the school? He'll make us close it down!'

Ed stopped, twirling around and grabbing my hand as if this was something to celebrate.

'So what?!'

After our meeting with the Chairman something about Ed was changed, his initial enthusiasm for Schools for Change displaced into a darker, almost manic obsession with Oxan and BNRC. He should have been overseeing the building works and doing his teaching, but instead spent his days meeting Aunik's activist friends in Chittagong or in the Internet cafe in Noton Bazaar composing lengthy emails to aid officials in Dhaka or to the media. The World Bank was backing the oil excavation, he furiously announced, returning after a long day in front of a computer screen; they had told him that local farmers would be adequately compensated and it would boost economic growth. The only person who seemed even slightly interested in the campaign was Dan Jameson, one of the advisers at the UK's Department for International Development, but he was currently away.

Whilst Ed had stopped teaching his classes, no one turned up to mine. For the first few days I managed to convince myself that the unusual absence of the five young women on whom I had been practising was caused by the unbearable heat, or perhaps one of the bouts of fever that occasionally gripped the village. Yet after three mornings spent waiting for them to arrive, I knew the worst: since Ed had not done as the Chairman had requested and stopped the campaign, he was preventing Schools for Change from functioning.

I sat in the bedroom, deciding what to do. Above me, the fan was clattering so energetically that I was half afraid it might whizz from its base and decapitate me. Holding down the ends of my flapping *orna*, I gazed unhappily across the small room: Ed's clothes, dumped on a chair; my rucksack stored on top of the wardrobe; books, piled on the floor. Once again, Ed was in Noton Bazaar. When I mentioned the classes he had merely shrugged indifferently; perhaps he too was being boycotted. Didn't he care that everything we'd worked so hard to establish was being thrown away? Or was it simply that campaigning against BNRC was a more pressing cause? In theory, I supposed he was right. So why did I have this ache in my chest?

Bracing myself, I changed into my smartest sari. If I could get the Chairman's mother and the other women in his house to listen, I reasoned, perhaps they in turn could persuade him that all we were doing was trying to help the people who had been dispossessed in Jhomgram. OK, so Chairman Roul was taking a cut from BNRC; it was a sensitive topic. But surely there must be some kind of compromise? Newly energized, I hurried down the steps.

Away from the bungalow's fan, the combination of heat and humidity was unbearable. Sweat poured over my belly and into the folds of my sari, down my back, from behind my knees. Breaking free of the trees, I progressed across the fields, my legs slithering against each other. It was going to be OK, I told myself. The village women loved me; I'd win them round.

If only it wasn't so bloody hot! As I reached the Chairman's compound I made gratefully for the pond, jumping down the ghat steps in my enthusiasm to cup the cool water in my hands. Dipping my fingers in the water, I splashed it over my face. I was trying to be matter-of-fact about the visit but I was horribly nervous.

'Auntie?'

Glancing around, I saw the Chairman's nine-year-old son standing behind me. Dressed only in a pair of shorts, he was hacking at a stick with a machete.

'Hello!' I smiled at him happily, relieved to be addressed with so much affection. 'What are you up to?'

The boy ignored the question. 'My grandma said to tell you she wasn't in,' he said, slashing at the stick.

I swallowed, my face burning as the meaning of his words sank in. 'What about your mother?' I said slowly. 'I wanted to see her too.'

'No one's in. They say we're not to talk to you because you're with Bush.'

'Bush?'

'Bush in Amerika.'

'Why would I be with Bush?' I said, trying to sound relaxed. 'I can't stand him.'

'That's what people say. That you're working for Bush and trying to make us into Christians.'

'*What?*'

'My father says you and Mr Edward are missionaries and we mustn't talk to you any more.'

'That's not true!'

Jumping up, I walked quickly away, tears of indignation prickling my eyes. I had a horrible, mortifying sense that the boy was laughing at me.

'Where are you going, Auntie?' he called. As I hurried out of the compound his home-made arrow landed at my feet.

I stumbled back down the path, towards Syeda's house. She would not care what the Chairman said, and even if she did, I could explain to her what Ed and Aunik's campaign was really about. Surely not everyone would take against us? Yet even as I reached the bamboo fence that encircled her small property, I was feeling sick. Ever since Ed's public meeting, no one – not even Syeda – had called to visit.

I found her squatting on the step, scaling fish with her dag. As she finished with one, she would toss it into her pot, then reach into the slithering pile beside her and start on another, dragging its silver scales over the blade.

'Syeda. *Oh, go Shonar!*' I cried, using the old village greeting that she had taught me, which always made her laugh. *Syeda, my Golden Mother!*

But rather than jumping to her feet and grabbing my hand her face was stony.

'*Ki kobaor?*' Jerking her chin enquiringly, she slowly stood up, wiping her hands on her thin sari. Mobed was asleep on a mat behind her, I noticed.

'I'm good. How are you?'

She didn't reply. Instead, she peered carefully at the path behind. 'Did anyone see you arrive?'

'No.'

'Good. Now come inside.'

Grabbing my arm, she led me inside her small earth-walled house, its one room dominated by the large, wooden-framed bed. Sitting me down firmly she took my hand between her rough palms and regarded me sadly.

'Bad things are happening,' she said gravely. 'There's too much danger.'

'What bad things?'

She jerked her head towards Jhomgram. 'Big people have been here,' she continued. 'They said we shouldn't talk to you.'

It took me a while to answer. I stared into her thin face, feeling the nausea wash over me. It was as bad as I'd feared, perhaps worse.

'What do you mean "big people"?'

She pulled a face. 'People from the government . . . Oxan people. They said if we did what Mr Edward said there would be lots of trouble.'

'And do you believe them?'

I was willing her to shake her head. All she had to do was whisper 'no' and I would be fine. But she did not answer. Instead, she stood up, dropping my hand. 'You should go home, Sister,' she said sternly. 'Go back to your country. It isn't safe here for foreigners.'

She did not have to say any more. As she spoke, I realized that the intimacy I thought we shared meant nothing. I was a blundering, foolish foreigner, and she was a poor rural woman, who would have no hope of surviving if she crossed the 'big people'. I'd romanticized our friendship, imagining we had a special bond which transcended culture and economics. But it was an illusion. We were too different, our circumstances mutually unfathomable. And now she was ushering me out of her house, terrified to be caught entertaining me.

At the bungalow, Ed had unexpectedly returned. As I trailed through the trees, I saw him sitting on the terrace, gazing at a newspaper that was spread over his knees.

'Hiya!' he called cheerfully. 'Don't look so pissed off! I've got something here to cheer you up!'

It was an article written for one of the English-language dailies by a journalist based in Chittagong. The piece took up an entire page, with the headline: *The price of progress. A special report by Anu Jalal.* Underneath this was a gory picture of a corpse wrapped in a funereal shroud, the dead man's eyes blackened, his lip split: the man who Ed had seen lying on the road perhaps. The BNRC had grabbed the land in Jhomgram without offering adequate compensation, the journalist had written. A local partner of the multinational, Oxan, BNRC had been acting without regard to international law or the public policies of Oxan. Because the villagers were poor fishermen, they had been easy targets; when they had tried to resist, there had been beatings and two deaths. In addition to this, the BNRC planned to take more land in the immediate vicinity: it had bribed local leaders to ensure that there was no opposition. Indeed, money earmarked for community development was being poured into their pockets. The article concluded with a brief interview with Ed.

> 'It's a human rights violition,' Mr Salisbury, a British aid-worker, opined. 'The sooner the outside world knows of outrages such as this in the name of economic growth, the better. What is even more sickening is that village leaders, who should be protecting the people in their communities, are happy to sell their souls for financial reward.'

I stared at the words in shock. How could Ed be such an idiot? If the Chairman saw it, and he surely would, we would have to leave Lalalpur.

'It's great, isn't it?' Ed was saying. 'Now that it's finally been made public, the donors are going to have to sit up and do something.'

'Yeah,' I said flatly. 'Well done.'

'And this is just the start! According to this guy who wrote the article, the issue is potentially explosive, much, much bigger than just the BNRC being a bit corrupt.'

'What do you mean?'

He smiled smugly. 'I can't tell you. I'm sworn to complete and utter secrecy. Let's just say that the highest levels are involved, and it could bring down the government.'

I glanced away from his gleeful face. He wanted me to press him for details, or at least share his excitement yet all I could muster was: 'Oh.'

'So?' he said after a pause. 'What's the matter?'

'Nothing.'

'Tell me . . .'

I sighed, sitting down heavily on the bed. 'It's just that I'm worried about the consequences.'

'What consequences?' Hovering above me, he folded his arms tightly around his thin chest.

'For the school and for us . . . I mean, supposing all we achieve through this campaign is to get ourselves thrown out? Shouldn't it be up to local people to fight their own battles? And if they're going to get compensation, then who are we to tell them what to do?'

'But they're not going to get proper compensation! That's the whole point!'

'How do you know? I mean, OK, so the chairman is getting a cut of the proceeds. Isn't that the way things work?'

Ed flinched. He looked so skinny, I thought with a lurch of pain. 'You have to stop being so negative,' he said quietly. 'Please, just trust me.'

Chucking the newspaper on the bed, he walked away.

After that something between Ed and I was fractured. I'd assumed I knew him, for in the intensity of Bangladesh our brief twelve months together had felt like years. Yet now he was like a stranger. We still communicated, but politely, like friendly acquaintances. At night he would kiss me perfunc-torily on the lips and turn over. Mostly he came to bed long after I had gone to sleep, working into the small hours on drafts of emails he planned to send. He always kept to his side of the bed.

Like sand pouring through my hands, I was losing him. Gone was the confident, playful man I had met in Dhaka. In his place was this troubled, ramshackle character, who barely spoke and spent all night writing secret missives. When I asked what he was doing he would stare at me blankly, as if he had forgotten I was there.

'Come on, honey, come to bed,' I said one night as he sat, hunched over his exercise book. Wandering to his chair, I put my hand on the back of his neck, rubbing it. 'You can do that in the morning.'

'It's too hot to sleep,' he murmured, not looking up.

'Then you can talk to me . . .'

Finally he turned, his slender fingers catching my arm and pulling me towards him. 'What about? I'm not exactly very entertaining at the moment.'

Plonking my behind on to his bony lap, I put my arms around

his middle, squeezing him with relief. 'I don't care! Tell me
about something other than Bangladesh. Tell me about India!'

He chuckled. 'I don't know anything about India. Er, it's
very big and there are elephants?'

Giggling, I shoved him in the shoulder. It was so long since
I'd heard him laugh. 'Duh! You don't get off the hook that
easily, mister! I know you know about India because you used
to live there.'

Shoving me gently back, he raised his eyebrows in bemusement. 'No I didn't.'

'Yes you did!'

'No, I *didn't*!'

Pulling away from him, I stood up. He wasn't laughing any
more, but frowning and drumming his fingers on the desk.

'But you said you worked there before you came to
Bangladesh,' I said quietly. 'I definitely remember you saying it.'

He blinked, his cheeks flushing.

'Well I don't want to talk about it, OK?' he said tersely.
'Why the hell can't you just leave me alone? Can't you see
I'm working?'

I stared at him. For some reason he was lying, I thought
with a wave of misery. And now I couldn't reach him.

EIGHTEEN

The next morning I was in Noton Bazaar, stocking up
on supplies. The market was particularly crowded today:
the lanes so packed that I had to queue on the pavement whilst the congestion ahead cleared, staring vacantly at
the clothes stalls: seconds from the Dhaka factories that
Primark and Hennes didn't want, frilly baby dresses, rows of
fake designer shades. I filed past chai stalls and sweet shops,
their windows filled with *gulab jamin* and samosas, then turned
a corner and was in the butcher's market, the grisly remains
of cows and goats hanging in lumps from hooks, clouds of
flies whirring around the congealing glut.

Normally I didn't mind the shoving, the overpowering stench
of rotting fruit or the guttural hawking of men, gobbing on the

ground. But today I was tetchy, wanting to complete my chores and get away. I couldn't stop brooding over the argument I had had with Ed the night before. I kept dredging up the conversation we had had in Dhaka, when we barely knew each other. He told me he'd worked in India, I was sure. He was a consultant, he'd said; before that, he was in India. I'd pictured him sitting meditatively by the Ganges. Why would he bother to lie?

I'd reached the electrical shops now, where piles of out-of-date batteries were heaped besides counterfeit hi-fis and Korean TVs. Yet as I turned to cross the heaving road, I was suddenly violently pushed from behind.

'Hey!'

There wasn't time to see his face. As the man jostled me against a stall, all I registered was the rough clutch of fingers on my bum, his white trainers and tobacco breath.

'Tell your husband Sadid needs him,' he whispered softly.

I gasped, about to shout out, but he had gone.

Back in Lalalpur Ed was slouched at his desk. Since our dispute the day before we had barely spoken. Now, he looked blearily up at me.

'I've got a message for you,' I said lightly. 'This man told me to tell you that Sadid needs you.'

'What man?'

'I don't know . . . He kind of bumped into me.'

Ed frowned. 'What do you mean he "bumped into you"? You mean he groped you or something?'

I forced myself to laugh. 'Of course not! It's just like I said. I was in the market, and he came up and said to tell you Sadid needs you.'

'He didn't actually do anything to you?'

'No, it was fine!'

It *was* fine. OK, so I'd been groped. It was upsetting, but I'd survive. Yet even now I couldn't shake off the queasy feeling of having been violated.

'And that was all he said?'

'Yeah. Who *is* Sadid, anyway?'

Ed stood up, shoving back his chair with a clatter and running his hands distractedly through his shaggy hair.

'I've never heard of him.'

'Are you sure?'

Picking up his notepad he started to leaf through it. He seemed to have stopped listening. 'Yup.'

'Wasn't there someone called Sadid at that brick field in Dhaka?'

'For God's sake, Sarah! Can't you give it a bloody rest?'

I literally bit my lip, nipping the jellied flesh until I tasted blood.

Later that day four strangers came to visit. I was sitting under the trees gazing across the fields as Ed paced around the bungalow, planning God knows what. As I watched the men tramp officiously along the path, an unformed dread curled in my stomach. They had the sheen of urban wealth about them: the man leading the deputation was wearing a heavy gold watch, his belly straining the fabric of his kameez shirt. His face was soft and flabby, babyish almost, and his hair was so badly dyed that I could see the stain of the henna on his scalp. As the men filed past the trees they did not salaam me.

'Ed!' I called. 'You've got some visitors!'

He appeared on the terrace, his face pale. Not glancing at me, he showed the men inside.

I stop talking. My story is becoming increasingly difficult to tell.

'It would have been alright if we could have fought it together,' I say to Alexandria. 'But Ed kind of clammed up on me. I was trying to avoid having the school closed down, but it was like he didn't seem to care about it any more. I don't understand why. I keep thinking it was my fault. I mean, that I somehow pissed him off, or something and that he felt he couldn't trust me . . .'

'Listen, Sarah, stop a moment.'

Alexandria places her hand on my arm, regarding me thoughtfully. 'There's a lot you probably don't know about my brother.'

'What do you mean?'

'Just that I doubt he told you everything. Oh, honey, don't cry . . .'

She shuffles closer, placing her hands around my head. I lean into her, shuddering.

'You mustn't blame yourself, darling. It's just that this isn't
the first time Eddy's disappeared.'

'What do you mean?'

'He's done this before. A few years ago.'

'But why?'

For a while she is silent. Then she says, 'Let's get you into
some warm clothes. Then there's somewhere I want to take you.'

NINETEEN

I lie in the bath, staring through the skylight at the drifting
London clouds. When I scrub my pale body, the final remnants
of my life in Lalalpur will be irrevocably removed: a strand
of hair that Ed's fingers may have touched, some grains of sand
between my toes. I slosh myself with Alexandria's expensive
lotions and am remade. When I have finished I find that she has
laid some clothes for me on her bed; she must have noticed my
lack of luggage and discreetly picked them out.

In the hall, Alexandria is standing tensely by the door. 'Are
you ready? I'll get the car.'

It's one of those retro convertible Beetles, in silver. She
drives through central London with the aggressive thrust of
a Londoner. She's lived here all her adult life, she says. She
grew up in the family place in Devon but the 'county' scene
was never for her: green wellies and hacking jackets are *so*
not a good look. I smile faintly, not sure whether this is a
joke. She keeps talking, but I'm not taking much in.

'The thing about Ed,' she says as she accelerates past Hyde
Park Corner, 'is that he can never really work out who he is.
He takes everything so hard. Carries this great bloody burden
of guilt around with him.'

'He likes to think he's doing good . . .'

She gives her head a little shake. 'There's more to it than that.'

I don't know what she means. I am thinking of the things
he used to tell me. We were meant to be together, he'd say;
some lucky force pulled us both to Bangladesh in order that
we could meet; now that we'd found each other, we never
need be apart.

I've started to cry again. I dab at my face with the sleeve of Alexandria's denim jacket, hoping that she hasn't noticed. If I'd known he was thinking of disappearing I'd have tried to stop him. I could have insisted on us leaving the village with Dan the night before the storm, or forced him to tell me what was really going on.

'Nearly there now,' Alexandria says, glancing at me.

I try to concentrate on our surroundings. We've reached an area of splendid town houses arranged around a series of gated squares. I stare mutely at the grand buildings, their fancy fronts as ornate as wedding cakes. With the blue heritage plates displayed by gleaming front doors, their vast sash windows and polished flagstone steps, moneyed confidence oozes from each carefully preserved brick. As Alexandria searches for a parking space we edge past rows of Mercedes, Jags and Porsches. Finally she backs into a space in the line of vehicles, nodding at one of the mansions. 'It's just here.'

I follow her across the road and up the steps of one of the smartest houses. Producing a key from her bag she opens the heavy front door and steps inside the cavernous entrance hall. I shuffle behind, glancing curiously at the blood-red walls and chequered tiles. Old paintings hang on the walls: long dead aristocrats who peer imperiously back. By the wall, a Chinese vase stuffed with roses rests on a posh little table, engravings up its legs. On the other side of the hall a polished wood staircase sweeps upstairs.

'I know it's silly, but I still have it cleaned every week and the flowers done,' Alexandria says, leafing through a pile of mail on the table. 'Even though there's no one here.'

'Is it yours?'

She glances round at me, smiling. 'No, darling. It belongs to Ed.'

She shows me into what she calls 'the drawing room': a huge space with a corniced ceiling covered in plaster grapes and cherubs. The furniture is similarly classy: a brocaded chaise longue and the type of leather settee that creaks when you sit down. A shining grand piano is placed under the window, its lid propped expectantly open as if only a minute earlier the room's cultured resident has been delicately plinking some classical tune on its keys. I trail after Alexandria, my senses jangling. I cannot imagine the Ed I knew in such a place.

'Bit stuffy, isn't it?'

I look around, not sure how to react.

'I wouldn't have thought it was really his style . . .'

'He inherited it from Ma and Pa,' she says, as if this was obvious, wandering across the room and peering through the window at the street.

'That, and the places in France and Devon that he sold. He decided to keep this, what with property prices in London going so berserk. He couldn't really be bothered to do anything to it, so he left everything the way our parents had it. It's a bit less fusty upstairs.'

She stops, watching me.

'He didn't tell you, did he?'

I suck at my cheeks, trying to control myself. How could Ed have owned such a place? Now that I am here, gazing around his front room like a day tripper in a stately home the differences between us that in Bangladesh had felt like a hair-line fracture, appear as a gaping ravine.

'If you mean did he tell me he had a house like this, then no, he didn't bother to mention it.'

Alexandria does not react. Folding her arms, she adds evenly, 'He used to get so embarrassed about our background. He'd go to ridiculous lengths to hide it. It explains a lot about the way he was.'

'It was obvious he was posh,' I mumble. 'He didn't need to keep it secret.'

Alexandria eyes me. 'Oh yes he did,' she says with a humourless laugh. 'Eddy had a lot of secrets he needed to keep.'

Before I can respond, she gestures at me to sit down. 'We'll talk later,' she says. 'In the meantime, you need to get some rest.'

Since I have nowhere else to go, Alexandria suggests I stay here. She has to pick up Joseph from nursery, she says. She'll come back later with supplies. As she leaves, she kisses me formally on both cheeks. I have the sense that she wants to be alone.

'We have to stick together,' she says. 'Otherwise nothing's going to make sense.'

I stand by the window, watching as she zooms off.

*   *   *

Upstairs is different from the ground floor, the antique furniture replaced by more functional, modern pieces, the walls white. I wander through the enormous rooms, trying to imagine Ed's London life. There's very little to go on. The few framed photos displayed on the shelves are of other people: a little girl in an old-fashioned tartan pinafore who might be Alexandria, a soldier from what looks like the First World War. The only hints of Ed are the books that cover the walls on the second and third floors. In contrast to the heirlooms in the so-called 'drawing room' there are no pictures.

On the far side of the bedroom is a low, oriental-style bed, with a black headboard and plain white covers. There are no rugs on the parquet floors and little furniture, just an oriental lacquered wardrobe decorated by a red dragon. I drift across the room, opening its heavy doors and staring numbly at the rows of suits that hang inside. It's hard to imagine my Ed in such clothes. He was naturally shabby, I used to joke; his hair was too long, his clothes frayed. It was one of the many things I loved. Yet as I reach into the cool interior and brush my fingers against the yards of linen and wool, pulling the jackets back to discover a layer of pristine shirts, each perfectly ironed, some still in their designer wrappings, I am beginning to wonder if the man I knew in Bangladesh is really the same person who lived here.

I've noticed something else: a heavy woollen coat, deep blue, the colour of his eyes. The label's Versace; it must have cost thousands of pounds. Pulling it out, I hold the expensive fabric against my face. I had no claim over the man who would have worn a garment like this; now that I am marooned in his mansion, our relationship seems as flimsy as a half-remembered dream. In Bangladesh he was merely flirting with poverty, gaining a vicarious pleasure from living the simple life for a couple of years yet secure in the knowledge of the family trust fund behind him. *This* was his real life, which he would have eventually returned to. And I didn't know anything about it.

I am so tired. Cradling the coat in my arms, I lie on the bed. If I close my eyes, I can still hear the roar of the aircraft, feel the weightless sensation of flying all those thousands of miles. Dragging Ed's coat over my body, I curl into a ball, tucking my hands into the silk-lined pockets for warmth. My thoughts slide into a half dream and once again the men are approaching the bungalow. They walk soundlessly through the coconut grove, their faces grim. The one that I am most afraid of has a gelatinous belly which protrudes through his kameez; despite his baby face, his eyes are bloodshot. As they push past me and into the building I realize that Ed is in trouble. I need to help him but my legs refuse to move. Inside Ed is shouting something, I can't hear what. I have to move quickly but am glued to the floor. Now someone is screaming, a ghoulish shriek, that hardly sounds human.

It's coming from me. I lie on Ed's bed, crying. I feel as if I am being mangled, my intestines forced through my mouth, my lungs twisted and scrunched. It's exhausting; I'm reduced to a mass of trembling flesh, an outpouring of snot and slime.

'Don't cry, love.'

Ed's hand is on my shoulder. I can feel his warm fingers, pressing into my skin. He has draped his body around mine, his face pressed into my hair.

'Stay here forever,' I gasp.

He shushes me, pulling me closer until the sobbing subsides. I can feel his breath on my neck, his arms clasped around my shoulders. If I could only stop these memories, I might believe it was real.

TWENTY

Lalalpur, May 3rd

It was blocking the path. I hesitated by the screen doors, peering at the mound of white rags that had been dumped by the trees: from where I was standing, it looked like a pile of laundry, splattered with something nasty. Stepping on to the terrace, I progressed slowly down the steps. My chest had gone very tight. I did not like the cloud of flies that covered the browning stains, or the jackdaws that pecked around. Something thick and gloopy had spilt on to the sandy track.

I got close enough to see Aunik's face staring sightlessly at a heap of coconut husks. He was lying on his front, his head twisted oddly so that he appeared to be perusing the bungalow. The top of his skull had a deep dent in it from which the bluebottles were feeding; blackened blood trickled down his waxy cheeks. They must have dragged him by his arms for his white jeans were stiff with dirt. As I stepped closer, the flies lifted from his remains in one body, a droning amoeba, zooming into my face.

My yelling must have been heard across the village, for within five minutes, a crowd had gathered. Word quickly spread: as we kneeled, weeping, by Aunik's body, people poured through the trees. Some were shouting that the police should be called and Aunik's mother fetched from Chittagong; others simply stared. When I felt arms around my shoulders, I realized that Syeda was beside me.

'Sarah, *beti*, come inside . . .'

'No, leave me alone . . .'

Batting her away, I slumped against Ed, who was stroking Aunik's head as if he was a child.

'It's my fault . . . it's all my fault . . .'

He was deathly pale; as he reached across Aunik's bloodied face and rearranged a black curl, his hands trembled violently.

'Mr Edward!'

Habib the tea shop owner and Mohammed Bokt the imam were pushing their way through the crowd, a wooden stretcher balanced on their shoulders. As they reached us, they gazed sadly down at the corpse.

'We must take him.'

'No!' Jerking around, Ed glared at them. 'Don't touch him!'

'But this is our Muslim law.'

These were not Aunik's murderers. We had eaten in their houses and played with their children; they were decent, digni-fied men, who had treated us well. Yet Ed was jumping up and shooing them away, as if they were our enemies.

'Leave him alone!' he yelled in English. 'Wait for the police!'

Laughing grimly, they lowered the stretcher on the sand. 'We can wait for the police,' Mohammed Bokt said quietly. 'But they won't help.'

They were right. When the police finally appeared they glanced at Aunik's remains and nonchalantly covered him up. The Superintendent who'd arrived, horn blaring, in an armoured jeep, strode around looking important but doing nothing. He didn't take our statements, just jotted Ed's name and address in his notebook. As his lackeys loaded the body on to Habib's stretcher he hung back on the path, smoking a fag and looking bored. Later on, he wandered towards the beach, fiddling with his mobile. It seemed that no investigation was going to take place.

Once the body was gone, the crowd drifted away. There was nothing to stare at, no more drama. Even Syeda, who for the last three hours had sat beside me, her hand in mine, had eventually risen with a sigh and moved towards the trees. It was early afternoon by now, the day deadened in the oppressive heat; my jasmine wilting lifelessly and the birds mute.

Ed flopped on the steps, his head in his hands. Crouching beside him, I clumsily looped my arm over his inert back, my fingers touching his shoulder blades through the damp fabric of his shirt.

'Shall I get you something to drink?'

He did not respond: he seemed hardly to be breathing. 'You have to drink, Ed, otherwise you'll make yourself ill . . .'

Finally he lifted his head. His face was grey and greasy with sweat, his forehead crossed by lines.

'He didn't fucking deserve it,' he whispered. 'They should have killed me.'

I shuffled closer, pushing my face into his hair. 'How can you say that?'

'Because I forced him to get involved. He didn't want to, did he? He *said* it was dangerous. But I ignored him. I thought I knew it all . . .'

I recalled Aunik's mortified expression when Ed had accused him of being a coward. 'It was his choice,' I said slowly. 'He could have told you to piss off.'

'I wish to God he had!'

'Ed, you can't blame yourself for what's happened. All you've been trying to do is help. It wasn't as if you knew that someone would end up getting murdered . . .' I stopped, too shocked to continue. The things I had dreaded happening as a result of Ed's campaign – that the school would be closed and we'd be asked to leave – now seemed utterly inconsequential. I had never once considered that it would come to this.

'Jesus!' Ed moaned. 'He supported his whole family with his wages . . .'

Despite the heat, he was shivering. Rubbing my hand over his back, I tried to pull him closer but he remained rigid.

'Who do you think did it?'

He shrugged. 'It doesn't really matter. Any number of people might want to warn us off.'

'What, you mean to stop the campaign?'

Wiping the hair from his face, he slowly looked up, his green eyes locking on to mine. There was something else, I suddenly realized, something he was keeping from me.

'What is it?' I whispered. 'Tell me!'

'It's better you don't know,' he mumbled.

'What do you mean?'

'I don't want you getting sucked in.'

'Sucked in to what? For God's sake, Ed, you have to tell me what's going on!'

There was a long pause which suddenly seemed loaded with significance, like a cloud growing darker.

'I think we should leave,' he muttered. 'It's not safe here any more.'

'You think we should go back to Dhaka?'

'Yeah.'

I stared into his pale face. I had poured everything of myself into our life in Lalalpur, stupidly believing that, like some kind of Development Studies fairy-tale, we could stay here forever, doing 'good' and being happy. But now, with a few fragmented phrases, the fantasy was over.

'I'll go to Chittagong tomorrow,' Ed continued. 'I'll book a flight.'

'Fine.'

Standing, I started to move up the steps. In an odd way there was nothing left to say.

'I'm a piece of shit,' Ed suddenly whispered. 'A dishonest piece of shit.'

'Why do you say that?'

'I'm not who you think I am, Sarah . . .'

'Who's that, then?'

'Someone who doesn't fuck everything up . . . someone good . . .'

I glanced at his skinny, shivering body. 'You *are* good . . .' I couldn't do this any more, I suddenly thought; no matter how much he needed me to reassure him, I had to be alone.

'No I'm not. I've been pretending to you. I'm a fraud . . .'

I had to get to the cool of the fan. I had to lie on the bed and close my eyes.

'Don't be silly,' I muttered, turning towards the door. 'Of course you're not.'

It was the last real conversation we had. Ed left for Chittagong at dawn the next morning, saying that he was going to visit Aunik's grieving family. I awoke with a migraine and spent the day in bed. By the time he returned, I was asleep.

The day after that, Dan Jameson arrived. I watched in surprise as his jeep bumped down the track, taking in the Dhaka registration plate. The driver was Bengali, but his passenger was Western, I noted, dressed in the short-sleeved white shirt and linen slacks favoured by aid officials. When the jeep finally stopped the western man jumped out, waving at me cheerily. Perhaps this was Dan Jameson, I thought with a rush of hope; after his long correspondence with Ed he had finally taken matters in hand and come to see us.

'Howdy!' he called. 'I've come to see Eddy!'

I held out my hand, grinning with relief. 'Are you Dan Jameson? It's really brilliant that you've come all this way.'

He nodded, taking my hand and shaking it warmly. 'It was the least I could do.'

'We'd kind of given up on everyone in Dhaka to be honest.'

'You should never give up!'

Not waiting to be shown the way, he leapt up the terrace steps. Ed had already appeared at the screen doors, his arms wrapped defensively around his waist. He looked so ill, his clothes hanging off his skeletal frame, his face gaunt. Earlier, I had heard him in the bathroom, vomiting. Now, he stared at Jameson so intently that he seemed almost mad.

'Ed!' I called. 'It's Dan Jameson, you know, from Dfid?'

Remembering his manners, Ed finally held out his hand.

'Hello Eddy,' Dan said. 'Haven't we met before?'

Ed frowned. What *was* the matter with him? 'I don't think so, no . . .'

'But there've been a *lot* of emails!'

Finally, he smiled. 'Yeah, sorry about that. I'm afraid I've got a bit fixated on everything . . .'

'I'm not surprised!'

Ed pulled a face. 'Let's go inside,' he said quietly.

Whilst Ed and Dan talked in the living room, I retreated to bed for once again my head was throbbing. I lay under the fan, a flannel held to my temples. As I listened to the murmur of their voices I drifted in and out of an uneasy dream in which Ed and I were at the Chairman's compound, sitting on his veranda. There were clothes strewn around the courtyard, I saw as I gazed around; they must have fallen from the line: an old green sari; a small girl's pinafore; a pair of white jeans, oddly stained.

'I can help you, I promise,' Dan was saying in the room next door.

I could not hear Ed's reply. I rolled on to my side, my eyes closed.

Oddly stained and twisted: once white jeans now the colour of rust. And from the outhouse a red stain, spreading like a slick of oil. Slowly the sand turned crimson, the gloopy wave reaching the garments and gently lifting them as it moved towards me. It was almost at the steps now, lapping at my feet. I wanted to get away, but I couldn't. I tried to stand, but it was impossible. Looking desperately around, I realized that Ed had disappeared. 'Ed!' I tried to scream, but the words wouldn't come.

An hour later we were eating dinner on the terrace. A storm was forecast, Dan was saying, it was going to be a biggie, we should return with him to Chittagong; he was planning to leave that night. He snorted dismissively when Ed mentioned the bandits on the highway that were rumoured to hijack vehicles after dark.

'You don't really believe that, do you?'

'It's a significant factor.'

He sighed, pushing back his chair with his muscled legs. 'Are you sure? They're predicting a grade one cyclone. I'd hate for you guys to be in danger.'

'Thanks for the offer,' Ed said slowly. 'But I don't think we'll take it up. There's a perfectly good shelter in the village. We need to show our commitment to the community and stay here. Isn't that right, Sarah?'

For the first time in weeks, something flashed between us: empathy, perhaps, or simply agreement. Two days earlier we had vowed to leave, but we were going to do it on our own terms, not just because of a storm.

'Ed's right,' I murmured, pushing my plate away. 'We're not going anywhere.'

What would have happened if we'd done as Dan suggested? As I lie in Ed's oversized London bed I wish to God we had. Yet at the time, ignorant of what was already whirling towards us across the Bay of Bengal, I had glanced into Ed's face, relief surging at the surprisingly cheerful glint in his eye. He looked better, I realized; lighter, almost. He and Dan were discussing some meeting of head honchos in Dhaka. The fate of the villagers in Jhomgram would be top of the agenda, Dan was saying. Ed could rest assured that as soon as the top guys heard about what was happening, Oxan and their local henchmen would be stopped in their tracks.

'I'm going to bed,' I finally said, picking up my hurricane lamp from the table. 'My head's killing me.'

As I passed him, Ed's hand brushed mine. 'See you later, yeah?'

A few hours later he shuffled through the mosquito net.

'You're awake then?' His fingers traced my face.

'Mmf . . .'

'What a complete tosser that bloke is! I couldn't get away from him.'

I chuckled. 'Ah come on, he's not that bad. At least he's trying to help.'

'He gives me the creeps.'

There was a long pause. When Ed eventually spoke his voice was husky. 'Sarah?'

'Yeah?'

'Do you love me?'

He sounded so small and vulnerable. I rolled over, bringing my fingers to his face. After so long not touching, it felt strange to have his chest pressed against mine, our legs muddled together. In that small slice of time, between his question and my reply, I finally understood how much stronger than him I had become.

'Of course I do.'

'So it doesn't matter about things I've done? I mean, all my fuck-ups . . .'

I placed my hand on his cheek. 'You have to stop blaming yourself, hon. I'll love you whatever you do.'

He seemed to relax. For a while we lay quietly in each other's arms. I did not want to speak, just to feel his skin against mine. In the fields, jackals were howling at the stars.

'Listen,' Ed said. 'I can hear the sea.'

I held my breath, taking in the faint slap of the waves. When Ed finally spoke his voice was so soft that I hardly caught the words. 'Tomorrow,' he said. 'Everything's going to change.'

TWENTY-ONE

London

Footsteps clatter up the wooden stairs. I grope my way out of the bedcovers, trying to work out where I am. My cheek has been resting in a pool of drool; wiping the spittle away, I push Ed's coat off my shoulders and glance around the dimly lit room. I must have been asleep for a while, for the street lights are on. Beyond the windows, I can hear the distant roar of traffic: not the cacophony of peeping and bells that I'm accustomed to in Dhaka but a deeper, heavier sound: a great number of expensive cars moving fast down well maintained roads.

'Sarah! Are you here?'

It's Alexandria. Stumbling from the bedroom I watch her appear up the stairs.

'There's someone I want you to meet!' she calls in a cheerful voice that I haven't heard her use before. 'Come on Joseph, stop fiddling with that silly thing!'

She steps aside, revealing a small boy lingering by the banisters. He's wearing what must be his kindergarten uniform: grey trousers and a grey jumper and is playing with an action man dressed in army combats. I gawp at him, my heart stopping. He has Ed's face: the same almond shaped eyes and shy smirk, and Ed's unruly mop of brown hair.

'This is Sarah,' Alexandria says. 'Uncle Eddy's friend, who I told you about?'

The child glowers at me. 'What's she doing here?'

Clasping his hand, Alexandria pulls him away from the

banisters. 'She's staying here for a little bit. Come on darling, say hello. You can watch some telly if you're good.'

'Hello.' With considerable expertise, he flicks the action man over the edge of the stairs. It bounces several times on the tiled floor, coming to rest underneath the table. Turning his back on us, he scoots back down the stairs to retrieve it.

'I haven't told him yet about what's happened,' Alexandria whispers as she draws level with me. 'I don't know what to say.'

She hands me a leather bag. 'Here are some clothes and whatnot to keep you going. I thought we could carry on talking. If that's alright?'

Joseph is settled in front of a vast plasma television that I can't imagine Ed either buying or watching, and Alexandria and I descend yet another flight of stairs to the enormous kitchen that looks out over the private back garden.

'I'm sorry I woke you up,' Alexandria says as we settle down over mugs of tea. 'You must be exhausted.'

I shrug. 'It's OK.'

For a moment she is quiet. Then she takes a deep breath, as if gathering courage. She is in her late thirties, maybe older; despite the dreadlocks and pink clogs, she's every inch the responsible elder sister.

'I need to work out what exactly happened,' she says slowly. 'You said Eddy was *running* towards the sea. You saw him? Yet there was this tornado. You said you saw it twisting towards you. So he must have known how dangerous it was . . .'

I nod. There isn't much to add.

'And things had become difficult for you in your village. Ed's campaign had upset people . . .'

'You could say that.' I give my head a little shake, dispelling the memory of Aunik's broken body. I don't want to tell Alexandria that part of the story, not yet. But she seems intent on hearing more for her large eyes fixed solemnly on my face.

'And what did Sadid say? He did know what was happening, didn't he? Don't tell me Ed kept it secret from him.'

I look up sharply. 'How do you know about Sadid?'

'Well, I suppose because I helped my aunt employ him. After all, he *is* the director of Schools for Change Bangladesh.'

I goggle at her. She is simply not making sense. '*What?*'

'Sadid Ahmed,' she says, enunciating her words carefully. 'Sweet guy. He runs the programme in Bangladesh.'

'But I thought Ed ran Schools for Change! He told me *he* was the director!'

At this, Alexandria simply chuckles. 'No, darling. Dear old Edward was telling you porkies again. Schools for Change was set up by our aunt, Sylvia de Beaufort, in the early 1990s. Ed was in Bangladesh because we sent him there.'

My jaw has gone stiff. I put down my tea, swallowing hard. So he *did* know Sadid: he was his boss. I recall the man in reflector shades that Ed was chatting to at the brick field. He never introduced me; now I understand why.

'You sent him there?' I echo. I am thinking of the burnt out school, the pebble pinging off my forehead.

'We had to,' Alexandria says with a snort. 'He was in such a state . . .'

'What do you mean?'

'Oh God, it's so complicated . . .' She pushes her mug away, drawing herself up.

Upstairs, I can hear the jangle of Joseph's cartoons. A police siren whoops closer, then is gone. With each of Alexandria's announcements I feel as if my tenuous grip on Ed is further loosened. Folding my arms, I stare at her drawn face.

'Go on.'

'The thing is, when I told you that this was Eddy's house, you probably got the impression that he lived here.'

'Yeah.'

'Well, he didn't. Or at least, he hadn't, for a long, long time.'

'Right . . .'

She pushes a finger into her dreadlocks, twirling a curl. 'For the year before he left for Bangladesh he lived in a squat in Dalston. Before that he had a "breakdown".' She wiggles her fingers in the air. 'He vanished for about six months. I don't know if he mentioned it to you or not . . .?'

I shake my head. 'Doesn't look like he mentioned very much.'

She smiles wanly. 'It was because our childhood was so fucked up by our parents dying and everything. And the money made things complicated for him too. He basically couldn't handle having so much. As a teenager he got pretty wild and by the time he was in his early twenties he was really starting to lose it. He worked for this music magazine for a bit, but that involved lots of partying, and his drinking was really getting out of control. Eventually he had what the psychiatrists call an *episode,* after which he went walkabout for about six months. I went spare trying to find him. In the end I managed to track him down to this place in Dalston and persuaded him to go into rehab.'

'He was in rehab?'

'He kept trying to kill himself,' she says simply. 'There was a phase when he couldn't be left alone.'

I have placed my hand over my mouth. 'He never told me . . .'

'No, I don't suppose he did. He wanted to forget all about it. That's why we thought he should go to Bangladesh, where Sylvia has this project of hers. He was trying to start again, to find an identity for himself, I suppose, so it seemed like a brilliant idea. At first it seemed to work. He said he was going to turn away from the booze and general debauchery and dedicate his life to helping the poor. He got straight, he cut his hair—'

'But he never drank a drop in Bangladesh!'

'He wouldn't have. Alcoholics can't go near the stuff. It was why Sylvia and I thought he should go to a Muslim country. By the way, Sylvia's really keen to meet you. I don't know if Ed mentioned it, but she runs this absolutely wonderful retreat in Sussex. It might be just the place for you to stay, once the dust has settled . . .'

I shrug. I am trying to summon up Ed's image. Why didn't he tell me about his past? Did he lie to make me love him more? Or were his stories of development consultancies and directorships a ruse, to keep me away? It's no good: I can picture patchwork fields and betel nut trees, the mosque and the school, but try as I might, I can't recall Ed's face.

'Have you seen Ed's website?' Alexandria suddenly says.

'You mean about the campaign?'

She nods. 'It's pretty disturbing stuff, isn't it?'

I shrug, assuming that she is referring to the atrocities of Jhomgram. 'I never looked at it, to be honest. We didn't have Internet access in the village, and it was kind of Ed's thing, that he was doing with these friends of Aunik's in Chittagong.'

'So you never saw Ed's blogs?'

'No . . .'

'You should take a look,' she says gently. 'They're . . . well, to be honest, they're pretty on the edge.'

'But that's because of what was happening!'

'I know that, darling, but the tone of his writing . . . it worried me.'

I chew my lip, recalling Ed's increasingly gaunt figure, his inability to talk about anything other than Oxan and the BNRC.

'And that's what you think happened, is it, that he's had another breakdown?'

She doesn't reply, just cups her perfectly shaped face in her hands and gazes at me with her beautiful green eyes.

'Mummy!'

She gives a little start, and turns around. 'Ye-es!' she calls.

'Can I have a biscuit?'

Joseph's short legs appear at the top of the stairs.

'I've upset you, haven't I?' Alexandria whispers, covering my hand with hers.

'*Mummy!*'

Joseph continues to stomp down the stairs. When he reaches his mother he flops over her knee, slapping her gently around the middle. 'I'm *bored.*'

'Alright, Poppet. We'll go home in a minute.'

Kissing him on the top of his head, she looks directly into my eyes. 'Are you OK?'

'Kind of . . .'

But I'm not OK at all. I feel dislocated and queasy, like being on a nightmarish roller-coaster that never stops.

'You really mustn't blame yourself,' Alexandria whispers. 'That's terribly important. What's happened isn't your fault. It was just that no matter where he is or however many people love him, Ed was never at peace . . .'

'You think he's killed himself,' I mumble. 'Don't you?'

She does not seem to hear. Rising from her chair, she is helping Joseph find his shoes.

After they've gone, I go upstairs and pull Ed's briefcase from under the bed. Its battered appearance is oddly comforting; for a while I cradle it in my arms, placing my cheek against the worn leather and imbibing its smell. The man I knew in

Bangladesh was real, not a lying fraud. Despite what Alexandria has told me, I have to hold on to the reality of Ed as I knew him: jesting with the kids on the beach, or teaching his class. If once he was different, or misled me about his role in Schools for Change, it doesn't matter.

I click open the briefcase, pulling apart the dividers and peering inside. Surely, somewhere here I will find the answers I need? Pulling out the printed out pages, I glance through them once more.

> *Dear Mr Salisbury*
> *Re: Meeting with Dan Jameson*
> *Thank you for your email. Dan Jameson is currently out of the country. He will be back in the office on April 30th and will contact you then.*
> *Yours truly*
> *Mrs Shuli Syed (Secretary)*

I've seen these emails before; they contain nothing I don't already know. Next is the newspaper article that Ed was so proud of: *'The Price of Progress: Mining Developments in the Coastal Area are Illegal, Campaigners Say.'*

Placing it carefully on the floor, I rummage through the notebooks. I thought I had thoroughly searched the briefcase in Lydia and Mike's house, but now I notice a zipped pocket, tucked into the back of the case. Reaching inside, my fingers pull out a wad of paper, neatly folded.

There are three pages of paper in all: more emails, printed out.

> February 24th
> Dear Faker
> This is the voice of your conscience: a blast from the past that you prefer to forget. I gather you've moved on since our last encounter? You've remodelled yourself, turned into a good person, all bright-eyed and squeaky clean. It must have been quite a trip, no?
> But before you disappear completely up your own saintly arse, remember this:
> I know who you really are.

March 15th
Dear Faker
What a great bloke you are! I'm SO impressed by your
blogs. How lovely that you care so very deeply about
all those poor, exploited people! I bet it feels good,
doesn't it, saving all those poor paupers from the evil
rich? Ain't it great to have a cause? There's just one
teensy little question I'd like to ask . . .
How do you sleep at night?

March 17th
Dear Faker
You don't dare reply, do you? But you must know who
I am and what I want.
Remember this: someone has to pay, you fucking fraud.

There's more, but the language is so violent that it makes me
feel sick. I hurriedly crumple the paper into the secret pocket.
Who could have written such venomous, vile stuff? And why
would Ed print it out?

I can't sit here any longer. A few moments ago the briefcase brought me comfort, but now it's been poisoned. Chucking
the thing on the floor, I jump up and walk quickly from the
room, climbing the stairs that lead to the second and third
storeys of the house. As I wander through room after room
of expensive antiques I'm trying desperately to stifle the wail
of anguish that is building inside me. *Someone has to pay,
you fucking fraud.* Who could have written such a thing? And
what was it that Ed was supposed to have done?

As I climb towards the roof, the stairs become steeper and
the rooms more cramped, a far cry from the grandiose sweep
from the ground floor. Here, at the top of the house, the rooms
are small and bare: the servants' quarters, I suppose. Ducking
to avoid the beams, I clank across the bare boards and gaze
through the dusty window at the rooftops below. Three storeys
down car lights flow like water. The dark city spreads out
beneath: tiny people scurrying down the broad pavements, a
glimpse of the park, Edwardian lamps, illuminating the streets.
This house belonged to Ed, yet it means nothing to me.

Moving back to the landing, I peer at the books. Even these
are stiff-backed antiques, their golden leaves filmed with dust.

Why couldn't Ed tell me the truth? I thought we were close but now I see that just like his impressive career, our intimacy was an illusion. Sliding a book from the shelf, I weigh the crumbling tome in my hand. What am I doing here? I think with a stab of anger. Everything in the bloody house is *dead*. I start to shove the book back into its slot, then suddenly stop.

There's a noise, coming from downstairs: the heavy click of a door being opened and closed. Crouching by the top of the stairs, I listen intently. On the ground floor, shoes are slapping across the tiles. Could it be Alexandria, popping back? Or the cleaner?

'Hello?' My thin voice echoes down the stairwell. 'Is anybody there?'

I stand motionless on the top step, holding my breath. I should clatter loudly and assertively down the stairs and introduce myself to whoever is in the house, but something stops me. Below me, the footsteps start to move up the wooden steps. Edging towards the banisters, I peer into the darkness below, but it's not possible to see beyond the first-floor landing.

My mouth has gone dry. The person has entered the room beneath where I am standing, I realize; their feet move softly across the floor of Ed's bedroom.

'Who is it?' I whisper.

What I am thinking seems impossible: a form of madness. Yet as I grip the mahogany rail, I can hardly breathe.

'Is that you?'

Silence. My palms have turned so clammy that I have to wipe them on my jeans.

'Ed?'

The noise has stopped. Could I have imagined his presence, like all the other times? Grasping the wooden frets I squint into the gloom.

'Hello?' I call again.

This time I'm sure of what I've heard: the clump of feet, walking swiftly across the tiles. Then suddenly the door slams and someone is running down the stairs. Shrieking, I hurl myself down the narrow steps.

'Wait!'

Gripping the banisters, I take the stairs two at a time. Beneath me, the intruder has reached the bottom. I leap on to the first floor landing, but it's too late. The heavy front door slams shut.

Skidding down the remaining stairs, I yank the door open, crash landing on the grand front step and peering desperately down the street. What I see makes my knees sag. Gripping the wrought iron railing, I feel as if I have been struck violently in the face.

Ed is running down the street. He's wearing the blue cashmere coat that I had left lying on the bed.

'Ed!' I scream. 'Come back!'

He must have heard me yelling, but he does not look round. When he reaches the corner, he jumps on a bus, and disappears.

TWENTY-TWO

I've always known it: Ed didn't drown in the storm. It hasn't taken Alexandria and I long to establish the basic facts. Within a few hours her lawyers have verified that he shimmied through Zia International Airport a mere thirty-six hours after the tornado. According to British Airways he travelled First Class, arriving in London at 0825 on May 7th, two days before my own bedraggled appearance from Emirates Economy. Whilst I was blubbering on Lydia Simmons' guest bed, he was quaffing champagne as he soared over Asia. As I lurched towards the brick factory, head bashing the canvas roof of the baby-taxi, eyes stinging at the fumes, he had already landed. The log of a taxi firm based at Heathrow showed that a Mr de Vaal paid £200 at 0915 to be driven in a limo into W1. After that, nothing.

I should be elated. Yet once the shock of watching the love of my life zoom away on the number 52 bus had dwindled, what I felt was bewilderment. It's true that during those first dizzying moments I was weak-kneed with relief. Not knowing what else to do, I'd grabbed the phone and gabbled the news to an astounded Alexandria. Laughing, I described how I'd heard Ed moving around downstairs and how he'd scarpered when I'd appeared. He's turned up! I trilled triumphantly. Everything's OK!

But after about an hour I was spreadeagled across his bed, sobbing. Why didn't he turn when I called his name? He must have heard my voice, but he ran in the opposite direction, leaping on to the bus to escape. Even if he was terrified of some external threat, surely he trusted me? I kept remembering our last conversation. He was going to the bazaar to call Biman Airlines, he claimed; he'd take his passport in case it was needed. But he was lying, just like all the other times. The reason he took his passport and credit cards was not because he was booking our flights to Dhaka, but because he was leaving for the UK. I huddled under the covers, bawling. This time I did not feel his arms around my shoulders or imagine his voice in my ear. I finally had definitive proof that he was alive, yet it felt as if he was more distant than ever.

He's been busy, that's for sure. Since returning to the UK he's withdrawn thousands of pounds from his bank. They don't have his address, we're informed; even if they did, they don't give out confidential information about their clients.

Then there are the emails. We find out about these when someone called Jon Salway rings from the British High Commission in Dhaka. Alexandria takes the call. She, after all, is Ed's next of kin. I watch her grip the phone, her bony knuckles translucent. She strains forward, her other hand clutching the window sill.

'Yes?' She says, her voice cracking with hope.

Ed has emailed Mike Simmons to say that he's alive and well. Because of this the British High Commission in Dhaka no longer considers Ed to be missing. As far as Salway is concerned, the case is closed. After she puts the phone down Alexandria has a little weep. When she finally looks around and sees me standing behind her, she wipes her eyes with the back of her hands and gives me a rueful smile.

'He's fine,' she says. 'He's been emailing people in Dhaka. He asked Jon Salway to let me know. It's going to be OK.'

But she's wrong. It isn't going to be OK. Her Ed may be alive and well, but mine is still missing, for the Ed *I* knew would have had no truck with first-class flights or limos. As Alexandria bustles around the flat, chattering about friends of his we should call, all I am able to muster are a few stilted words. He must have somehow got to Noton Bazaar and then caught a bus to Chittagong, I murmur, not looking her in the eye. Or perhaps he was in the cyclone shelter all along, and I never noticed. Perhaps he was deliberately dodging me. I feel as if a rock is lodged in my chest; it actually hurts to breathe.

He's done a runner. With the news that he's emailed his

contacts in Dhaka and sent messages to Alexandria, it becomes crushingly simple. Unable to cope with what was happening in Lalalpur, Ed has run away.

'This Salway person is going to forward his email,' Alexandria is saying. 'I gave him my Hotmail address. Let's turn the computer on.'

I rise to my feet, my face set in a rigid smirk that makes my cheeks ache. Everything was perfect until the BNRC's rent-a-thugs torched Jhomgram. Ever since then the man I love – or *loved* – faded, becoming someone unreachable. Aunik's murder was obviously the tipping point. The day afterwards, when Ed told me he was visiting Aunik's family, he must have been booking his first-class flight to London. Like his other lies he was fibbing during our final night when he said everything was going to be fine; it was a fairy tale, hastily whispered in the gecko-clicking dark so that I wouldn't prevent him from leaving.

After her initial elation, Alexandria's mood has darkened. Her brother must have slipped into his old habits, she says, frowning as her computer whirrs into life; it's just like before. We huddle around her glowing screen, our mooning faces reflected back.

'He was always such an email aficionado,' she murmurs as she opens Outlook Express. 'When he was first in Dhaka he used to send me two or three a day.'

'It's weird he's emailed people in Dhaka but not you,' I say faintly. 'I wonder if he's been in touch with Dan . . .'

The email is already there: 'As discussed, Mike Simmons forwarded this to me this morning,' Salway writes perfunctorily. 'Best regards, Jon.'

Ed's email lies below, a few short lines that rent my heart apart.

Dear Mike
Thought I should write to assure you that despite impressions to the contrary, I'm very much alive and well. I had a bit of a lucky escape in Lalalpur (in more ways than one!) and have decided to return to the UK for a fresh start. Please let my sister and everyone at BHC Dhaka know that I'm OK. Sorry if you've been dragged into any unpleasantness
Ed

I stand behind Alexandria, my cheeks burning. When he writes 'in more ways than one' is he referring to our relationship? We were together for almost a year, yet he hasn't even bothered to name me. The offhand tone of the message confirms everything I was dreading: he's walked away from our life without even bothering to look back.

'It's a bit bloody casual, isn't it?' Alexandria says after a while.

I don't trust myself to speak.

'He could at least have written directly to me,' she mutters. 'It's incredibly inconsiderate.'

Leaning over the keyboard, she bashes 'send message':

Ed, Little Bro, Whatever you're going through, please, please be in touch A

Glancing around, she grabs my hand. 'Oh darling, don't look like that. I'm sorry. That was untactful of me. He should have written to you, too, of course he should have.'

'I don't actually have an email address . . .'

It's too late. I'm trying to hide them by pressing my fingers to my cheeks, but tears are sliding down my pallid skin. Swivelling around, Alexandria places both hands on my shoulders so that I can't avoid looking into her heavy-lashed green eyes. She reminds me so much of Ed.

'He's got into a panic,' she says. 'If we can find him we can make things between you alright again, I promise.'

She's lying. It's the nicest kind of fib, made to make me feel better, but a fib just the same. The truth is flickering on the screen behind her head: ultimately Ed felt so little for me that he doesn't even use my name. Instead, I am glossed as 'any unpleasantness'.

'Perhaps he thought I wouldn't care,' I gulp. 'We hadn't actually been getting on that well . . .'

'I'm sure it's not that,' Alexandria says briskly. 'Perhaps there's no obvious way of contacting you. He might not even know that you're in London.'

'So why didn't he mention me to Jon Salway?'

She doesn't know how to respond. She stares into my face, looking sad. Eventually she sighs and stands up.

'Please don't give up on him, Sarah. I know it looks different from the outside. We must seem so privileged and everything –' she gestures vaguely around the flat – 'but the reality is that Ed finds life very difficult, and he was clearly in a real mess . . . he probably wasn't thinking clearly.'

I glance away from her face, fixing my eyes on her designer ceiling lights in an effort not to cry.

'I'm going to pick up Joseph,' she's saying. 'Why don't you come along? It would do you good to get some fresh air.'

I shake my head. I want desperately to be alone. 'It's OK. I'll just stay here.'

When the front door has finally slammed shut I sit in front of Alexandria's Apple Mac. Taking a breath, I type 'Oxan Mining Bangladesh' into Google.

I find the website immediately. It's after an engineering report produced by Oxan and an article on a financial website commenting on Oxan's recent investments in Bangladesh.

> StopOxan.blogspot.com
> The atrocities in Jhomgram are just one in a line of human rights violations undertaken by imperialistic multinationals who aim to squeeze every last dollar of profit from the South. Today I watched in horror as BNRC aka Oxan henchmen moved their equipment to fields south of the Jhomgram site, where as I've written in my earlier blogs, the blood of powerless fishermen and their families has been spilt in their fight to save their homes. Now we hear that the BNRC, rotten to the core, are bribing local leaders to prevent any indigenous protest from taking root . . .

I skim the rest of the article, which is followed by Ed's name and the date, April 30th, 2003, a few days before Aunik's murder. Flicking backwards, I see that he added to the blog almost daily. The home page has links to Oxan's website, which presumably Ed was hoping people would bombard with messages and an electronic version of the newspaper article that he showed me in Lalalpur. For the first time, I clock the journalist's name: Anu Jalal. Scrolling to the bottom, I see that he has an email address. Without thinking, I click on it. I'm immediately in Alexandria's Outlook Express programme.

The message takes me less than a minute to write:

To: Jalal@hotmail.com
Subject: Ed Salisbury
Dear Jalal
Sorry to contact you like this. I got your address from
Ed's website. I'm trying to find out what's behind his
disappearance from Lalalpur during the cyclone last
week. Do you have any information that might help us
understand what has happened to him?
Best wishes
Sarah

After I've pressed 'send', I feel slightly foolish. Ed is alive and
well and living somewhere in the UK. Why would a journalist
based in Bangladesh know where he was? I get up, stretch, and
move towards the kitchen, where I flick on the kettle. Alexandria
was right: I should get some fresh air. Wandering back to the
computer, I click the mouse, ready to close the thing down and
see that Jalal has already replied.

To: AlexandriaSalisbury@talktalk.com
From: Jalal@hotmail.com
Can U meet?
Jal

Punching 'reply', I write: Hi Jalal, that would be great, but
I'm in London! Any chance of talking over the phone?
I wait for less than a minute, and then I get his answer:
I'm at the Royal Bengal Curry House, Hackney Road. C U
@ 2?

TWENTY-THREE

I take the tube to Old Street, then walk. I'm only a few miles
from Covent Garden but this is a different London, of
thundering traffic, boarded-up shops and dingy hostels,
advertising rooms for twenty quid a night. Hurrying past the
dealers who loiter by the tube, I stride past a row of scruffy
shops with grills on their windows and turn east. I'm probably

being neurotic, but I can't shake off the sense of being
followed; even in Covent Garden the skin on my back prickled
self-consciously. When I finally give into my paranoia and
glimpse round I see two guys in hoodies strolling ten yards
behind. The larger one returns my anxious glance with what
I interpret as a malicious grin; when I cross the road, he bursts
out laughing. I *have* to calm down.

The Royal Bengal is about half a mile along the Hackney
Road, sandwiched between a Pound Shop and Ladbrokes. It's
an odd place for Jalal to want to meet: surely no self-respecting
Bangladeshi ever eats in such a place? I step inside the restaur-
ant, looking around nervously. The room smells faintly of spilled
beer. With its swirly red carpet, plastic flowers and piped sitar
music, it could be one of thousands of British curry houses. I'm
hoping to see a man sitting in one of the booths. I imagine Jalal
as an older version of Aunik, probably dressed in thick beige
chinos, sensible lace ups and a jacket for the London chill. But
besides a waiter folding napkins by the till, the place is empty.

'We open at six,' he says, glancing up.

'I'm actually meeting someone . . . can I wait here?'

'What's the name?'

Sighing grumpily he moves towards a plastic backed ledger
resting on the bar. He must be making a show of looking for
a booking, for it's hard to imagine the place full.

'Jalal,' I say. 'Anu Jalal?'

He visibly starts. 'You know Anu Jalal?'

'He said to meet him here?'

'Sit down please.'

Giving me an odd look, he waves at one of the booths. 'I'll
get him.'

I wait in my allotted booth, fiddling with the menu. I'm so
tense that it's hard to sit still. Plucking a packet of salt from
the stainless-steel tray in the centre of the table I tear at it
fretfully. Since returning to Britain I had forgotten the urgency
in Dan's voice when he called me in Dhaka. Don't talk to
anyone, he'd said; it might be dangerous.

'Sarah?'

Looking up from the salt I see one of the kitchen staff standing
before me: a slim, youngish man with a large apron wrapped
around his waist and a stained white cap. He must be a washer-
upper, for he is in the process of peeling rubber gloves from his

hands. I smile tepidly, wondering how he knows my name. Perhaps Jalal has asked him to pass on a message. But to my surprise, he squeezes into the seats opposite.

'You found it then?' he says, holding out his hand.

'Yeah . . .'

'When did you arrive from Bangladesh?'

'About three days ago.'

'And it's OK if we talk here? No one saw you come in?'

The penny finally drops. Here in London, Anu Jalal, respected journalist and campaigner, is doing the washing up.

'I don't think so . . .' I say, grimacing. 'I'm sure it's OK.'

'Do you want tea? Or a coffee?'

I shake my head. There's a brief pause; there's so much to discuss that it's hard to know where to start. As Jalal pulls a cigarette from his pocket, I glance covertly at his face. He's probably in his mid-thirties, and unlike most Bengalis has a South-East Asian slant to his features, suggesting Burma or the Chittagong Hill tracts.

'I didn't know you were in London too,' I eventually start. 'When did—'

'I had to get out,' he interrupts. 'It was getting too dangerous.' Pinching the cigarette between his fingers, he glances around for a match.

'You mean because of what happened to Aunik?'

'Not just that.'

There is no match. Laying the fag on the table, he taps at it distractedly. 'I heard what happened to Ed,' he says. 'I was surprised, to be honest. I didn't think they'd want to be implicated in a foreigner's disappearance.'

I place my hands on my lap, trying to keep calm. I'm not going to tell him that Ed is alive, at least not yet.

'Who's "they"?'

He snorts. 'Take your pick. Oxan. The Bangladesh Natural Resource Company. The government.'

'The government? Why would they care?'

He glances at me with what I interpret as pity. As I gaze back, I'm freshly aware of the depths of my ignorance.

'You don't know about the Mizaram pipeline?'

'Not really, no . . .'

He takes a deep breath. Then he leans over the table and starts talking fast.

'Right, I'm telling you this because Ed was a great guy, and you're his wife. OK, he was a foreigner but he was one hundred percent sincere. And now he's disappeared, Aunik's dead and I'm here, but only because I had enough cash to get to London, otherwise I'd be gone too. You know they ransacked the newspaper offices, the day the article came out?'

'No, I—'

He's not interested in my answer. 'I left that night,' he continues. 'My friends arranged the passport and papers and smuggled me out. But now I'm here my hands are tied. I'm just another asylum seeker who your government want to deport. They won't listen to me, and even if they did they wouldn't do anything about it because they're backing what's going on. And I can't write anything on the Internet because if I do, my family will be harmed. So whatever I tell you, it didn't come from me, OK? In fact you've never met me.'

'OK . . .'

Picking up the cigarette, he taps it on the table, and then, without seeming to notice what he's doing, snaps it in half.

'You've been living in Bangladesh for what, a year or so, right? You know about the fighting and assassinations and strikes that go with our politics?'

I nod, remembering the general strikes in Dhaka. At Mahila Shadinota Shamittee, the office had been constantly buzzing with talk of politics: opposition MPs arrested, protests and rallies planned, campaigners murdered. The general strikes sometimes lasted for days, in which no one dared go out for fear of being stoned. My friends had lived through military dictatorships and now they were living with this strained version of democracy in which violence and corruption were never far off. All they wanted, they said, was stability. Yet whilst the newspapers that Ed occasionally brought back from Noton Bazaar were filled with stories of demonstrations and riots, in the village the troubles seemed distant, unconnected to the slowly revolving seasons or long days in which time was marked only by the call of the azan.

'And you also know that this last year, the opposition has been growing very strong?' Jalal continues. 'You know of the bombs let off at the February 12th demonstration at Dhaka University?'

'Umm . . .'

'Which of course the government were responsible for, even though they've tried to pin it on the opposition! So that's just made the opposition parties even more determined to bring the government down, right?'

I'm doing a kind of non-committed nodding, despite only having a dim understanding of what he's talking about.

'So the government's getting scared. The opposition are calling for a national uprising to topple them and they know that if and when that happens, they're going to end up either dead or in gaol. They can't even trust their own army. What they need is strong military backing, but they don't really have anything to offer . . .'

I've been looking at the salt scattered table, but now I glance up. I have just remembered what Ed said when he showed me Jalal's article. 'It could bring down the government!' he'd remarked jauntily, like a school boy playing spies.

'Except for oil . . .'

'That's right!' Jalal finally smiles. In his enthusiasm, his cap has slipped down the back of his head, making him seem slightly tipsy. 'Except for oil – which Oxan have been prospecting for in the area for years. And now they've found it, big time! So the government tells everyone that they should celebrate, because it's a huge national resource and will make the country rich. They even make a show of having a national company to mine it on Oxan's behalf. Meanwhile they make a deal with India to pipe the stuff straight to them, in return for military help.'

I sit up, finally focusing on what Jalal is saying. 'So this pipeline is going to India?'

'Sure.'

'Leaving nothing for Bangladesh?'

Leaning back against the fake leather seat, Jalal slowly shakes his head. 'Not a drop. Meanwhile Oxan takes the lion's share of the profits, and the government gets an unlimited supply of arms.'

'Which isn't exactly something they want made public . . .'

'Can you imagine the uproar if people knew that our country's natural resources were being virtually given away in return for keeping the government in power?'

'What about the donors? Couldn't you get the international community involved?'

Jalal laughs bitterly, his face twisting in contempt. 'They're right behind it! That's why none of them would support Ed.'

'But why would they be behind it, when the oil can help boost Bangladeshi development?'

His head twitches impatiently. 'Because it's not about development, not as you and I understand it. It's about keeping the region politically stable and friendly to the West. The UK and US are terrified of the government falling and the far-right Islamic parties getting in. They'd rather have a corrupt state than an Islamic one.'

For a moment, I'm quiet. So *this* is why Dan advised me to leave Bangladesh. No wonder he said it might be dangerous.

'How do you know all this?' I eventually ask. Jalal frowns. 'I can't talk about that.'

'And Ed knew everything?'

He nods. 'He wanted to write about it on his blog, but we persuaded him that it was too dangerous for the story to be linked directly to him. What we wanted was to get the international media involved, to link up with global campaigns – that's what he was going to try to do.'

'And then Aunik was murdered?'

I remember Ed's despair the day we found his body. It was *his* fault, he said. Perhaps he thought that by leaving me, he would make me safe? Jalal frowns, placing his fingers over his eyes and rubbing them exhaustedly. I can only guess at how it feels to leave one's home and family in fear for one's life, only to land up scrubbing scummy pans in a curry house in East London.

'I don't know who Ed talked to,' he says quietly. 'Perhaps he didn't talk to anyone. Or perhaps he talked to the wrong person.'

'He didn't even tell me,' I whisper.

If he notices the pathos in my voice, he doesn't react. 'You'll be reporting his disappearance to the British police?' he says, sitting up. 'There's a case?'

'It's a bit complicated . . .'

'They won't do anything about it, not when they realize that Ed was protesting against Oxan. The British High Commission in Dhaka will put them off the scent. The best thing you can do is to go to the British press. But whatever you do, don't mention my name.'

He has started to lever his slight frame from the gap between the table and seats. 'I have to get back to work. My boss will be here . . .'

He holds out his hand. I should have told him that Ed isn't dead, but it's suddenly too late. Or perhaps I'm afraid of the conclusions he might draw. 'I'll email you,' I say. 'Or can I get hold of you here?'

'Please don't contact me again,' he mutters, grasping my fingers. 'It isn't safe.'

Then he's dropped my hand and is gone.

TWENTY-FOUR

I walk south, steering myself in the direction of the river from the dull glow of sun behind the watery clouds. There's so much space to pass, all of it filled with buildings and roads and people who push past, their eyes fixed to a point somewhere beyond my head. I trudge on, eyes averted. Ed knew something that, if it were made public, might topple the government. He was passionate and committed, but he was not one to bite his lip. Might he have told the wrong person? I dodge between wheezing buses, cutting through empty streets in which tower blocks loom; I pass rows of shops, each one either protected by a heavy metal grille or boarded up. Now I understand why he was so secretive for the Ed I loved would have wanted to protect me. What I'm still trying to fathom is why he disappeared without saying goodbye. The Ed I loved would never have done that.

When I reach a railway line, I take a detour through a housing estate, jogging past the kids that circle the tarmac on their chopper bikes. Perhaps I have turned into a ghost, for no one notices me. I've been trying so hard to work out the reasons for Ed's vanishing act. Yet as I cross the road I realize that in a way, the whys and wherefores are irrelevant. All that really matters is that, for whatever reason, he's gone.

The memories pierce like arrows: Ed and I on the beach, the sand cool and damp beneath our backs, the moon as bright as day; that soft patch of skin behind his ears, which I liked to stroke; his tuneless singing – old Smiths' songs usually; he knew the words by heart. I miss him so much. And despite everything I've learnt today, a part of me blames myself for losing him. I keep remembering my mistakes. Every thought returns to the same swirling pattern, followed by the inevitable suck of the whirlpool, dragging me down. 'If' has gained great status in my head, whipping everything else into shape. *If* I had been more supportive of him from the outset, he might not have lied; *if* I had insisted on him telling me exactly what was going on instead of detaching myself from the campaign, I might have persuaded him to act differently. *If* I had been more understanding, less critical, more proactive, less idle, he might have confided in me, and his disappearance averted. There I go again, hands flailing as I'm dragged down.

I'm finally approaching the City, the unforgiving glass buildings reflecting my inconsequential figure. I want to remain a foreigner in this place, for the employment agencies, sandwich bars and newsagents to remain alien, part of a culture that isn't mine, but the disjunction I experienced on my return to Heathrow has worn off and it's all as bleakly familiar as the mizzling rain that's falling: bitter, spitting stuff that isn't worth wiping away. All those things I'd acquired in Bangladesh, the experiences, insights and sensations, are sloughing off me, like dust from a butterfly's wings.

It's getting late, the streets filling with people on their way home. The bustle propels me forwards, my elbows jogged by office workers, sharply dressed young women, clicking impatient heels, students in jeans. I need to keep my mind moving in a direct line. Return to Kensington. Call Alexandria. Make some kind of plan. But it keeps getting snagged on disconnected images that I can't control. There's Ed, as usual, running down the beach. Then the fisherman, dragging me away. There's the Chairman's roof, popping off, and our own demolished bungalow, the papers spread around.

The whirlpool's pulling me closer; I can feel it sucking on my heart. We should have escaped with Dan, I think. We should have forgotten our romantic nonsense about showing solidarity with the locals and got the hell out of there. Why didn't I insist?

By the time I push my key into the door of Ed's house, it's past eight. I've been walking for most of the day and my feet are covered with blisters. Kicking off my trainers, I move towards the stairs. Perhaps I'm still jet-lagged, for I'm suddenly desperate for sleep.

Yet as I place my foot on the step, I hear something odd: the creak of a floorboard, as if someone's moving across the room. My muscles tightening, I hold my breath, waiting for more. There it is again. This time the sound is more deliberate: a muffled footstep, approaching from the palatial sitting room, with its old masters and oriental rugs, followed by what I imagine to be the creak of the leather armchair as someone sits down. And then, a cough.

He's returned. Ed has finally returned. Turning shakily away from the stairs I hurry across the chequered tiles. He's waiting for me.

The door to the drawing room is ajar. Pushing it open, I step inside the room. I can feel the blood pounding in my veins.

'Ed? Is that you?'

His back towards me, he's standing by the window, the lower part of his body blocked from my vision by the grand piano.

'Sarah!'

It's *his* voice: that same warm tone that greeted me whenever we were reunited after a brief separation, the hint of laughter, poking through. I gasp out loud, my heart about to explode. In that glancing moment, everything that's happened seems to hurtle away: the tornado, our arguments, his strange disappearance, my desolation. All that remains is this single, shining truth: my Ed has returned.

'Oh my God,' I whisper. 'You've come back . . .'

Yet as he turns to face me, my heart plummets. For it's not Ed who is laughing and moving across the room, his hand stretched out.

It's Dan.

TWENTY-FIVE

'Are you OK?' Dan says anxiously as he clunks over the floor and kisses me formally on both cheeks. 'You look like you've seen a ghost.'

I step hastily away from him, grabbing on to the side of the sofa to steady myself. How could I have possibly mistaken his voice for Ed's? Here in London he looks so different from when I last saw him: he's shaved, had his hair cut, and is wearing smart trousers and a stripy shirt, like the Sloane he always was.

'What are you doing here?' I manage to say. 'I thought you were in Chittagong.'

He bites his lip, regarding me. He's retrieved Ed's brief-case from the bedroom, I notice, plus a pile of his smartest suits, which he's spread over one of the chairs.

'I had to come back to London,' he says. 'Ed asked me to.'

'Oh!'

As I gaze into his fretful face I am finding it hard to breathe.

'It's great to bump into you,' he continues, as if we were guests at a cocktail party. 'Ed said you were staying here. I was just popping in to pick up some things for him.'

'Where is he?'

He winces. 'Afraid I can't tell you that. I'm sworn to secrecy.'

'What, even with me?'

He exhales, gazing at me with concern. 'It's kind of compli-cated, Sarah,' he says gently. 'Why don't you sit down?' He points to the creaky leather settee, where I perch expectantly. 'Now you're here, we should probably have a little talk.'

Pulling up the ends of his trousers so that they don't crease, he sits down. 'I know I should have been in contact earlier, but I've been really tied up.' He pauses. I wish he would stop looking at me so pityingly. 'It's actually quite an incredible story . . . When I got back to Chittagong, after dropping you at the airport, I found Ed outside my hotel. He was in quite a state: barefoot, his clothes all torn. He was ranting and raving like a lunatic. It took me ages to calm him down.'

'Why didn't you tell me he was alive when you called me in Dhaka?' I butt in. 'I was going out of my mind!'

'Wait a sec,' he says placing his large hand on my arm. 'I'm going to explain everything.'

I swallow, not taking my eyes from his face.

'What he told me was that he didn't go into the sea at all, but ran along the beach until he got to the road. I can't work out all the details, but it seems that he managed to find some kind of shelter in one of the government buildings on the highway. When the storm eventually died down he just kept walking until someone picked him up. From what he says, he eventually hitched a lift to Chittagong.'

I'm trying to grasp the image: Ed running towards the waves. And then, in the whirling sand, he was gone.

'But how did he know where you were staying in Chittagong?'

'Because I was hoping you guys would have a last-minute change of heart about the storm, so I'd given him the details ... Anyway, he kept going on and on about how he had to get out of Lalalpur because of some danger he was in. He was completely freaking out, saying that he was going to be murdered. He made me promise on my life that I wouldn't tell anyone I'd see him.'

'Not even me?' I hate the way my voice cracks when I say this.

'Actually, especially not you,' Dan says quietly. 'What he did ask me to do, however, was to call you in Dhaka and make sure that you got out of Bangladesh as quickly as you could.'

I look away. I am trying to control my features.

Dan draws himself up, speaking more briskly. 'Basically, the long and short of it is that, as you know, Ed's upset some very powerful people involved in this Oxan affair and he's seriously afraid for his life. Ever since we got back he's insisted on completely changing his identity. He's terrified he might be traced.'

'But why? I mean, now that he's back in the UK and he's not involved in the campaigning, what harm can possibly come to him?'

'To be honest I'm not entirely clear. But something's making him very, very afraid.'

I bite my lip, thinking of my meeting with Jalal. 'It's because of this thing with the pipeline,' I whisper. 'Jalal Anu told me all about it.'

Dan blinks. 'That's right,' he says quietly. 'I didn't think you knew.'

'I've just met with him in Hackney ... he had to leave Bangladesh too.'

'It's all extremely delicate,' Dan interrupts. 'I wouldn't advise that you get involved. You also need to be very careful about who you trust. I mean, this Jalal chap is probably fine, but I'd be very wary of getting too close to the Bangladeshi contingent . . .'

'I don't understand why he'd cut me out of his life, just like that,' I continue, only half listening. 'I mean, I can just about accept that he found out something he shouldn't have. But why turn away from *me*? He must know I'd never in a million years do anything to hurt him!'

Reaching across the sofa, Dan places his large hand on my shoulder. 'I know that, Sarah. But I'm afraid Ed is . . .' He stops, looking at me in a way that makes me feel as if the air is being squeezed from my lungs. 'Look, let's put it like this: he's keen to start a whole new life. And that means cutting himself off completely from his old relationships.'

I look away from his face, my stomach plunging. 'Even from me?'

'That's very much the impression I have.'

Ever since seeing Ed's retreating back as he escaped from the house, I've known it: our relationship is over. Yet even so, Dan's words make me feel as if I've been punched in the stomach. I gasp, clutching my hands around my mouth as the words sink coldly in. 'Oh!'

'I'm so sorry,' Dan's saying. 'I've obviously been trying to convince him that he's making a huge mistake and that if there is anyone he should trust it's you, but I'm afraid he's adamant.'

I look down at my hands. I'm still wearing his ring: since he gave it to me that night in Dhaka, I've never taken it off. As soon as Dan is gone, I think, I'm going to wrench it from my finger and throw it in the bin. Then I'm going to gather up my things and leave.

'So that's it, is it?' I say faintly. 'He doesn't want any more contact?'

There's a long, loaded pause, in which Dan doesn't take his eyes from my face. Then he says quietly, 'He'd very much prefer it if you stopped looking for him.'

I am unable to reply. I close my eyes, trying to rein myself in. When I open them, Dan is leaning forwards, gazing at me sympathetically. His hand is still on my shoulder, and now he squeezes it comfortingly.

'I'm so sorry to have to be the one to tell you,' he says. 'But it would make things a lot easier for us if you could accept that whether Ed wants to or not, he's had to move on.'

Jerking my shoulder away from Dan's kneading hands, I stare at him. 'Who's "us"?'

'How do you mean?'

'You said "it would make things a lot easier for *us*". Shouldn't you have said that it would make things a lot easier for Ed?'

Dan blinks at me. 'What I meant was that firstly, it would make things easier for Ed and secondly, it would make it easier for us at the Foreign Office ...'

I sit up straight, shuffling an inch further from his meaty hands. 'The Foreign Office? I thought you worked for Dfid?'

Dan smiles, but he cannot stop his brows from twitching in irritation. 'Both departments work closely together, I'm in a kind of bridging position ...'

'Anyway,' I continue. 'Why should you be putting so much energy into helping him? I thought you were meant to be organizing emergency aid for the coastal area? Isn't coming all the way back to London with him a bit beyond your job description?'

Dan smirks at me patronizingly and I am suddenly struck by how much I dislike him; after the tornado I'd thought of him as a friend, but now his Hooray Henry loafers and air of superiority repulse me.

'Yes,' he says with a little chuckle. 'I suppose it is a little beyond my usual job description. But Ed is in a rather special position, isn't he? You have to remember that the British government gives a great deal of aid to Bangladesh, so we're obviously very concerned about the developments with Oxan. And since it was Ed who alerted us to the problems there's a general sense that we should look after him. And that job fell to me. Luckily there was a chap in Dhaka who we've drafted in to do my old job.'

'I see.'

There's a long silence, in which Dan eventually leans over and places a meaty hand on my knee. I wish to God he would stop touching me. 'This must be very hard for you, Sarah,' he says gently.

I am sitting very still and thinking very hard. If what Jalal told me about British support of the Mizaram pipeline is true, then why would the Foreign Office put so much effort into helping Ed when he was threatening to expose the whole affair? I can't believe Jalal was lying; even Mike Symmonds implied that Ed's campaign had got snared in something far greater than a bit of local corruption.

'Are you OK?' Dan whispers.

I shrug, dabbing at my eyes as if I'm weeping. Dan's jacket is lying on the back of the pretty Georgian chair by the door; a white linen affair to match his preppy chinos.

'I'm feeling a teensy bit faint,' I say in as pitiful a voice as I can muster. 'Would you mind awfully if I was alone for a little bit?'

He leaps up, nodding ingratiatingly.

'Of course not! You poor old thing! Let me get you a cup of tea. Where's the kitchen?'

'Downstairs.'

He tiptoes out of the room, closing the door softly behind him, as if I were a mourner left with the deceased. He doesn't pick his jacket up.

Jumping to my feet, I bound across the room and grab it, rifling desperately through the pockets. I'm in luck: his wallet is here. My hands yank it open, revealing the usual stack of plastic: Mastercard; AmEx Gold; membership of some gym. The name's the same on each: not Dan Jameson, as I was expecting, but G.A. Montgomery or, on the gym membership: Giles Montgomery. Dan's face smirks from the photo in the corner. Apart from this, there are no other pictures, or receipts, or crumpled rail tickets and I can't find any trace of an address.

Snapping the wallet shut, I stuff it back into the pocket. I am about to place the jacket back on the chair, when I notice something inside the silk lining on the right-hand side. Scrabbling around I locate a hidden compartment, from which I withdraw what feels like a clunky necklace. As I pull out the long metal chain, I gaze down at my find.

It's the type of security pass one wears around one's neck. There's no name or photograph of the employee but the name of the company is printed clearly across the front, over the magnetic strip: *Oxan*. For a moment or two, I gawp at the pass, turning it over in my hands. Then I stuff it back in the hidden pocket and sit down.

Five minutes later I am drinking Dan's tea and promising to give up my search for Ed. I love him, I say, but I agree to be strong and let him go. He can take Ed's suits, I add, nodding

at them. I've kicked the briefcase under the sofa; thankfully
Dan seems to have forgotten about it. At last he leaves. I wave
him goodbye with what I hope is an expression of anguish.

I'm relieved to be shot of him. As he clumps down the steps,
I lean against the front door, my mind working furiously.
Everything has changed. I'm afraid, angry and confused, but
I'm no longer mortally wounded. I'm not going to collapse,
sobbing on the floor and nor am I going to be sucked into the
whirlpool. Blaming myself for what has happened is a complete
waste of time. For whilst I still don't know where Ed is, or
what's happened to him, what I am sure of is that Dan Jameson,
or Giles Montgomery, or whatever he's called, is lying.

Alexandria, who despite her dreadlocks and artistic tattoos,
has a sweetly innocent faith in the British establishment, thinks
we should go to the police. I rang her as soon as Jameson
had left the house, rendered so breathless by the strange
mixture of hope and alarm that currently grips me, that I could
only splutter a few strangulated words.

'Dan Jameson's turned up,' I blurted. 'We have to talk.'

She came straight over.

'We need to get the police involved,' she announces after I've
described my meetings with Jalal and Dan. She's pacing around
the sitting room, frowning and twirling her locks with a pencil.
'Did you get a contact number for this Dan Jameson person?'

I shake my head. 'I forgot. I'm sorry.'

She shrugs. 'If I've followed you right,' she continues,
'then what you're implying is that because of this deal that
the Bangladeshi government have made with India, Oxon
or the Foreign Office, have got Ed and are keeping him
against his will. Is that right?'

I grimace. She's right: it sounds preposterous. Throwing
herself on the sofa, she stretches her long fingers over her
cheeks, tugging at the skin. She's looking particularly thin
this evening: her pelvic bones stick out of the top of her low
slung jeans and her arms are skeletal. Her face is drawn, too,
her eyes ringed by bruises of exhaustion.

'I don't know exactly what I'm implying,' I say. 'I know
it sounds bonkers, but what other explanation could there be?'

'Perhaps this Bangladeshi guy, Jalal, was lying to you? Or
perhaps he's simply wrong about what's happening with the

oil? People are always accusing their government of heinous crimes. Perhaps he's a conspiracy theorist who gets off on making up grand theories about the evil doings of the government he obviously opposes . . .'

'So why would he be forced to escape from Bangladesh?'

She looks at me as if I'm an idiot. 'Darling, wouldn't most Bangladeshis prefer to come and live in Britain?'

I bite back my retort, which is that she's being racist. 'Even if the stuff about the pipeline was untrue,' I say carefully, 'why would Dan Jameson tell me that the Foreign Office are helping Ed change his identity? They're obviously in close contact with him. How else would Dan have the keys to this house? The more I think about it, the more convinced I am that either Oxan or the Foreign Office sent Dan down to Lalalpur to get Ed to stop causing trouble. And now they're somehow keeping him captive, or something . . .' I trail off, glancing at Alexandria's dubious face.

'Perhaps Ed's been helping them,' she says gloomily. 'Perhaps he's decided he can do more good by working with them . . .'

I stare at her, my irritation swelling. 'But why would Ed want to help Oxan? You know what he's like. He hates anything to do with capitalism.'

She sighs pointedly. Clearly, it's not just me who is growing exasperated. 'I know you were with Ed for a year,' she says. 'But I'm not sure you saw every side to him.'

'What do you mean?'

'Just that he can be very complicated. And he has a penchant for walking away when things gets tough. He likes to reinvent himself . . .'

'So what do *you* think's happened?' I mutter.

'I don't fucking *know*!' She's weeping, I realize, the tears making track marks in her make-up. She sits motionlessly before me, not bothering to wipe them away. Ed was always talking about how much he adored her. She was a complete brick, he said. When we finally met, we were sure to be friends.

'Let's not fight,' I say, taking her hand. 'It's like you said the other day. We're in this together.'

This is what we decide. We both need to get a good night's sleep. Then tomorrow Alexandria will drum up a friend of a

friend who works for the Foreign Office, and I'll call
Bangladesh and try and find out what I can. After that, I have
to travel to Sussex for my promised visit to Sylvia.

As she leaves, Alexandria gives me a little hug.

'It's going to be alright,' she whispers. 'We're going to get
him back.'

TWENTY-SIX

Ed is perched on the end of the bed. I've been aware of
his presence for a while: his bony buttocks are jutting
into my feet and every ten seconds or so, he sniffs loudly.
But only now, as I slowly become conscious, do I realize it's
him. As I open my eyes and peer at his slouched figure, I see
that he's sobbing.

For a while I simply gaze at him. He looks quite comical:
he's wearing the torn cotton trousers and 'Fuck The Machine'
T-shirt that he had on the morning he disappeared, but over
these has pulled one of the smart Ralph Lauren shirts that
Dan Jameson took yesterday evening. He has it back to front,
and the sleeve is torn.

'What's the matter, honey?' I say, pushing myself up from
my pillows. 'Why are you crying?'

He's mumbling something; it's hard to work out what, for
his face is hidden in his hands. I want to shuffle to the end
of the bed and put my arm around him, but for some reason
I'm finding it hard to move.

'You mustn't be sad,' I say. 'The main thing is that you're here.'

Finally he looks up. The sight of his face takes my breath
away: his high cheekbones, those worry lines that dig into his
forehead; his mop of tangled hair and dark green eyes, which
now, as they stare back at me, glisten with distress. How could
I have forgotten those eyes?

'I'm not who you think I am,' he says.

'What do you mean? Of course you are . . .'

He's shaking his head, and as he does, something terrible
is happening.

'I'm a faker,' he whispers. 'A fraud . . .'

His face is caving in. As I reach out to him his eyes slide down his face and his nose collapses, like a melting jelly.

'Ed!'

There's nothing left, just a mush of skin. And although I'm trying to scream his name, no sound comes out.

I open my eyes. It is morning, the room infused with the murky grey of an overcast sky; from the street below I can hear the screech of a braking bus and the rumble of cars. For a moment or so I lie motionless, trying to purge the image of Ed's disintegrating features from my thoughts. It was just a dream, I tell myself; it didn't mean anything.

I get up, padding across the room and out on to the chilly landing. I need to talk to someone or listen to the radio, for in the silence of Ed's vast house it's hard to shake off the sense of his presence. Humming loudly I clatter down the stairs. In the kitchen, I switch on the old Philips radio that sits above the sink. A man is being interviewed about a forth-coming cricket match in Jamaica. I turn the volume up, comforted by the normality of the voices. I am going to have a cup of tea and then I am going to use the mobile phone that Alexandria has lent me to call Bangladesh. The timing is perfect: six a.m. in London, midday in Dhaka.

The first call is the easiest. Luck is on my side: Jon Salway is in his office, and the line is as clear as if he were in London.

'This is Sarah Jeffery,' I say. 'I'm a friend of Ed Salisbury? You spoke to his sister Alexandria yesterday?'

'Yup, that's right.'

He sounds bored; he's probably hoping I'm not going to take up too much time. I imagine him sitting in his air-conditioned office, a framed picture of the Queen on the wall behind. Most of what he eats will have been flown from the west, and everything he wears manufactured in South-East Asia, but purchased either in London or the Bangkok branch of M&S. When he's off duty he'll drink beer in the British High Commission club, play tennis and swim in the heavily chlorinated pool. He could be anywhere in the world.

'I was actually caught up in the tornado myself,' I say care-fully. I must have been spending too much time with Alexandria: my voice sounds clipped and upper class. 'I'm trying to get in touch with someone called Dan Jameson who works for Dfid . . .'

'Yup. I know Dan.'

'He very kindly drove me back to Chittagong,' I go on. 'I was wondering if you had his contact details?'

'Not to hand I'm afraid. Your best bet would be to call Dfid directly. There'll be a staff directory.'

He gives me the number of Dfid's Dhaka office and rings off.

I call Dfid in Dhaka. The woman on the switchboard says that Dan is currently out of the country but she can put me through to his voicemail. When I request a mobile number she sniffily replies that the personal details of Dfid's staff are never given out over the phone.

'Can you tell me where he is, then?'

'In Bangkok.'

'Really? I thought he was due back from there at the end of April.'

There's a pause. Then the woman says, 'He's been delayed.'

I ask to be put through to the voice mail. 'It's Sarah,' I say to the machine. 'Whenever you get this, please could you call me back?'

I recite Alexandria's mobile number, then put down the phone.

After I've rung off, I spend a minute or so sitting at the table staring into space. I should be making notes, or concocting a plan, but I'm finding it hard to focus. I rest the nib of my pencil on my notepad, tracing a few faint lines on the empty page. Either the receptionist on Dfid's switchboard was lying or Dan has misled his colleagues about his whereabouts. If only I could contact him directly.

There's one more call to make, but for some reason I am more nervous about it than the others. When I eventually reach for the worn piece of paper, with its smudged numerals, my pulse jumps skittishly. I dial the numbers.

Miraculously, the connection works. The phone rings a few times, and then I hear Syeda yelling, '*Salaam e-lekum!*' down the line.

'It's Sarah,' I shout back, giddy with the shock of being transported so immediately back to Lalalpur. I can picture her as clearly as if she was standing before me: her small brown hands clutching the phone, her bony wrists, each bearing a yellow plastic bangle, her crinkly black hair, which she would

oil then twist into an ingenious, pin-free bun. She was at least
a foot smaller than me and very thin, but far stronger, grabbing the spade that I was ineptly attempting to dig my garden
and shoving it competently into the soil with a few swift
thrusts. *Look at your hands!* She'd laughed. *So weak!* Where
is she now? I was picturing her standing in her yard throwing
seeds for the ducks, but that's not possible, for my final glimpse
of her house was of a collapsed wreck of straw and wattle,
her family's few belongings flung around the surrounding
fields as if a giant child had thrown a tantrum.

'Ma!' she cries. 'I've been praying for you!'

The line is very faint, and as with Jon Salway, there is a
disconcerting echo.

'How are you?' I ask, my mouth stumbling over the words
that only two weeks ago flowed so easily. 'How is everyone
in the village?'

'God has willed for us to live . . .'

'Have people come to help you?'

'No, Sister, no one has come . . .'

I take a breath, trying to steady myself. 'My husband, Mr
Edward . . .' I pause, cursing my lack of fluency. I'm not sure
how to phrase the question. 'There's something I don't understand. You said something about him being dead, the morning
I left? You said, "May his Soul Rest in Peace." But why did
you think he was dead?'

'That man said.'

Have I understood her correctly? It couldn't have been Dan
who told her; he can't speak Bengali. I am digging my pencil
into the paper with such force that the nib snaps and my fist
bangs into the table.

'What man? Do you mean the fisherman that brought me
to the shelter? Or was there someone else?'

It's too late. Whatever Syeda's said was not something she
intended to let slip.

'What man, Syeda?' I yell at her silence. 'Tell me! How
did he know that Ed was dead?'

'I'm going now, Sister,' she whispers. 'Pray for me.'

The line breaks off.

For a few seconds I remain at the table, the broken pencil
clasped in my fingers. The force of the wind was so great that
I could hardly stand; even now, in the subterranean quiet of

the kitchen I can hear the roar. Before me, the swelling sea rose in crested plumes; I had seen Ed run towards those waves and now he was disappearing into a mist of swirling sand. Whatever happened between our last matter-of-fact kiss and those moments on the beach to cause him to disappear?

Rising, I wander across the room, glancing through the tall windows at the back garden. The morning's telephone calls have left me sea sick with doubt; I'm trying to steady myself in the truth, but it keeps tipping sideways, leaving me disorientated and nauseous.

Alexandria's mobile is ringing. It's her, calling from her landline.

'Any luck?'

'Not really. Dfid say Dan's in Bangkok but they won't give me his contact details. How about you?'

'No headway at all. The police refuse to register Ed as a missing person as he sent those emails to people in Dhaka, and the Foreign Office guy my friend knows is sticking to the line that Oxan's programmes in Bangladesh are completely pukka. He thought the idea that Ed had been mixed up in some complicated plot to siphon the oil to India was ludicrous.'

'So what do we do now?' I say after a pause.

'I'm not sure . . . I thought maybe I'd go over to Dalston and see if Ed's turned up in that house where he was squatting before. He had quite a lot of friends there . . .'

'OK.'

'Aren't you going to see Sylvia today?' Alexandria suddenly says. 'She said she was sending a car.'

'Oh God, I completely forgot!'

Bang on cue, I hear the distant chime of the front-door bell. So much has happened since yesterday, when the visit was arranged, that travelling down to Sussex to meet Ed's aunt is the last thing I want to do.

'Can't it wait?'

'Darling, I really don't think so. She's desperate to talk to you, and she has terrible problems with her back so can't easily get to London.'

I want to say that all I'm interested in doing is finding Ed, but there's a steely edge to her voice that makes it hard to demur. 'Anyway,' she goes on. 'What else are you going to do today? You'll have a lovely time. It'll help take your mind off things.'

Upstairs the door bell rings again.

'I'd better go,' I say resignedly. 'It sounds like the car's already here.'

'Oh, and can you leave my phone on the table?' Alexandria adds. 'I'll pick it up later.'

She rings off without saying goodbye.

TWENTY-SEVEN

Sylvia's house is at the end of a high-banked lane, tucked behind a screen of fir. It's a beautiful place, covered in purple wisteria that clings to stones the colour of honey. It's huge, too. There must be at least ten rooms on each of the three storeys, and what looks like a converted stable block tucked around back. Asking Sylvia's driver to drop me by the gate, I linger for a while at the top of the gravelled drive. Before approaching the main door I need to gather my thoughts.

My fingers trail the lavender that grows in clumps by the gate. For days I've been giddy with shock. Not knowing what to believe or who to trust, my emotions sway sickeningly between hope and despair. If Ed was dead, I would know how to feel. But as I vacillate between half formed theories – that Oxan are holding him against his will, that he's on the run, or that he has simply given up on Bangladesh and walked away – I am unable to stop my thoughts from spiralling into ever more confusing constellations. Despite what he said, Ed was a good person. He loved me, or I thought he did. I need to keep myself steady, to remember how things were in Lalalpur. Yet after talking to Jalal and Dan I feel as if my grasp on him is slipping, like fingers prised from the edge of a cliff.

I tramp across the gravel. The early-morning grey has cleared and for the first time since returning from Bangladesh I'm warm. Bees drone around the lavender; the clover's blooming. Alexandria mentioned that Sylvia's house was a 'retreat', and now I notice that in front of the house a group of people wearing tracksuits and Maharishi pants are practising Tai-Chi. I watch their dreamlike movements: entranced limbs, moving together. Bracing myself, I approach the entrance to the house.

The door is open. Stepping into the entrance hall, I take in a huge stone Buddha placed against the wall. His eyes are beatifically closed; a rose lies in his folded hands. The flagstones are bare, the wall covered with an oriental hanging: bright squares of fabric inscribed with Tibetan prayers. On a board opposite a list of the day's activities is displayed: Monday, May 6th: 6-8 a.m. Morning Rise Meditation with Sally; 10-12 p.m. Tai Chi (garden); Dervish Dance (Great Hall). I gaze at the schedule, not taking it in. Over the last two weeks I have learnt that if repeated enough times, words lose their meaning, like staring at something for so long that the image blurs. Ed was dead but now he's back. Ed loved me once, but now he's gone. What do the phrases actually mean? They're just sounds, placed in a certain order, to achieve a certain effect. If I repeat them quickly, again and again and again, they turn to mulch.

'Sarah! It *is* Sarah, isn't it?'

A woman has appeared from the main stairway, one hand outstretched in greeting, the other leaning on a cane. She has long silver hair which swings down her back, and is wearing flowing clothes: loose lilac trousers, covered by a silk dress, thick Birkenstock sandals. A soft shawl is wrapped around her shoulders. It matches her eyes: light blue, the colour of the sky. I nod at her, smiling. So here is the real founder of Schools For Change: Ed's aunt. Would he have ever introduced us? Or did he never intend for our relationship to go that far?

After staring intently into my eyes for an embarrassing moment or so, Sylvia links her arm through mine and leads me into a large reception room.

'Did you have an alright journey? I hope it wasn't too much of a drag coming all the way.'

'It only took a couple of hours.'

'I really appreciate you making the effort, dear. Lexie told you about my silly old back, didn't she? I can't sit in a car for more than about half an hour. It's such a bore.'

After the shady hallway, the reception room is filled with so much sunshine that I am temporarily dazzled. Despite the stick, Sylvia moves with purposeful verve across the floor.

'This is our meeting room,' she says brightly. 'We come together as a community here every evening for our meditation.'

Now that my eyes have become accustomed to the light I can see that the room has the cheerful, functional appearance of a friendly hotel, or an upmarket nursing home: an exclusive establishment for the artistic elite. Leather sofas and chairs are placed in welcoming clusters, the wooden floors covered with Turkish rugs. The leaflets displayed on the table are for yoga courses and walking holidays; the walls covered with modern art: colourful swirls, landscapes, tribal designs. The air smells faintly of incense. Alexandria was right, I think. If I had stayed in London I would have spent the day obsessively trawling through my memories and the lapping panic would have engulfed me.

'Would you like me to show you around? It's only the first year we've been open, so I do still love to show it off.'

'I don't mind . . .' I say faintly.

'Perhaps later,' she says, eyeing me thoughtfully. 'In the meantime we can sit here. Everyone's busy doing classes, so hopefully we shan't get disturbed.'

She leads me to a window seat that overlooks the gardens: an overgrown lawn surrounded by banks of foxgloves and hollyhocks which slope towards a river that divides the property from the fields and woods beyond. As we sit down Sylvia is still clutching my hands with her soft fingers.

'Shall I get you something to drink? We've got some rather wonderful Green tea that one of our guests brought from China . . .'

She's peering at me so closely that I have to look away, flustered by her intensity.

'I'm fine,' I mumble.

Leaning her cane against the wall she pulls her long legs up to her chest and wraps her arms around them, like the hippy child she once was. She must have been stunning in the Sixties, with her long blonde hair and high cheekbones.

'Now I've got you in the light, let me have a proper look at you,' she says, peering intently into my face. 'Eddy must have adored you,' she whispers after a moment or so. 'You're so lovely.'

I grimace. 'Am I?'

'Of course you are. Eddy told me *everything* about you in his emails, you know. He said you were the best thing that ever happened to him.'

I blink away hot tears. 'Did he?'

'Yes, dear, he did.'

She sits quietly beside me as I pull myself together. In Bangladesh Ed had only mentioned her in passing: his 'wacky' aunt, who had stepped into his mother's shoes; now I am beginning to grasp how close they were.

'I'm sorry,' I say, sniffing. 'I didn't mean to cry . . .'

'Why not? We really oughtn't fight grief. It's part of the healing process.'

'But how can I grieve when Ed's not even dead?'

She does not reply, just stares at me sadly.

'If only I knew what's happened to him!' I cry.

'I think you do know, Sarah,' she says gently. 'It's in your eyes. And the way you stand. You're so open. Like everything's exposed . . .'

I'm not going to ask what she means. I shake my head, glancing away from her. 'He's not dead,' I whisper.

I glance through the window, dabbing at my eyes. In the garden, a group of people are setting up easels. A breeze has picked up, and they're having trouble attaching the paper to the wooden struts. Clouds scatter skittishly across the sky as a girl laughingly chases a sheet of paper.

'I saw him,' Sylvia suddenly says.

I jerk around. 'You *saw* him? When?'

'It was just before Lexie called to say he was missing. He was standing by this very window, looking at me.'

I can't breathe. I ogle her, trying to remain calm.

'He said he was sorry for everything that had happened,' she continues. 'Then he faded away.'

The disappointment is so suffocating that all I am able to do is open my mouth, sucking at the air like a fish.

'So it wasn't actually him?' I eventually whisper. 'It was like, some dream?'

'I suppose you could say that, yes.'

For a while I'm unable to speak. All day I've repressed it, but now I remember my own dream. Ed said he was a fraud. And then his face caved in.

'I'm sorry if I've upset you, dear,' Sylvia eventually says. Reaching out, she gives my hand a squeeze. 'I suppose we all have our own ways of coping with what's happened . . .'

'It's OK . . .'

I return the pressure of her hand. I *am* upset, but I don't mind, for she radiates a calmness that draws me towards her, like a moth seeking light.

'Now look,' she says in a more businesslike voice. 'I know a bit about Eddy's campaign from Sadid, but I wanted to hear your version of things.' She gazes into my face, her eyes narrowing. 'I gather it's led to a lot of problems for our project?'

I nod, relieved to be able to discuss something practical. 'It's been a disaster. The school in Dhaka was burnt down and I don't think we'll be able to operate in Lalalpur now—'

'This is what I was getting from Sadid . . .'

I give her a brief summary of everything that has happened, including Chairman Roul's involvement with BNRC, Aunik's murder and Dan Jameson's visit to the village.

'Poor Eddy!' she exclaims, when I describe how obsessed he became with stopping Oxan. 'This is my fault! Knowing Bangladesh, and knowing my nephew, I should have predicted this. I just hoped that being somewhere so completely different from everything he was familiar with would help him sort all his problems out . . .'

'But it did!' I cry. 'You mustn't blame yourself! He loved Bangladesh. Before the thing with Jhomgram he was doing brilliantly. He was a fantastic teacher, everyone thought he was great. It was all going really well . . .'

'And then?'

'Then it all got messed up . . . we didn't realize how complicated the local politics were. We went charging in without working out what the implications were and everything exploded in our faces. I wanted us to back off, but Ed categorically refused. He felt it was his duty to stand up against Oxan.'

'Poor, poor Eddy,' Sylvia repeats sadly. 'He was trying so hard.'

'It was just that he wanted so badly to help people.'

'He's always had a problem with balance,' she continues. 'He used to throw himself one hundred and ten percent into things; he could never get himself on an even keg. To tell you the truth I used to sometimes feel that he was acting out a role rather than allowing the real Eddy to emerge, whether it was being a drop out in East London or saving the world.'

I gaze at my hands. I always thought I knew the real Eddy, but maybe she's right. Maybe even in Lalalpur he never existed.

'Now look, you sit here,' she continues. 'I want to show you something.'

Sliding off the window seat, she grasps her cane and starts to move across the room. 'I'll be back in a sec.'

The would-be artists are finally organized. Easels in place, they place their stools in a semicircle, facing the river. Most have started to paint, but one man sits, slightly apart from the group, arms by his sides, staring at the ground as if deep in contemplation. He's balding; the breeze keeps flicking back the strands of hair that he's combed over his tonsure to reveal a smooth pink oval. I stare at him until my eyes blur.

'Here we are!'

Glancing around, I see Sylvia hobbling across the room, a box file in her arms. Placing it on the seat beside me, she pulls open the binders to reveal a stack of photos which she starts to shuffle through.

'I wanted to share these with you . . . Here we are. Edward in 1973.'

Beaming, she places the picture in my lap.

It's a formal christening photo. He is being held by his mother, who is sitting on a chair in the middle of a very grand room. She's wearing a long flowing dress and is gazing adoringly down at her baby. She looks very young.

'Is this your sister?'

She nods. 'My darling little sister, Alice. You know she died of breast cancer at thirty two?'

'Ed told me.'

'It broke my heart.'

She hands me another picture. It's of Ed and Alexandria, sitting on a bench in front of what looks like a fig tree. He's about ten or eleven and is smiling broadly, his hands spread over his knees like a footballer in a team shot. Alexandria's a teenager, dressed in a puffy blouse and flares. Unlike her brother's toothy grin, she glares sulkily at the camera.

'They've had such a tough time,' Sylvia goes on. 'Losing their mother when they were so little, and then their father . . .'

'What actually happened to him?' I murmur, brushing my fingers affectionately over Ed's ten year old face. If we'd had children, is this how they would have looked?

'Suicide. Shot himself with one of his hunting rifles.'

'Oh, God!'

I put the photo down. Ed had told me he'd died in an 'accident'. The way he'd said it made it clear he didn't welcome further questions.

'I was absolutely furious with him!'

'How old was Ed?'

'About eight or nine. Luckily he was away at school at the time.' She pauses, staring into space, then gives herself a little shake, extinguishing the memory. 'After that, I did what I could for him and Lexie, but staying with your aunt during school holidays isn't the same as having your own parents, is it?'

'No . . . the poor things . . .'

'They inherited all the family money of course. Their father was extremely rich, so materially they've always had everything they want. But Ed has had a difficult time, much more than Lexie. The money made him aimless. He got to Oxford but didn't seem to care whether or not he came out of it with a degree. He was always so influenced by the people around him; that was partly the problem. In his twenties he got in with the wrong sort of friends who I'm afraid took rather a lot of drugs. Then he had his breakdown and decided to become a dropout . . .'

She hands me another picture, which I greedily receive.

'He never seemed to know what to do with his life,' she says. 'He went from one mad fad to the next. That's why we were so pleased when he agreed to go to Bangladesh.'

The photograph was taken recently. Ed sitting under a tree, his arms wrapped around his knees. He's looking directly at the camera, smiling in that way he has: as if suppressing a great belch of laughter. He looks exactly as I remember him: a kind, gentle man, not the sort who'd walk away.

'This one will amuse you,' Sylvia says, pushing another picture my way. 'Eddy always loved a party . . .'

I don't want to stop looking at Ed sitting under the tree, but I can't let Sylvia's hand remain hanging in the air so I reluctantly take the final picture. It shows a group of young men, posing for the camera. It must have been taken at a May Ball or possibly a wedding; they're dressed in the full white tie regalia. There are eight or nine of them, arms splayed theatrically, all in various stages of inebriation: the guy at the front is glugging a magnum of champagne; another swings a bottle of vodka. Ed stands in the centre. I gaze at his lovely face for a while, my heart catching. His face is boyish, his hair spiked and sprayed pink and he's grasping a bottle of champagne. On his face is the same jocular expression that I fell for in Bangladesh. He's pulling a pose, laughing at himself.

'Balloil May Ball, 1993,' says Sylvia.

'Looks like they're having a good time.'

She beams. 'He was a great socializer. He got it from his mother.'

'Who's that?'

I point to the young man standing next to Ed. He's taller than Ed, with long brown hair, arranged in a comical top knot on the top of his head. He has stuck a sprig of what looks like Rosemary in the button of his tuxedo and is wearing an extravagant cravat. With one hand, he salutes the camera. With the other, he clasps Ed's shoulder.

'That's his best friend, Giles Montgomery. They were inseparable all the way through Oxford. He was a bright spark, a real joker.'

She starts talking about various other people in the photograph, but I have stopped listening. *Giles Montgomery.* Wasn't that the name on the cards in Dan Jameson's wallet? I scrutinize his image, as if it might yield Ed. It must be a coincidence, I decide; it's a common enough name, though God only knows why Jameson is using it as an alibi. I am just about to hand the photo back when I notice something else.

My eyes fix on a figure hovering on the edge of the group. He's trying to push himself into the picture, but a section of his body has been cropped by the frame. There's something slightly desperate in his stance: his smile is so bright and the LA gangland sign he's making with his outstretched fingers so pathetically pretentious that one might almost feel sorry for him. I gawp at the image, my fingers gripping the paper. I am finding it hard to breathe.

It's Dan Jameson. He's grinning inanely in a way that I can't imagine his more adult self doing, and has not yet acquired the bulk of muscle, but has the same sandy coloured hair and the same bland sheen. What the hell is *he* doing here?

'Are you alright, dear?'

I'm unable to respond. I'm recalling the way Ed greeted Dan on the terrace. Dan had gone striding up the steps just as Ed was emerging from inside. They'd shaken hands, talked about the condition of the road. Then Dan asked if they'd met before, and Ed said they hadn't, despite exchanging so many emails. Could it be they didn't remember each other? But if it's as simple as that, why has Dan or whatever he's called, got the name of Ed's best friend on his credit cards?

'Who's that?' I say breathlessly, pointing at Jameson.

Sylvia glances at the picture, pulling a face. 'No idea,' she says distractedly. 'Just some hanger-on.'

TWENTY-EIGHT

I don't remember much about leaving Sylvia's house. I didn't tell her about Dan Jameson. I was too confused, my emotions splattering everywhere: dismay pooling on the carpet, confusion streaking down the walls, a lump of terror landing on my lap. She wanted me to stay for a meditation session, but I was desperate to return to London. Giving her a hug, I told her I'd be in touch. Perhaps I should have tried to explain everything, but I needed time alone, to think.

Now, as her car speeds towards London, I'm frantically trying to make sense of what's happened. Why is Dan Jameson using the name of Ed's friend? The only reason I can think of is that in his search for an alias, he's grabbed a name he remembers from his past. But why would he need an alias? And if he and Ed knew each other at university, why make a point of saying that they had never met? Or did they want to give the appearance of never having met?

I'm unable to think straight. Everything has become so jumbled that all I can process are a series of discombobulated images. There is Dan, sitting on the over-stuffed sofa in Ed's Kensington house, murmuring his condolences. He was picking up Ed's clothes, he said; the Foreign Office was helping him. So why carry an Oxan identity card? There's Dan's jeep, parked on the village road. He'd been so friendly, so insistent that he could help. 'Howdy!' he'd called, grinning at me as he appeared through the trees. 'Come for a chin wag with Ed!'

There's the tin roof, popping off the Chairman's house, and the fisherman, running ahead of me, mud slicking down his muscled calves. Here come the men, four of them, kicking off their flip-flops disdainfully and marching up the terrace steps. The leader has hennaed his hair orange; his belly wobbles as he walks.

I huddle in the back of the car trying to stem the flow, but it's impossible. Here's Aunik, curled like a sleeping puppy on the path. As I approach him the dark stain of flies that obscures his face lifts into the air. It's the whirr of wings that makes my stomach turn.

I have to stop the images. I open my eyes, rubbing them. I need to concentrate on Dan Jameson, but can no longer focus. There is Ed, peering at my overturned rickshaw as I lie in the dust. He'd appeared from nowhere, like an angel. 'Are you OK?' he'd said, trying not to laugh. Then he'd taken me to his house and bandaged my hand as gently as if I was a baby. He'd come from nowhere, and then he'd disappeared. Who *was* he?

'I'm not being funny or anything, love,' the driver suddenly says. 'But are you alright?'

Glancing up, I catch his eye in his mirror. Despite the purplish blush to his cheeks and overripe drinker's nose, his face is kind. I'm crying I realize, wiping at my cheeks with the back of my hand. It's just as Sylvia said. Skin pulled back, flesh bared to the elements, I'm completely exposed.

'Yeah, I'm fine . . .'

'Whatever he did, he ain't worth it. Plenty more fish in the sea for a pretty girl like you.'

I attempt a smile. 'Thanks.'

'So where we going? Back to Kensington?'

'Can you drop me in the City?'

I leave the taxi outside Moorgate and walk the rest of the way. It's good to be outside after so long confined in the stale atmosphere of the cab. Even if the air that I'm pulling into my lungs smells predominantly of exhaust it makes a change from car air-freshener. I walk fast, pretending I know where I'm heading.

I pace past grand Victorian banks and 1960s office blocks, peering at the numbers. I Googled the company and wrote their London address on the back of my hand before leaving for Sussex: 160 Needlemaker Street. The road turns to the right. I stride on, trying to look like an executive on her way to a meeting. Dressed as I am in jeans and trainers, and with my hair flopping messily over my face, there's not much chance of that. What I actually resemble, I realize as I notice my reflection in a shank of corporate glass, is a down and out. I stop in shock, gazing at the person I have become. I had not realized I had grown so thin, or that I walked in such a broken, cowering way. Pulling back my shoulders, I try to smooth down my hair, deleting my hunted expression with a false grin. I keep trying to practise my patter, but my mind bucks away from the task, cantering back relentlessly to those terrible images. The roof: like a champagne cork. Aunik's white jeans: sticky brown; Ed, running away from me towards the waves. Over and over and over again.

It is late afternoon. The sun has slipped behind the high-rise buildings, leaving this slice of the street in the shade; despite walking with gusto, I am shivering. As I cross the road, peering up and down the street, I am unable to formulate a plan. Only one string of words comes to mind: *I have to find Ed.*

I pace another block, drawn instinctively towards a large, showy building, fronted by marble pillars and sheets of dark glass. I am muttering the name like a prayer: *Frank Carswell.* I remember his name from the emails. *Director of Corporate Social Responsibility.*

When I reach the building I see that a tree is growing in the cathedral-like lobby. Behind this, water cascades over fake boulders. The name is there, in giant letters that seem to drop from the sky like Da Vinci's hand of God: **OXAN**.

I am so tense that my shoulders brush my ears. I try to relax, taking a deep, steadying breath, but feel as tightly bound and terrified as a kidnap victim wrapped in tape. Pushing my way through the rotating doors I walk purposefully to the reception desk, where I attempt a polite smile.

'I wonder if I could speak to Mr Frank Carswell?'

The uniformed guard stares at me impassively. 'Do you have an appointment?'

'No, but it's really urgent.'

His face deadpan, he picks up the phone and dials a number. He is chewing a wedge of gum, pushing it into the back of his mouth and masticating as he speaks. 'Coleen? Got a young lady here who wants to speak to Mr Carswell. Says it's urgent.'

I look away, feigning nonchalance. I cannot stop my fingers from drumming on the desk.

'What's your name love?'

'Sarah Jeffries.'

Eventually he puts down the phone. 'He'll be leaving the building in about ten minutes, you can catch him as he comes out.' Indicating an area of seating by the waterfall, he waves me away. 'Wait over there.'

I sit by the tinkling water, trying to stop shaking. It feels even colder here than outside; despite the gloomy London evening, air-conditioning pumps through the wall shafts. I have pulled a copy of *The Economist* on to my lap and opened the pages, but am staring at them unseeingly. I feel as if I am balancing on the icy ledge of a mountain. Everything that's happened cascades around me, an avalanche of disconnected images, fragments of conversations and memories. I want to escape from them before I'm crushed, but I can't move.

It's so, so cold. Ed wouldn't leave me, I keep thinking. No matter how difficult things had become, he said he loved me. I have to remember him as he was in Lalalpur. He cared deeply about the village and he loved his school; he was outraged at injustice. The idea that he and Dan were working together in Bangladesh, either for Oxan, or for British interests, is preposterous. Yet now that I'm trying to picture him, all I can remember is my nightmare. He's a faker, he says. Then his eyes start to slither down his face.

'Sarah Jeffries?'

I look up. A man in a suit is standing before me.

'Yes?'

'Frank Carswell. Reception said you wanted a word.' He holds out his hand. A youngish guy, with heavy framed Jarvis Cocker specs and a pinstriped jacket.

I gawp at him, rising unsteadily to my feet. I have temporarily forgotten where I am. I can remember looking for the building, but not coming inside or sitting down.

'I hope it's something quick. I've got a train to catch . . .' His eyes glide almost imperceptibly over my trainers, a faint smile flickering on the edge of his thin lips. I take in his elegant loafers, the fashionable cut of his suit. 'How exactly can I help?'

'Can we talk in private?'

'Not really. I'm in a real hurry.'

'OK . . .' I glance at the seats, but Carswell remains standing.

'I'm a close friend of Ed Salisbury's,' I say slowly. The words feel lumpen, bunging up my mouth. 'We've been living in the coastal zone in south-east Bangladesh, where your company has been drilling for oil. I think Ed contacted you?'

Carswell makes a tiny gesture with his chin which I take to be a nod. He's starting to look faintly annoyed.

'As you know, Ed was involved with this campaign to stop your partner company, the Bangladesh Natural Resources Company, from illegally evicting people . . .' My heart is skittering nervously. 'He was working with this journalist, Anu Jalal, and our friend, Aunik Chowdhury . . .'

A constant flow of people are passing over the marble floors of the lobby, waving their security passes at the guard and squeezing through the turnstiles into the bowels of the building; the place echoes with the slap of their shoes, and the fake, urinal-like trickling of the waterfall.

Carswell folds his arms resignedly. 'Are you one of these anti-globalization people? Because if so, I'm going to have to call security . . .'

'Aunik was murdered. They dumped his body by our bungalow.'

I stop. I'm picturing the flies again. They'd been feeding on the gunge coming from his head, but as I approached, they lifted into the air, butting my face with their filthy wings.

'Look,' Carswell says. His expression has turned blank. 'I'm sorry to hear about all this, truly I am. But I'm not really sure why you're here. Oxan has got absolutely nothing to do with any of it. We're completely scrupulous about our dealings with our Southern partners. If you want to know more about our Corporate Social Responsibility policies take a look at our annual report . . .'

'The police didn't even bother to investigate the death,' I continue. 'They just stood by whilst people's houses were being torched.'

Carswell is holding out his smooth white hands, trying to placate me. 'I really don't have time for this . . .'

He's trying to walk away, but I grab hold of his arm. All the way from Sylvia's house, the question has been simmering inside me. Now finally it bubbles up.

'Do you know Dan Jameson?'

He shrugs. 'Doesn't he work for Dfid?'

'Has he visited you here?'

'I've never met him.'

'What about someone called Giles Montgomery?'

'Never heard of him,' he murmurs, pulling his arm away from me, and pushing past.

'I think you have! I think he's working for you! He's got an Oxan identity card. You've hired him to stop Ed's campaign!'

Carswell turns, glancing at me with disdain. 'Having an identity card doesn't mean someone's working for us. This is a huge corporation. Hundreds of people come through the building every day. This person was probably just visiting. What you're suggesting is ridiculous.'

He's trying hard to remain impassive, but as he speaks I am filled with bile at the superior moue of his mouth, the way he is standing, arms crossed, scrutinizing me with barely disguised contempt.

'What have you done with Ed?' I say, my voice rising. 'He's disappeared!'

'I beg your pardon?'

'Ed's vanished – they warned him not to get involved but he wouldn't listen and now he's gone!'

Frank Carswell has started to back away. 'I've got absolutely no idea what you're talking about . . .'

'Jameson's got Ed, he's brainwashed him or something . . .'

I did not mean for this to happen, but I realize that I am shouting. People are turning and staring; behind his desk, I notice the security guard put down his paper and stand up.

'Look, calm down . . .'

Gripping me by the arm, Carswell propels me towards the revolving doors. 'You need to go home,' he says. 'We can't help you here.'

'Where's Ed?' I cry. 'You have to tell me what you've done to him!'

'It's alright,' I hear Carswell muttering to the security guard, who is loping towards us, like an overfed bull. 'She's just leaving.'

He hustles me into the swinging door, still holding onto my elbow. It's just as well, since my legs are buckling.

'Please help me,' I wail. 'I have to find him!'

But Frank Carswell is shaking his head. 'Go home,' he says, almost kindly. 'There's nothing to be gained in hanging around here.'

I sit on the pavement, bawling. No one comes near. Probably they're afraid that I'll jump to my feet, muttering that they're the devil, and knife them. I don't blame them. I'm just the same as all the other crazies, my hair wild, my chin smeared with snot.

As far as I can see, I have no reason to carry on.

TWENTY-NINE

I am slumped on the pavement, head down and arms around my legs. When I hear the engine and the squeak of brakes I don't look up. The car door clunks shut, followed by the beep of the locks. Footsteps approach.

'Sarah!'

Someone is bending over me; a hand grips my shoulder. When I eventually raise my head I see Alexandria bending over.

'Sarah, darling, what's the matter?'

I glance into her face. Despite her puffy eyes, she gives me a hesitant smile.

'Thank God I've found you!'

Allowing her to pull me up, I slowly stand. I have been sitting in this position for so long that I have to slowly unfurl myself like an old woman.

'How did you know I was here?'

'We got hold of Sylvia's driver. He said he'd dropped you in the City. I guessed this is where you'd come . . . what the hell's happened?'

'I've had a slightly traumatic day.'

Her face furrows in glancing bemusement. 'There's news,' she suddenly says. 'Look at this.'

She thrusts her phone in my face. I stare at the illuminated screen for a while, trying to focus on the message.

Auntie, Mr Edward is found. Come now. Bye, Jamil.

'Who's Jamil?' Alexandria is asking. 'Is he from Bangladesh?'

'He's my friend Syeda's nephew. He lives in Lalalpur . . .' I cannot stop staring at the message. *Mr Edward is found.* Is it a joke? 'She must have got him to send it,' I say faintly.

Alexandria gazes at me ponderously, her pale face caught in a pool of piss-yellow light. Her white dreadlocks are coiled around her head like ropes; her skin, normally so artfully made up, is pink and blotchy. Standing before me in her padded parka and plastic clogs she looks less like an avant-garde fashionista and more like an overgrown Dutch girl.

'So he's gone back to your village . . .' she says slowly.

'Looks like it.'

I straighten up. *Mr Edward is found.* I still don't understand what this means, but the heavy ache that has been lodged in my chest since the tornado has lifted. *Mr Edward.* I picture him, standing in the fields, his umbrella balanced on his thin wrist, grinning. He used to play cricket with the village boys; they'd call him 'Uncle' and invariably bowl him out. Everyone had a right to education, he said; it was a source of light. All that work. The lists and plans, the half-built school and tenderly garnered classes, held in the Chairman's yard. Of course he's returned to Lalalpur. It's where we have our life.

'How did she get my number?' Alexandria's saying.

'I rang her on your phone the other day.'

'Can you call her again?'

'Sure . . .'

I bend over the mobile, fiddling. Ed must have had a change of heart, and gone winging back to the village assuming I'd be there. As soon as I retrieve Syeda's number, I press 'call'. My hands are trembling so violently that the phone keeps slipping through my fingers. Yet however many times I press the shiny buttons, the response is always the same: the line is dead. Alexandria twitches on the pavement beside me. It's clear that she wants to grab her phone from my incompetent

hands and ring the number herself, but she's too well brought
up to mutter anything other than: 'Any luck?'

'She's either turned the phone off or is out of range,' I eventually say, passing the mobile back. 'I can't get through.'

'I don't understand why he'd go back to Bangladesh . . .?'

I turn to her, trying not to smile too widely. *I do.*

'He loves Bangladesh,' I say. 'He made it his home.' *He's
looking for me.*

She glances at me sceptically, folding her arms and toeing
a fragment of dirt on the pavement. 'There's something wrong
about this,' she murmurs. 'Something's not right.'

I don't want her to continue. Her uncertain face is like a
chilly breeze, when what I crave is warmth. All that matters
is that Ed has returned to Lalalpur; his presence there rendering
everything that has happened in the last few weeks irrelevant.
Glancing away from her I focus on Jamil's message. I want
to luxuriate in the words: such a simple arrangement of letters,
which changes so much.

Mr Edward is found. Please come.

Perhaps Dan was telling the truth: Ed really was trying to
escape from some threat. But now it's been removed, so naturally he's returned to Bangladesh. Perhaps that's why Dan had
the Oxan security pass; he was visiting them in an effort to
sort the problems out. It's odd that he hasn't called Alexandria
directly, or tried to find me in his Kensington house; perhaps
there wasn't time. If there are more glitches in this shining
new version of events, I'm going to ignore them.

'The only way we can find out what's happening is if I go
to back to Bangladesh,' I say excitedly.

'Go back to Bangladesh?' Alexandria echoes doubtfully.

'I've got a return ticket. Remember?'

'But don't you think it would be better to get Interpol to
investigate first? Or the British High Commission? It all seems
so odd . . .'

I shake my head impatiently. 'The British High Commission
will be useless. They don't even accept that he's gone missing!'
I stand up, not wanting to counter any more objections. 'Please,
Alexandria,' I say, gripping her arm. 'This is something I have
to do. Don't try to stop me.'

I'm smiling beseechingly, trying to make her return my
gaze, but she just bites her lip. For a moment I think she is

about to say something. Then suddenly she steps apart from me, giving her head a little shake.

'OK,' she says with a sigh. 'We'll do it your way.'

I head east, crossing deserts and mountains and time zones to return to my love. I'm fixated on the computerized map that blinks on the screen before my seat, willing the miles away. For too long we've been apart, but now the distance is finally closing: Turkey, the Black Sea, Iran; all are behind us. As we reach Pakistan, a golden glow appears beyond the plane's wing. Somewhere in India, the sun is rising. I don't sleep or eat the food they bring me on the plastic trays.

I keep picturing the scene. I'll hire a rickshaw, to take me to the outskirts of the village. Once I reach the track that leads to the beach I'll walk, picking my way through the long grasses, so the seeds don't stick to my *shalwar* ends. Step by step I'll return. It'll be steamy hot; as I move closer to the sea, my body, so taut and chilled in Britain, will relax, like melting ice. If I concentrate, blocking out the roar of the aircraft engines, I can already hear the constant burbling of village voices, like water running over stones; the call of the magpie robins as they hop amongst the trees, the tireless cicadas. Respectfully circumnavigating the bull that Jamil Ahmed keeps tethered by the track, I'll skirt around Syeda's compound, smelling the wood smoke and water lilies and, as I approach the beach, the stink of drying fish.

I'm almost there. Traversing Syeda's pond, where her poor hen once pecked, I'll turn down a narrow mud path that leads through the patchwork fields and head for the bungalow. Like the times we returned from Chittagong, the kids will quickly spot me. 'Auntie!' they'll call, scampering across the fields. 'What've you got in your bags?'

Somewhere, on the other side of the coconut trees and banana plants, my Ed is waiting. I'm going to take it easy. I'm not going to run or call his name. I'm going to stroll up the path, inspecting my tomato plants and the jasmine that curls around the fence. Only when he bounds down the terrace steps will I put down my bag.

'Hi honey,' I'll say, as I step into his open arms. 'How've you been?'

We enter an area of turbulence, the aircraft rattling and

bumping through the freezing air. Closing my eyes, I lean my head against the polyester pillow. With every second that passes, Ed grows closer. I imagine him appearing in the empty seat beside me, his blurry image solidifying into flesh and bone. After my dream it was getting hard to remember his features but now my mind replays every contour of his face: the high cheekbones and dark green eyes, his mischievous lips and his forehead that's getting crumpled. I want to trace each gulley with my fingertips, smoothing his worries away. If I keep my eyes shut, I can feel his hand on my arm, sense his mouth brushing my ear. It's been so long since he's touched me. Moving closer, I rest my head on his shoulder.

THIRTY

Bangladesh, May 20th

The bus drops me at Noton Bazaar. It's over forty-eight hours since I boarded the plane in Heathrow and I stumble down the rusty steps, staggering as my feet hit the hot tarmac. The reek of rotting garbage and faeces rises from the gutter; peering at the hairy object that's brushing my legs I realize that I'm about to trip over a goat. Shoving the creature away I glance down the shabby street, taking in the chai stalls with their mounds of sticky sweets and samosas, a booth selling *beedis* and paan and, in pride of place over the crumbling mini-roundabout, a billboard advertising Grameen Phones. An old man, bent almost double, is hobbling towards me, his hands clasped in supplication as his wavering voice calls for alms. Taking in his frayed prayer cap and begging bowl I wearily hand over a ten-taka note. The air is tacky with heat; the sky murky with oncoming rain.

Ever since landing in Dhaka, I've become increasingly tense. Whilst still in the air, the fantasy held. I would glide into Lalalpur as effortlessly as a kingfisher flitting over the village ponds, my turquoise feathers flashing in the light. The village was undamaged, nothing had changed, and Ed would be waiting for me, just as Syeda's message had implied. Yet the moment

I stepped into the airport with its creaking carousel and sparrows fluttering in the ceiling, the thin skein of my trance was burst. The tornado had flattened Lalalpur as effectively as a boot stomped anthill, I remembered. Ed could not be waiting for me in the bungalow, for the bungalow was no longer there. As I flopped into the 'De-Luxe Chittagong Express Bus', with its broken springs and blaring horn, my anxiety shifted gear, edging into fear. I don't want to think about it, but I keep remembering Alexandria's comment when she showed me Jamil's message: *Something's not right.*

A fleet of rickshaws hovers expectantly. Nodding at one of the drivers, I climb into the back of his rickety vehicle. He's a child really, his chin smooth, his shirt torn. Fastening his *lunghi* between his legs, he jumps athletically onto the bony bicycle seat, calf muscles bulging.

'Lalalpur,' I say, pointing in the direction of the track.

'*Lalalpur nai!*' he says, spitting red paan onto the sandy road. *There is no Lalalpur.*

'I don't understand?'

'*Lalalpur shersh!*' He grins, turning the cycle towards the track. *Lalalpur is finished.* '*Apni bujjen na?*' *Don't you understand?*

'Take me there,' I say curtly, pursing my lips and pulling my *orna* around my shoulders as the rickshaw gathers speed. How can Lalalpur be 'finished'? Despite the damage done by the tornado, the village obviously still exists. The boy must be pulling my leg.

We set off down the track, my adolescent chauffeur bellowing out a devotional song as he cycles.

'Ah Baba! Take me across the river in your golden boat!'

I have started to feel unpleasantly light-headed, as if the top of my skull is about to shatter. Each time the rickshaw jolts across a pothole I gasp, grabbing the plywood sides. I keep trying to grasp the images that filled me with hope during the flight, but they've vanished, as insubstantial and transitory as faces in the clouds. *Mr Edward is found. Please come.* The message was sent from Syeda's phone, or at least from the number she gave me for unlike the young men in the village, who were constantly shouting at each other down their phones, I had never seen her use a mobile; perhaps it belonged to Jamil. If only I had spoken to her, but despite my attempts the phone was either out of range or switched off.

Swallowing down my anxiety I take in the upturned trees and smashed thatch houses that have started to appear by the road. In Noton Bazaar there was little evidence of the tornado, but now that we're moving closer to the sea, the destruction it left in its wake is unavoidable.

Please come. For an instant, before I can block it out, another phrase pops into my head: *It's a trap.*

Peering across the open countryside I try to orientate myself. The track is cutting through open land, the fields stretching into the horizon, but the landscape has dramatically changed. A month ago the patchwork fields were scattered with houses yet all I can see now are humps rising from the soggy land like molehills. By now the graceful tower of a minaret should have appeared over the smashed-up trees, but there's nothing, just the gaping sky. The paddy is ruined, I notice, the newly planted shoots uprooted and flattened by the storm.

As we pass through more villages I gaze around with dismay. The stone buildings are largely intact, but the mud and straw huts have been razed, their remains piled haphazardly in what's left of their yards. There are no trees, just their fallen remains. Dragged from the thoroughfare, twigs and leaves surround the corpses like pools of drying blood. Shelters constructed with plastic bags and tarpaulin hug the sides of the raised road. At a village called Digolbar we pass what looks like an army distribution point, in which sacks of rice are arranged on a low trellis table, surrounded by a long queue of people clutching bowls and plastic bags. High-booted soldiers keep them in line, batons twitching at their thighs. I lean forwards, tapping the driver on his damp shoulder.

'Is Lalalpur like this?'

He glances around, displaying his broken teeth.

'No, Auntie! Didn't I say already? Lalalpur is finished!'

We lurch forwards, the boy's bare feet pumping the pedals. In places the road becomes impassable and he has to hop from his seat and push the rickshaw around the craters. By now I am rigid with apprehension, my nails digging into my arms. In London I was desperate to reach the village but now I have started to dread my return. The churned-up mud is increasingly indented with tyre marks, I notice. I stare at the tracks, imagining ambulances and army jeeps.

It's started to spot with rain, the warm water splattering my forehead, but when the boy stops his pedalling to pull the rickshaw's stiff covers over my seat, I shake my head.

'You like the rain, do you, Auntie?' he shouts, laughing.

I smile weakly. I can't think straight enough to formulate a coherent reply.

We're nearly there. We pass through the edge of Santigao, a large village about a mile away from Lalalpur to the west of Jhomgram. For some reason the trees here have survived, their dense foliage shading the road and protecting us from the rain. I am thinking of the number of times Ed has walked along this track. Perhaps he's on it now. Perhaps Alexandria has finally managed to contact Syeda and he's coming to meet me. Peering into the drizzle, I try to conjure up his image: a youngish Western guy, hair a little too long, muddy feet curling over the edges of those high tech Nike sandals. He'll be wearing a *lunghi* and one of his old T-shirts, each as hilariously inappropriate as the other: 'Punk isn't Dead', or 'Fuck the Machine'. 'You can't go out in that!' I'd cried, choking with laughter as he set off down the steps. 'Don't worry!' he'd called, swinging his briefcase jauntily. 'A bit of anti-establishment propaganda is just what this place needs!'

But there's no one who looks remotely like Ed, just a couple of men in blue overalls and yellow helmets who stare at me in surprise as the rickshaw jolts past. They must be construction workers here to rebuild the place. Turning a corner, we come to an ornate pink mosque which, like the mango and banyan trees, has miraculously escaped the storm. As we pass the courtyard, a bearded man in Arab robes looks sharply up from the trough of water where he's washing his feet. He does not return my hesitant smile, just frowns and turns his back.

Any minute now the road will curve south and we will break from the trees into an expanse of paddy, followed by the scattered compounds of Lalalpur, each surrounded by a cluster of betel nut trees and banana plants, the way it always was. Wiping the water from my face, I grip my freezing hands in my lap. Any minute now, I'll be back. Yet as the rickshaw bumps around the final bend and the track breaks into open country, my heart plummets. We must have taken a wrong turn, for what lies ahead is not Lalalpur but some other place: a waste land, filled with trucks and diggers that swarm around a long, deep ditch which slashes through the fields.

I stare ahead in shock. The rain is increasing in intensity, falling like a curtain that separates me from what lies ahead. In a moment I shall step through it into this unknown place. There are no houses, no bulls tethered by the path and no trees in which the magpie robins can twitter and hop. The murmur of voices has been replaced by the grind of diggers, the shouts of children by the rumble of trucks.

'Here's your Lalalpur, Auntie!' the rickshaw driver shouts. 'Do you like it?'

He steers me along the main track, where I see that next to the forgotten foundations of our school a building has been hastily erected with breeze blocks and sheets of tin. Outside this, more yellow helmeted men mill around. I remain rooted to the seat of the rickshaw, gawping. On the other side of the road, where the Chairman's compound once stood with its mango trees and the fancy stone arch on which his grandfather's name was engraved, an area of two or three acres has been flattened. The remains of the buildings are heaped by the road; beyond this, a bulldozer slowly traverses the ploughed-up yard. A pile of concrete cylinders is heaped to one side, awaiting installation.

'Oil!' the boy proclaims, using the English word. 'Have a look at the drill . . .'

He points across the wrecked fields, where a crane is lifting something into the air. They're digging a pipeline, I realize. It's exactly as Ed predicted.

'Where is everyone?'

The boy jumps onto the road, wiping his wet forehead.

'Gone!'

But he is not entirely correct, for as I gaze around I notice that further along the road a small shanty of makeshift hovels has appeared opposite the school, an echo of the shelters built by the people of Jhomgram a few months earlier. Handing the boy a one-hundred-taka note, I leap from the rickshaw and hurry towards them. The rain is drenching but I barely notice. As I pass the prefabricated building I return the construction workers' curious gazes with a scowl. The sign on the building reads: 'Bangladesh Natural Resources: A partner of Oxan, UK'.

When I reach the huts I pause, looking awkwardly around. I had dimly imagined that the people living here would be my old village friends, doggedly clinging on to their homes.

When they saw me they would rush out to greet me, and I would finally discover where Ed was. Yet now that I am standing beside the ragged lean-tos, with their banana leaf roofs and plastic sheet floors I am unable to step from the road into the desolate shanty. Who am I to barge in, demanding help? I pretended that Lalalpur was my home but I will never have to live in conditions like this. Whilst I was scuttling back to the comforts of London, the place was ripped apart.

'Sister!'

A man has appeared from one of the huts. He's wrapped in a shawl, and squints at me through the rain, his face creased into a grin. It's the fisherman who rescued me from the tornado, I realize with an unpleasant plunging sensation.

'You've come back, have you?' he calls. Were I not familiar with the direct, humorous way that village people speak, I'd think he was mocking me.

'I've come back.'

It's harder than I expected to control my voice. I suck on my lips in an attempt to repress the sob. I've come back, but everything has gone.

'Your Englishman is over there,' he suddenly says, jerking his chin in the direction of the beach. 'He's waiting for you.'

I stand before him, swaying. My eyes are fixed to his crinkled face, but everything else has receded. I can no longer hear the trucks' wheels churning through the mud, or the pounding of the diggers. Rain is driving into my face, but I don't feel it. All that remains is the imprint of his words in my head and the hammering of my heart.

'I'll go and find him,' I whisper. '*Kudah Hafiz.*'

Turning hastily away I run back down the road, past the oil workers' building and the school and towards the track that leads towards the beach. I forgot to ask about Syeda, I remember as I reach what was once a grassy path but is now a jagged thoroughfare slicing through the empty land like a wound. Her house should be a short distance ahead, but all I can see is a mound of broken bricks. I start to pick my way through the mud. There are more bulldozers ahead and a jeep, parked beside a deep ditch. A heavy, rotten odour hangs in the air.

I do not feel the way I should. My hands are so clammy that I have to keep wiping them on my sleeves. I wish that Syeda would appear, hurrying across the desolate landscape to meet me, but there's no one around. Even the bulldozers are abandoned to the rain. As I pass the jeep I glance inside, noting the mud sprayed down its sides. It has a Dhaka number plate and a brocaded tissue box on the dashboard: a smart vehicle, probably driven by one of the BNRC engineers.

The rain is falling so steadily that it's becoming hard to see. Stumbling past the remains of Syeda's compound I pause for a moment, still vainly hoping to find her there. The diggers have not yet reached this far into the village; the destruction is natural rather than man-made. The pond is still intact, with its painted stone ghat and the slippery steps where I watched her wash her clothes, but the betel nut trees have been blown down, and only one wall remains of her wattle and straw house.

'Syeda!' I call. 'It's me, Sarah!'

There's no reply, just the sound of the rain splashing in the pond.

I hurry on. *Mister Ed is found. Please come.* The closer I get to the beach, the odder the message seems. What was it that the fisherman said? *Your Englishman is here. He's waiting for you.* Why did he grin like that? His expression had seemed almost malicious.

I have almost reached the glade where the bungalow once stood. By now my body is openly rebelling, my heart thumping hard, my knees weak. This is meant to be the scene where I am finally reunited with Ed. I shouldn't be feeling like this. 'Please, God,' I hear myself whisper. 'Let it be alright.'

I had imagined myself strolling past the coconut trees and up the sandy path. As I passed the jasmine, Ed would come leaping down the steps, and I would crumple into his outstretched arms. Now, as I stumble past the few trees that remain, I gaze at the space where our home once stood. The sight turns my stomach: the shattered skeleton of the building, its steel rods sticking up like fractured bones; the twisted roof, smashed into pieces and strewn across the path; the toilet, still squatting uselessly amongst a heap of coconuts and palm fronds that have accumulated around its base. The sticks that litter the trampled grass must be the remains of our furniture, the soggy rags that flop dispiritedly from the ruins, our clothes. At my feet is the empty husk of the computer; shards of glass lie everywhere.

In the time that I've been away, our possessions have rotted. The papers that eddied at my feet during that terrible night have either blown into the surrounding bushes or turned to mush, the wicker settee where I sat is soaked and sagging. Weeds have already started to appear amongst the rubble, grass to push up through the broken bricks. Wiping the rain from my face, I glance at a runty goat that's chewing something in the mud.

I'm going to faint. Squatting down, I hang my head between my legs and wait for the dizziness to recede. Despite the shivering I'm sweating profusely, my soggy clothes clinging to my skin. Summoning up what remains of my strength, I eventually manage to stand, turning away from the bungalow towards the sea. I'm going to take it one step at a time. He's waiting for me on the beach. That's what the fisherman said.

When I reach the place on the path where Aunik once lay, I gulp down a wave of nausea. They dumped him as we slept; an early-morning surprise. And now I'm here again, the bait taken. Stepping over the sand, I fix my gaze on the screen of bushes and upended palm trees that separates the track from the beach. In the distance I can glimpse a strip of blue and above the horizon, a crack in the clouds where the sun pokes through. The rain has stopped, vaporizing into a fuggy steam.

Your Englishman is on the beach, the fisherman had said, his eyes glinting with a meaning I had been unable to grasp. *He's waiting for you*. If this is true, by now I should be running along the track, calling out Ed's name. But instead, I can barely bring myself to move. As I drag myself towards the sea, I remember the way the man grabbed my arm in those moments before the tornado hit. He saved my life, pulling me away from the deathly water and into the shelter. So why, just now, did his teasing eyes fill me with such dread? Brushing past the fleshy leaves of the banana plants, I break free of the thin layer of wilderness that separates the fields from the beach. Now that the sun has reappeared, the air is as sticky as glue. I step on to the sand.

The Englishman is there, just as the fisherman said. He's sitting beside an upturned boat, gazing out to sea. The sight of his back, glimpsed in the slanting light, knocks the breath from my lungs. Yeah, he's there alright. And now, as I stagger across the treacherously soft sand, I finally understand. I must have cried out, because as I step towards him, he turns around.

THIRTY-ONE

'Jesus Christ!' he breathes, gawping at me. 'What are *you* doing here?'

He looks so different that for a moment I'm unsure I'm regarding the same person. It's not simply his dishevelled appearance: Punjabi shirt soaked with sweat, mud streaked down one side of his face, slacks caked with filth. He's dyed his hair and is wearing the kind of stiff cotton kameez that Indian politicians favour, a vote-winning rustic style, cream coloured and decorated in embroidery.

I glance away from him, towards the brilliant sea. If I closed my eyes I might imagine that everything was normal: the churn and grind of the diggers overtaken by the steady suck of the waves, the sun warming my face. Nothing has really changed, I could tell myself: the farmers are in the fields, the fishermen at sea. But it's too late for fantasies. There are no dhows riding the lulling waves; instead, the beach is scattered with their decaying remains. And rather than the neat, workaday coils of rope and netting that usually rest on the sand, all that's left is a torn net, flopping by the shore.

'What have you done with Ed?' I say to my 'Englishman'. He has stood up now and is holding out his hand, his eyes still fixed to my face. What an idiot I was, to ever believe in him.

'I haven't done anything to him,' he says. 'He did it to himself.'

As I stare at his jagged fingernails I remember the half moons of dirt I had noticed there on the day of the tornado. He'd gone to get help, he'd said. But now I know that like everything else he's ever told me, he was lying. A moment earlier I was winded with fear, but now a new emotion is taking over: fury, as pure as fire.

'Don't give me that bollocks,' I say evenly. 'Just tell me where he is.'

My feet sink in the shifting terrain. I dig my heels in, not blinking in the blazing light. Leering self-consciously, Dan Jameson steps back. Is he dressed like this because he wants to look like Ed? If so, he's deluding himself, for Ed would never wear those preppy chinos, nor would he cut his hair so short. Now he's fussily brushing grains of sand off his trousers, as if Ed would ever care about a bit of dirt. He pretended to be *helping* me, I remember with horror; I thought he was my friend.

'It was *you* I saw at Ed's house, wasn't it?' I say quietly. 'You were wearing his coat.'

It's a random guess. But rather than denying it, Dan smirks, as if I'm finally acknowledging how clever he's been. 'It was a good fit, wasn't it? I was really rather pleased.'

I ogle him, my mind reeling at the implications. 'And it was you who took the money from Ed's account . . . you stole his credit cards . . .'

Dan shrugs. 'I was doing him a favour. I figured that since he was now the great saviour of the world's poor, he wouldn't need all those extra millions he had lying around.' He snickers, his fat lips curling. He's sweating so heavily that the dye from his hair has started to trickle down his forehead. 'Poor Eddy! He's been trying so hard out here in Hicksville, hasn't he? All that pretending must have been such a strain.'

'What's that meant to mean?'

'Just that if you knew what Ed was *really* like, you'd have seen straight through his stupid performance . . .' He waves his hand in the direction of the village. 'He's a fraud, Sarah! A spoilt little rich boy . . .'

'You don't know the first thing about him!'

He snorts. 'Oh yes I do. It's *you* who doesn't know him.'

I can't stand it any more. I lunge towards him, raising my arm in a feeble attempt at violence, but he simply reaches out his large paw and catches my wrist mid flight, as if it was as light and harmless as a shuttlecock.

'I'm the only person who understands what Eddy's really like,' he whispers. 'We go *way* back.'

'That's crap!' I cry. 'He didn't even recognize you!'

He's still holding onto my arm. As I try to tug it away, he squeezes tighter, his face twisting. 'He was playing his idiotic games. He's full of shit!'

Pulling back my head, I do something I haven't done since I was six. I hawk up a frothy mouthful of spit, and gob it into his face. It works a treat. As Dan jumps back with a yelp of disgust, I barrel into him, my knuckles bashing into his chops with a loud thwack which momentarily causes him to sway, clutching his mouth. The impact has grazed my fingers, but blood bubbles from his fleshy lips. Hurray for Ed's ring.

I'm not sure of the order of what happens next. It's too fast and fierce for my mind to process into logical thought. The only thing I clearly register is that Dan's voice has changed. Gone is the lofty disdain of a few moments earlier, that upper class drawl that, I now realize, was utterly affected. Instead, he has an estuary twang.

'You stupid cow!'

My hair is yanked so hard that I can feel it tearing from my scalp. At the same time, something – a fist, I suppose – crunches into my face, knocking me backwards into the sand. My mouth fills with blood, the warm liquid splashing over my hands and down my front.

'Why the *fuck* did you have to turn up?' Dan Jameson, or whoever he is, yells. Giving me a final shake he pushes me back down. 'I warned you not to get involved!'

Standing, he dabs at his mouth with the sleeve of his ridiculous Punjabi. I sprawl on the ground, eyeing him. OK, so he's stronger than me, and nastier. But he hasn't won yet.

'You were at Oxford with Ed, weren't you?' I mumble through a mouthful of bloodied spit. 'And you've got his friend's credit cards . . .'

Dan tries to sneer, but it's a difficult gesture to pull off when one's lip is split. 'The stupid prat. He should look after his things.'

Dragging myself onto my elbows I force my face into what I hope is an expression of haughty contempt. I'm desperately trying to recall that moment, two weeks ago, when 'Dan' jumped from his jeep and strode up the path to meet me. Did he introduce himself? Or was it me who said his name first?

'You're not Dan Jameson, are you?' I whisper.

Dan keeps smirking, but his eyes flick from my face. I have just recalled those letters, hidden in the side pocket of Ed's briefcase. 'It was you who sent those weird emails, wasn't it?' I slowly say.

I want to smash your face against a wall and make you squeal, he'd written. *Someone has to pay, you fucking fraud.* These weren't the words of an employee of The Department for International Development; they were the words of a lunatic.

'You're nothing whatsoever to do with Dfid . . . you're a fake.'

He folds his arms, his head cocked back. The key to the Kensington house must have been on the fob that Ed hung from a hook next to his desk in Lalalpur. Dan must have fingered them when he came for dinner.

'The only thing I don't get is how Oxan are involved,' I continue.

Jameson snorts. 'Oxan? They're just a nice multinational doing their bit to drag this dump into the twenty-first century. The only way they're involved is through Eddy's pathetic campaign. If it wasn't for his website, I'd never have found him.'

'So why do you have a security pass to their London offices?'

'Because I went to see them. I was doing my research.'

'But what about Aunik? Who killed him?'

He shrugs disinterestedly. 'Don't ask me. The local heavies, I suppose. That's what your precious boyfriend said happened. Why the fuck should I care?'

I don't take my eyes off his face. 'Why do you hate us so much? What's Ed ever done to *you*?'

His mouth is still bleeding. Wiping it clumsily with the back of his hand, he smears half the stuff over his cheek. He's quivering, I realize, and his normally ruddy cheeks are grey.

'He betrayed me,' he murmurs. 'I'd have done anything for him, but he turned his back . . .' His face contorts. 'Yeah, well, he might think it's fine to drop his real friend for a bunch of cunts like Montgomery. He can afford to fuck other people over, can't he? He's got his money. He can do what he likes . . .' He glances around the beach, his features twitching. He's spitting out the words, as if they were poison. 'He can even set up a nice new life for himself and pretend to be some kind of saint, helping the needy of the Third World, then bragging about how much he's helping "empower" the poor on his fucking website! It makes me *puke*.'

For a moment I think he's going to hit me again. He looms over me, face clenched, fists flexed. I glare back at him, trying to look as if I don't care. He's completely deranged. It's incredible I didn't spot it earlier.

'You want to know what he's really like?' he whispers. 'About how he fucked me over? When it really comes to it, your wonderful Eddy doesn't give a shit about helping people who need him . . .'

Suddenly his face changes, as if he's just remembered who he's pretending to be. He takes a breath and gives me a lopsided smile.

'Anyway,' he says, his voice returned to the suave calm of the Dan Jameson who drove me to Chittagong. 'Now that we've met up like this I'm going to give you what you've come for.'

'What do you mean?'

'I'm going to take you to your darling Edward.'

Turning, he starts to stroll across the rippled sand towards the area where the tea stalls and fishing boats once shimmered in the distance; beyond the mashed planks and squashed jute is the road that leads to Noton Bazaar. I can't help myself. Despite everything that I know, I limp after him, my face flashing with pain.

'Where are you going?'

'You want to see Eddy, don't you?' he calls over his shoulder. 'Come on, then! He's waiting for you.'

THIRTY-TWO

*T*his isn't what's supposed to happen. I'm the victim here, the one in need of an apology. So don't blame me for this mess. I wasn't the instigator: it was you. People keep jerking me around, you see. They lie to me, betray me; treat me like shit. And when you're pushed into a corner, you're forced to lash out.

For years I've kept the lid on. I'd been hurt really badly, but I managed to cope. I'm a strategist – an opportunist, some might say – I use my wits to survive. But then, when I was least expecting it, I saw Montgomery. For years I'd blocked him from my mind and then suddenly there he was in this bar in Piccadilly. His face had sagged and he'd got fat, but it was definitely him: the same braying voice, the same air of arrogant entitlement, pushing people out of the way as he ordered his drinks. For a while I sat motionless on my stool, staring. He was so busy leering at the tart he was with that he didn't notice. But when he took a call on his mobile, I sidled up behind and lifted the wallet from his show-off Armani suit. As usual he was talking too loudly, yelling to some poor minion on the other end.

My encounter with Montgomery was a shock. Like I said, I'd done a pretty good job of forgetting what happened in '93, but now I started remembering. Over the next few days everything came back: how I'd given you my friendship, how you betrayed me and how I lost everything. Like I said, I'd done my best to erase our final encounter but now that I'd started to remember, it was with me all the time, even in my dreams. I needed closure, I realized: to put the thing to bed. So I started looking for you. I thought we should meet and talk. To be honest, the trusting, honourable side of me was hoping for a reconciliation. We'd meet, I thought, and, recalling the good old days, would decide to let bygones be bygones. 'I'm so sorry,' I naively imagined you saying. 'You've been terribly let down. Let me make amends . . .'

I began to get excited about meeting you again. You'd be in London, I thought, or maybe lording it up in the countryside. I could stay with you; perhaps you'd need me to help you with whatever career you had carved for yourself. We were so much older now; we could start again. So when I Googled you, and found you were in Bangladesh, I was amazed. But there you were, pretending to be some frigging saint defending the world's poor against the evils of multinationals without a hint that you were from one of the richest families in the UK!

Never mind. Perhaps you were trying to make amends for your youthful misdemeanours. I'd write to you, I decided, see what you said. Yet the more I studied your blog, the more disturbed I became. By this stage I'd moved from my sentimental nostalgia into something different; perhaps I was finally facing up to what a fraud you've always been, pretending to be so good and kind. How dare you lecture people about globalization when your ancestors owned most of the East India Company! Yeah, that's right. I may not have had your education Eddy, but I know my history. And how dare you pontificate about the poor when you know sweet FA about how it feels to go hungry, or to have people look at you like you're a piece of shit they've discovered on the sole of their shoe? That's an *experience I would have avoided if you'd stuck by me. How dare you take the moral high ground, after all you've done? So I wrote a different kind of email than the one I'd originally planned, one that was rather more honest. Yet even then, rather than showing me the respect I deserved, you didn't even bother to reply.*

That's when I began to get upset. I'd been honest enough to lay bare to you the depths of my emotions and once again you'd blanked me. All I could think of now was your betrayal. For weeks I couldn't eat or sleep, all I could think about was you.

In the end I resolved to give you one more chance. I'd take a leap of faith and pay you a visit, I decided. I suppose part of me was hoping that our friendship might be saved. I blew the last of my cash on getting to you, Eddy. I travelled for three tortuous days. But what did you do when I finally arrived? You stood by, whilst your stupid girlfriend introduced me as someone else. I was yearning for you to acknowledge our true relationship, but instead you shook my hand and didn't say a word.

All I wanted was your loyalty, Eddy. That's what friends are for. They stick together. They don't take fright and dump each other at the first sight of trouble.

But when I reminded you of how badly you'd behaved, you didn't even apologize. Instead you did what you always do. You lied and denied and turned away.

You fucker. You've had this coming a long, long time. You've forced my hand, pushed me to the limit.

Now there's only one way out.

THIRTY-THREE

Gasping, I stumble over the hillocks of sand, trying to catch up. I'm moving like a crab, falling onto my hands and knees and clambering lopsidedly over the dunes. Ahead of me, Dan moves swiftly. He's so confident that I'm following that he doesn't bother to look round. Finally, just when we've almost reached the road, he dodges into the undergrowth that presses around the edge of the beach. Then he disappears.

When I reach the place where he was swallowed by the

dense foliage, I straighten up, peering into the dark. Trees and bushes press tightly into the wilderness; it's odd how the tornado has left these small pockets of land untouched. There's no obvious path, just a tangle of knobbly roots which jut from the muddy ground. As my eyes adjust to the light, I can make out the shapes of trees. Some have fallen in the wind, leaving gaps in the canopy where dusky sunlight falls in spirals. I walk slowly inside the scrappy jungle.

'Where are you?'

There's no reply. Gripping on to the slim tree trunks for support, I move further into the foliage. The heat is suffocating, the steam enveloping me. There's a strong smell of fungi, mixed with the stench of stagnant water. Mosquitoes and midges billow in the faint light. Dan said that Ed was waiting for me. I know I can't trust him but his words draw me inwards, moving closer to what I'm praying I'll find.

There's no sign of Dan. Does he assume that I'm following him, or has he deliberately vanished? At the crack of a twig, I jump round, scanning the elephantine leaves and fleshy lipped flowers that mass behind. Something is lurking there: an animal or a person, for there's a rustle of movement, a brush of sound that could be footfall. My palms are sticky, my stomach knotting.

'If you're trying to scare me, it isn't working!' I call into the gloom.

The only answer comes in the form of a heron, which rises from its perch in the trees, large wings flapping languorously.

I don't understand where Dan has gone, but I'm beginning to suspect why he's led me here. I was an idiot to follow him, I suddenly realize. I have to get out. Turning sharply, I stumble back the way I came, pushing creepers from my face as I head for the chink of light ahead. I keep tripping on the roots, and am covered with mud and slime, but I'm almost there. I can hear the waves now, and glimpse the sun, which falls in slanting shafts a few hundred metres ahead, illuminating thousands of tiny bugs that wiggle and twirl dazedly in the rays.

'Ed?' I stupidly call. 'Are you here?'

There's no answer. How could there be? As I stand, swaying with uncertainty in the dank half light, I finally grasp what, deep down, I have always known. Despite my denials, the instant I saw him running towards the sea it was clear that I would never see Ed again. For Ed is dead, murdered by a deranged loser, who for reasons I still don't fully understand, has come rearing out of his past to snatch him away. And now, as I crash towards the beach, I finally understand Jamil's message. *Mr Edward is found*. It was his body they meant, not him: that would explain the odd wording. Someone must have told Dan too: perhaps his 'driver'. Not wanting word to get out that Ed was dead, Dan must have rushed back here to stop the locals from talking.

He's going to stop me from talking too. Gasping with sudden terror, I clamber over the fallen trees, my feet tripping on the roots. I'm nearly there: the bright sunlight and flashing sea are only a few metres away. But suddenly there's a crack of twigs and as I leap backwards, Dan steps into my path.

'In a hurry, are we?'

I have to get away. Staggering backwards I attempt desperately to reverse, but it's too late. Grabbing my arm, he jerks me towards him.

'You and Ed make me *sick*!'

'What have you done to him?' I screech.

Putting his hand over my face he pushes me into the mud. 'He turned his back on me!' he yells. 'I was going to die!'

Even if I tried to speak it wouldn't be possible for my mouth is mulched into the ground. Gripping me by the hair, Jameson yanks me up, twisting me around and pressing his face into mine. His breath smells rancid: it's repulsive.

'If you'd kept out of things this wouldn't be necessary.'

I gaze dully back at his contorted face.

'Do what you like,' I mumble. 'I don't care.'

Dragging me up he grips my throat with his fleshy fingers. In the moments before he starts to apply the pressure, I hang limply in his hands, like Syeda's mangy fowl. Without Ed, there's no reason to fight back, even if I was able. All that awaits me now is obliteration, the thankful dark.

Dan squeezes tighter. I have started to choke, yet despite my lungs' panicked attempts to gulp oxygen, I can't breathe. They are going to explode, my eyes to pop from my skull. I don't want to live, but instinctively my hands flap at the air, trying to get a grip on my attacker's arms in a feeble attempt to pull him off. It's impossible; I'm tearing at the rough material of his kameez, but he doesn't even notice. As my vision dims, I feel myself falling backwards. My head's detaching from my inert body and I'm hurtling upwards, sucked towards a rainbow so bright it's blinding. I'm surely about to die.

Yet instead of the blackness I was anticipating, the dazzling colours soften and I realize that I'm standing in a pool of light looking out at the fields. I can feel the rough floor beneath my soles and hear the familiar shriek of the myna birds. Smoke from someone's *chula* drifts through the trees.

I'm standing on the terrace of the bungalow, regarding Ed. He's sitting sideways in his wicker chair, long legs flopping over the sides. He's gazing at me with an expression that I'd forgotten: exasperation intercut with disbelief. He's got the 'Fuck the Machine' T-shirt on, and his trousers are ripped. I wish he'd cut his toe nails. In the split second that I comprehend where I am, I remember that we're having an argument.

'You can't let the bastards win,' he's saying heatedly. 'You've got to fight back.'

I'd forgotten his green eyes. They're peering into mine, seeking me out. He hated it if I disagreed with him, not because he has to be right but because he can't bear for us to be apart. I step towards him, extending my hand, which he catches in his. Tugging me closer, he pulls my fingers to his mouth and kisses them.

Then suddenly he's gone and I'm under the trees again, Dan's knee pressing into my belly. In the second or so that the memory of Ed sitting on the terrace dissipates, I suddenly realize that I don't want to die. Ed's obstinate refusal to counter objections was difficult to live with, but he was right. We can't let the bastards win.

Twisting myself abruptly around, I ram my knees as hard as I can into Dan's groin.

'Oof!'

For the brief moment that his hands loosen their grip, I manage to suck in a little air. As Dan jerks backwards, I roll to one side, trying desperately to escape, but his hands are on me, grasping me around the middle and dragging me back.

'Forget it!'

He's grabbed my neck again and this time he's not going to mess around. Twisting his hands with brutish efficiency, he pushes his face so close to mine that I can feel his foul breath on my skin. I try to scratch his face, but without effect. Wrenching my hands from his face, he pins them to the ground, leaning on me with his entire weight.

'Fuck you, bitch!'

I'm going to blank out. Everything's fading: Ed and Lalalpur, Alexandria, my poor parents. Will they discover the truth about what's happened or will Dan return to London to spin more lies? Now Ed's friendly face is peering into the Dhaka gutter as I roll in the dust. Green eyes; a garland of jasmine; the pir, wailing into his mic. Everything is slipping from my grasp, never to return. Gold bangles flashing on my wrists; Ed's diamond ring. Copper, silver, drenching red. It's all just colours now, bleeding into each other; I think I've reached the end.

But something odd is happening. A figure has emerged from the bushes and is standing over us, swinging something through the air. I'm too far gone to make out the details: just a faint outline, and a swishing movement. My forehead registers a blob of something warm and suddenly my windpipe is no longer being crushed. Instead, Dan's body flops heavily over mine: a disappointing lover, come too soon. I'm covered with a sticky substance, too. Gasping for air, I manage to swivel my trunk from under his inert body. For a moment or two I'm overcome by wracking coughs. I lie in the mud, retching as my eyes refocus. I don't understand what has happened to Dan or why he's stopped strangling me but as I dab my fingers in the slicking wetness that covers my cheeks I realize that it's blood. It can't have come from me, I don't feel any pain. Now, as I gradually sit up I see that a curved blade is embedded in the back of Dan's head. His body is twitching in a strange way, and he's groaning softly. What I also see is that Syeda is standing beside me, panting.

'He wasn't a good man,' she says leaning over and pulling her dag from Dan's head. Wiping the blade on her sari, she flashes me one of her smiles.

THIRTY-FOUR

*M*y body isn't moving like it should. I want to stand up and make things right, but there's this terrible slashing pain in my head, and an odd sensation in *my face, a kind of numbness, like something's been sliced off. The light seeps from my vision; something's pouring out.*

I didn't mean to hurt you, Eddy, that's what I'm trying to say; it's just that sometimes my emotions get so intense. I thought that if I could finally talk to you alone, away from all the distractions, we could sort things out. That's why I got you on the beach; I thought we could drive off together, take shelter from the storm. But when I reminded you who I was, you yelled at me, told me to 'move on'. That's what I couldn't take; that, and the look in your eyes.

That is you standing over there, isn't it? Now you've returned, please don't play tricks on me again. I thought I'd killed you, you see. I didn't mean to do it, but I got carried away. You said I should 'move on'; then my hands went around your neck and they squeezed and squeezed until you stopped moving. But now you're here I realize it was just a nightmare. Everything's OK. You've come back.

Hey old pal, where are you going? Please don't leave me, not again. I don't like the way it's getting dark. There might be snakes and leeches hiding in the grass; I can feel them now, slithering over my body, up my legs and over my flesh.

Please don't turn your back on me Eddy. I'm begging you to help but you're not listening. Eddy, my dearest, oldest friend, why are you walking away?

THIRTY-FIVE

Ed
May 5th, 2003

Eleven p.m.: a still, sultry night, in which the only sign of the oncoming storm was the swollen orange moon. Ed was sitting on the terrace, watching the glow moths flicker by the steps. He was supposed to be discussing Oxan with Dan Jameson, but despite nodding in a distracted kind of way he wasn't concentrating on what the guy was saying. To be honest, these days he rarely concentrated on what anyone was saying.

'This is exactly what makes my post worthwhile,' Jameson
was burbling. 'The sense that I can actually make a *difference*.'

Ed gazed at him without replying. The guy gave him the
creeps, but he was unable to formulate why, for as usual, his
thoughts were stuck in the same sticky terrain: Aunik was
murdered, Schools for Change destroyed, and it was all his
fault. The guilt was suffocating: a thickening mass of self-
hatred that had clogged his mind for weeks. Round and round
the thoughts twirled, a terrifying carousel that he could never
get off. He had pushed Aunik into supporting the campaign,
ignored the warnings from Sadid and now he was so deep in
shite he couldn't breathe. From the moment he opened his
eyes to his tortured attempts at sleep, the whining guilt was
continually with him: a greedy dog, ravenous for grub.

Without warning, Jameson had suddenly produced a flask of
whiskey from his rucksack, which he was pouring gleefully
into two plastic cups, despite Ed muttering that he didn't drink.

'Be a devil,' Jameson chided reprovingly. 'You only live once!'

Reluctantly receiving the cup from the guy's meaty fingers,
Ed placed it obstinately on the table. He wasn't even going to
pretend to sip it. What was it about the guy that made him feel
so wary? He'd been amazed when he had turned up out of the
blue, even more so when Sarah introduced him: his last email,
sent from some conference he was attending in Bangkok, had
seemed like a polite brush-off; Ed had never considered that he
might come all the way down here. Jameson reminded him of
someone, he thought, as he eyed him across the table. When
he'd first arrived, he had been instantly struck by a jolt of recog-
nition. Yet try as he might, his befuddled brain refused to make
the connection. It was someone he had known a long time ago
. . . something nasty had happened. What the hell was it?

It wasn't important. As Jameson chucked the whiskey down
his throat, smacking his lips with a rapaciousness that was
utterly repellent, Ed's thoughts returned predictably to the mire.
Jameson was blabbing about something, but he'd long stopped
listening. If he hadn't lied to Sarah about his lowly role in
Sylvia's project then perhaps he wouldn't be in this mess; he
could have admitted how ignorant he was, as well as how scared.
But at the time it hadn't seemed a big deal. He had wanted to
impress her, so he had told one simple lie. He was the director
of Schools for Change, an old India hand. Why put her off with

the truth? Incredibly, she had swallowed his pretensions whole, seeming genuinely to believe that he was an experienced and knowledgeable Bangladeshi Wallah rather than a disgustingly wealthy Trustafarian who'd been rescued from the brink. After so many years of wanton debauchery, it was a revelation to be taken seriously. Within a matter of weeks he morphed from Eddy up-your-arse de Vaal, into Ed The Great Expert, the role encasing him, like stepping into concrete.

Perhaps that was why he'd been so keen to start the campaign. He'd had enough therapy by now to recognize that when things became difficult he had a propensity to walk away. Not from Sarah, he would never do that, but from his role in Schools for Change, where his pathetic lies were waiting to be discovered. And so, by increments, he had slipped into this God-awful mess. His mistakes were too multiple to list, but the greatest was that he'd acted without grasping local politics, which, as Sarah had warned, were as dense and deeply rooted as the jumble of jungle that screened the fields from the beach. Unlike Sarah, he hadn't bloody listened. Unlike Sarah, who'd picked up the local lingo with incredible speed, he couldn't grasp half of what the locals were saying! Recalling how, in the early days, he'd pretended to be fluent the guilt dog wagged its tail and licked the memory up.

Jameson was asking about the school, so he started falteringly to give him the official low-down. Six months earlier he had cared passionately but now even the phrase 'functional literacy' made his heart sink. Even as he spoke, his mind was crammed with the usual stuff: Aunik's broken body, the smouldering ruins of the school in Dhaka, what Tasneem had screamed at him.

'Basically it's academic now,' he said briskly. 'There's no way we can work here any more.' Flashing Jameson a fake smile, he pushed some project documents towards him, hoping for a respite from his jabbering.

'Fab!' Banging his cup on the table, Jameson propped the file on his knee and started to leaf through the papers in a manner that indicated that he wasn't actually reading them. His ignorance of the situation was incredible; he'd obviously not looked at the various emails that Ed had sent: something that once would have infuriated him but now no longer mattered. Folding his arms over his chest, Ed returned to his brooding.

*   *   *

He'd travelled to Dhaka the day after Aunik's murder, in a state of total panic. He'd even lied to Sarah about this, telling her he was going to Chittagong. Instead, he'd caught a flight to Dhaka and travelled by baby-taxi directly to the brick fields. As the kilns and factories edged closer, the diffuse dread solidified into something more tangible. He could have prevented disaster, but he hadn't. Stubborn sod that he was, he'd continued with his hopeless campaign, as if trying to prove a point.

Now it was going to be too late. Leaning forwards, he motioned at the taxi driver to slow down. He was so nervous by this time that it took him a while to remember his Bangla. *Jalal Bricks? Just a little way down here?* Gripping the hand rail as the car weaved through the traffic he stared grimly at the hulking factories that edged the road: 'London Fashions', 'Chowdhury Garments International', 'Shah Milk Products'. Hordes of young women trooped down the narrow pavements, bright scarves draped over their heads. He didn't even glance at them. He was fixated on the road ahead, where a pall of blotching smoke hung over the buildings.

They'd torched the school that morning. Sadid had phoned him a week earlier to say that some men had arrived at the brick field, roughing him up and making threats. If the campaign against the BNRC continued, they'd warned, Schools for Change would be forced to close. Sadid had begged him to stop his activities but Ed had laughed it off. Things couldn't be that dangerous, he'd retorted; surely Sadid was exaggerating? Now, as he sprinted towards the smouldering remains, he had to fight down the tears.

'Leave us alone!' Tasneem shrieked when she saw him in the yard. She was picking over the remains of the classroom, her *shalwar* kameez smudged black with cinders, hair swaying wildly in her face. 'It's you who's done this! We didn't need you in the first place! Now you see what you've done!'

After that, he found himself another taxi and went straight to the Hilton, the only place in Dhaka where one could get a drink. Once there, he sat at the dark bar and downed one whiskey after another, the first booze he'd touched in three years. He felt as if he was plummeting into a place so dark and vile that the only possible action was to obliterate all sensation. Shivering in the air-conditioned cavern, he drank himself into oblivion, until the tinkling water feature and heavy red curtains, the velour bar stools and 'rustic' wall hangings merged into an undulating, blurring whole and he passed out in the lap of a Japanese businessman.

Now Jameson was mouthing off some old shite about Dfid's pledge to 'give charity to the poorest of the poor', which was not only mind-bogglingly old fashioned but quite unlike the current policy documents Dfid had published on their website. Ed stared at him sardonically. He'd started out with such high-minded ideals, but although he'd tried to hide it, had lost faith both in his dreams of 'community development' and his abilities to facilitate such a thing, were it to ever exist. What did he know, after all? The only thing he had learnt from Lalalpur was that he was an outsider. It wasn't about aid workers or donors or how many millions of pounds were spent on a project. It was about power.

'So what do you say?' Jameson was murmuring. He had the ingratiating keenness of a car salesman, Ed thought vaguely. It was a surprising departure in style from the other donor execs, who, when they deigned to answer his emails, behaved as if they were doing him a huge favour. 'We could leave first thing in the morning, and by close of play on Monday, the money's yours.'

Ed stared at him, puzzled. The offer was both wildly optimistic and completely inappropriate, for the one thing he'd never lacked was money.

'Thanks, Dan,' he said, standing to signal the end of their exchange. 'That's a great offer, but given the current state of affairs I think we'll pass. If you give me your card, we'll look you up when we're next in Dhaka . . .'

He led Jameson down the steps, towards the place under the trees where his jeep was parked. Not only was the guy a plonker but for reasons he couldn't quite nail, his presence was making him increasingly uncomfortable.

'You're sure you don't want to come with me to Chittagong and get out of the path of this storm? Whatever her indoors might say?' Opening the door of the jeep, Jameson raised his eyebrows suggestively. It was such an odd remark that for a moment Ed merely blinked.

'Like I said, there's a shelter in the village. We'll be OK.'

'Fine,' Jameson answered huffily. 'It's up to you.'

They shook hands. Despite being past midnight, the air was sticky. On seeing his employer approach, Dan's driver had switched the jeep's headlights on, illuminating the bugs that flitted in their beams. In the distance, the jackals were screeching.

'Thanks a million for coming to see us. Let's hope we meet again.'

'Yup.'

He watched as Jameson climbed into the jeep. The guy must be strangely insecure, for he seemed to have taken offence at Ed's refusal to travel with him to Chittagong. It was in the handful of moments that Ed was considering this, as he took in Jameson's stony face that he realized who he reminded him of. *As Good As Anthony!*

Jesus! The memory barrelled into him, like a train he had not noticed approaching. It was years since he had thought about As Good As. The name evoked an uneasy sensation, a kind of dread that he couldn't yet source. He and Giles had never called him that to his face, had they? What the hell was he actually called?

Its tyres squelching, the jeep edged down the track.

'Have a safe journey!'

Anthony something or other: the guy who pretended to have got a scholarship to Balliol to read law but who turned out to be working in some crummy supermarket. He'd been friends with him for a whole year, before Giles had found him out.

'Thanks for coming!'

Ed watched the jeep bump into the distance, his mouth hanging open. Could it really be the same bloke? He'd put on a lot of weight, but the similarities were incredible. Perhaps Jameson was his doppelgänger. After all, if it really was As Good As, wouldn't he have recognized Ed? Or perhaps it really was a weird coincidence: both had ended up working in Bangladesh and both had forgotten they were once acquaintances.

Turning, he started to retrace his steps, taking care not to step on any toads. He should try to forget about As Good As; the similarities with Dan Jameson were a fluke. Yet as he moved towards the bungalow his all familiar high pitched anxiety was overlain with something new: a malevolent, creeping dread. There were those letters, he remembered, with a little pitch of fear; that freaky hate mail that he'd assumed was sent by a crank.

It wasn't As Good As. It couldn't be. There was no reason on earth why As Good As would pitch up here. He glanced across the darkened fields, noting the retreating lights of Jameson's jeep with relief. Within a few hours he'd be in Chittagong. There was no reason he and Ed need ever meet again.

THIRTY-SIX

I t was one of those accidental friendships, picked up in Ed's first term at Oxford without realizing, like a ball of dust clinging to the hem of one's clothes. For some reason he had started chatting to a geeky guy standing alone in the corner during one of the many parties held during Freshers' week. Ed had a memory of As Good As firing a heap of questions at him with an earnestness that he'd found endearing. What subject did he do, he wanted to know; where did he go to school? He was gawky then, far skinnier than now, and wearing a polyester blazer that made Ed determined to be kind. In the end he had invited him back to his room for a smoke and a drink; the party had been a dud, filled with Sloaney girls and the rugger crowd.

Over the next weeks As Good As became a regular in Ed's rooms, where he took to sinking into the battered college armchair and rolling joints with Ed's prime quality Lebanese Black. There was no doubt he was clever. He'd got five As at A level, he let slip with a little yelp of self conscious pride, and a scholarship to read History: the subject that Ed was supposedly doing. He was just a comprehensive kid, he added coyly; it was amazing he was even here. As they smoked the dope, Ed told him about his own background, enjoying As Good As's rapt attention. He wished *he* was a comprehensive kid, he laughed, taking a toke on the reefer. He was only here because he'd had the kind of education where even at nursery school getting into Oxbridge was a fait accompli. He hated the family money, he added; it made him feel a fraud.

During that first term, Ed and As Good As formed a strangely mismatched friendship in which As Good As worked hard at becoming indispensable. Whilst Ed lounged in bed, As Good As attended the Part I lectures, bringing back sheaves of notes, or fetching him books from the library. He had a knack of plumping Ed's fragile ego with a stream of compliments that Ed initially found hard to resist: Ed had such good taste; he was so well read, so cosmopolitan and witty. 'Thank Christ we found each other!' he kept saying. 'Apart from you, this place is dead!' For his part, Ed enjoyed the idea that simply by hanging out with him, he was somehow 'helping' As Good As to find his feet. He was charmingly eccentric, he decided. It was true that his high-pitched laugh had started to grate, but he was one of those refreshing 'characters' that enlivened the Oxford scene.

By the end of Michaelmas term Ed was wondering if As Good As really needed to spend so much time in his rooms. He had met more people by this point, most of whom, like him, had a penchant for drugs and partying and wouldn't be seen dead in a polyester blazer, for Chrissakes. He started to avoid returning to his rooms at the times when he thought As Good As was likely to call. When he arrived back late one night with Giles and found him hunched on the steps outside his room, he'd winced with embarrassment, for in Giles' presence, As Good As no longer seemed like an entertaining eccentric, but a clingy creep. They let him in, but Giles made it clear he shouldn't stay.

Yet despite the obvious cooling of their relationship it was almost impossible to shake As Good As off. Throughout the Easter term he continued to turn up uninvited at Ed's rooms or would find out where the crowd that Ed now hung out with were partying and gatecrash. By this stage, Ed could no longer remember why they had ever been friends. He'd developed a strange, fake laugh and dressed as if he was fresh from the set of *Brideshead Revisited*, with a straw boater and a blazer that didn't quite fit. And this was 1993, when the rest of them were trying to look like Kurt Cobain! The problem was, wherever Ed went, As Good As turned up too. He was like pubic lice, Giles said. Having infested Ed's life, he kept clinging on.

Ed started to jog back to the bungalow, his unease at Dan's uncanny resemblance to As Good As swelling. Perhaps it was his old friend the guilt dog; he had a nasty feeling that in the end he and Giles hadn't been very kind to him. His mind rummaging through his fragmented memories, he tried to recall

what had happened. For the rest of the year he had continued
to tolerate him, letting him hang out in his rooms, even cutting
him lines of charlie. There were always people dropping in to
Ed's place by now: he had firmly established himself at the
core of the A-list party crowd. Yet despite these kindnesses, As
Good As had grown increasingly irritating. The compliments
that Ed had originally enjoyed warped into an ingratiating
manner that was increasingly knocked off course by an undertow
of anger. One afternoon he'd returned from a supervision to
find a furious note pinned to his door: *Where the fuck* are *you?*
I thought we were having lunch? Dumped underneath was a
bag filled with cheeses and a bottle of port.

The crunch came when Giles discovered that As Good As
was a fraud. It was the summer term by now and to Ed's relief
he hadn't visited for a while; perhaps he'd finally got the
message. Then Giles had spotted him working on the till at
Somerfield. Enjoying the espionage, he had waited for his
shift to finish and discreetly followed him to a bedsit in the
far reaches of the insalubrious London Road. Later that day
he and Ed checked the college roll and found that Anthony's
name wasn't included. So *this* was why he hadn't wanted Ed
to visit his rooms. He wasn't a member of the college; he'd
faked everything. Ed dimly remembered a scene at a party –
or was it a May Ball? Giles had drunkenly confronted him.
He couldn't recall the details, only As Good As being cornered
at their table. Giles had asked him why he was working at
Somerfield's and living on the London Road, if he had a scholarship. Then someone had drunkenly plucked the cheap carna-
tion from his lapel and chucked it in his face.

'I may not officially be at Oxford,' he muttered, his cheeks
flaming. 'But I'm *as good as . . .*'

It was probably the coke, but they had all cracked up.

Jesus, what arses they'd been. All Ed could hope was that
if Dan Jameson really was the same person, he had forgotten
all about Ed. It was, after all, a long time ago. Surely he
wouldn't have sent those emails?

Leaping up the steps to the bungalow, he flapped through
the thin terrace doors. The building was hushed, so he crept
quietly across the creaky wooden floor, wanting Sarah to be
awake but trying not to wake her. Even if they were relevant,
which they surely weren't, his memories of As Good As had

only strengthened his resolve. Tomorrow, they would leave Lalalpur. But first, he had to tell Sarah the truth.

She was lying on her back, gazing up at the motionless fan. It had been so long since they had touched and now he was desperate to put his arms around her slim waist and pull her warm body against his.

'You're awake then?'

Lifting aside the mosquito net, he clambered on to the bed, his fingers reaching for her smooth cheek. He loved her so much; he prayed he hadn't ruined everything. Turning over, she placed a sleepy hand on his shoulder. 'Mmf . . .'

'Sorry to come to bed so late,' he whispered. 'That bloke's a complete tosser. I couldn't get away from him . . .'

He would tell her about As Good As Anthony tomorrow, he decided. She'd almost certainly fix her calm, sensible eyes on his and tell him he'd made a mistake. If it really was the same guy he'd have recognized Ed, wouldn't he? And why on earth would he have changed his name? It was a typical Ed story, she'd say, rolling her eyes: he was so full of bullshit. Then she'd give him a little push and he'd start to tickle her, something he hadn't done in months.

'He couldn't stop talking . . .' she murmured sleepily.

He didn't want to think about Jameson a moment longer. He wanted to push his hands into her thick yellow hair and kiss her. But first he had to tell her everything. He'd been an idiot, he'd say. He'd lied to her about the extent of his experience; because of him Aunik had been murdered and the brickfield project closed. He'd made terrible mistakes, but it needn't mean he'd reached the end. If she could forgive him, they could start again.

'Sarah?' He meant the question to sound casual, but his voice was trembling.

'Yeah?'

He should have said, 'There're some things I have to tell you, some stupid things I've done . . .' but he couldn't. He opened his mouth and closed it. *I'm a shit. I've ruined everything.* It would be easier if he could write it down. They lay together in silence. *Can you still love me?* He wanted so much to touch her; he could feel her warm body stretched alongside his.

'You mustn't worry any more,' he eventually said, placing his hand on her waist. 'It's going to be OK.'

'Is it?'

Of course it was going to be OK. It had to be. He pulled her towards him, terrified of puncturing the silence with the wrong words. 'I hope so.'

She rested her head against his shoulder, her arm draped over his tummy. It didn't matter about his stupid lies or the mess with Schools for Change. He'd make it up to Sylvia and Sadid; he could sell the Kensington monstrosity and they could have a hundred schools. Then he'd start a new organization, his own, which dealt head on with land evictions. And finally he would prove himself to Sarah.

'Listen,' he said, leaning over to kiss her. 'I can hear the sea.'

THIRTY-SEVEN

May 6th, 2003

He woke early, like he always did. Eyes open, mind whirring, he treasured the first moments of consciousness, when the day was still fresh. He'd lie on his back in the pale light and the thoughts and plans of the previous day would sweep back in, like the tide. Sarah was different: she could sleep for England. Leaning over her sweet, dreaming face he brushed his lips on her flushed cheek then climbed from the mosquito net.

He felt so different. For weeks, he had been ensnarled in terrible anxieties which twisted around his ankles, tripping him up. He'd tried hard to disentangle them, but every thread he tugged merely tightened the knots. But now, after the decisions he had taken the night before, he was filled with purpose. Padding across the wooden floor he pushed open the terrace doors and stepped into a blush of sun. Already it was peeking over the horizon, haloed by a smudge of pink cloud. Taking a deep breath, he arranged his lanky limbs into Greet the Sun, pushing his palms together and raising them Buddha-like above his head. If she spotted him Sarah would invariably take the pee, but she was asleep and even if she unexpectedly stuck her chortling face around the door, he didn't care. 'You look like a complete knob head!' she'd guffawed the first time she'd caught him in this pose. He'd just crossed his eyes and stuck out his tongue.

Yoga was the perfect way to start the day. Like so many good intentions over the last few months he had allowed his routine to slip: thirty minutes of Astanga, followed by a glass of hot water and a bowl of pineapple. No *beedis*, bed by ten, and absolutely no booze. It shouldn't have been difficult; the nearest place you could get a beer was Chittagong, two hundred miles away, and even there only in a few upmarket hotels. Yet he had let himself down.

Exhaling, he slowly turned, bending his knees and staring upwards, his gaze falling on a large spider's web that stretched over the top of the door. His bones were a little creaky, but it felt good. From now on Astanga was back on the agenda and the debilitating guilt that for weeks had crushed him into a frenzy of ineffective activity a thing of the past. First, they had to get out of Lalalpur. From Dhaka they would return to London and talk to Sylvia and Alexandria. And then, Inshallah, the real work would begin.

Stretching his arms higher, he placed the sole of his right foot inside his left thigh. It was incredible how the dragging weight that for weeks had been lodged deep in his chest had lifted. Sarah would forgive him, he thought with a shiver of nervous excitement. OK, so he had lied. But after their reconciliation last night, he knew he could trust her.

As he placed his wobbling foot back on the floor, there was just one niggling doubt. Last night he'd deliberately pushed Dan Jameson to the back of his mind, but now he remembered his uncanny resemblance to As Good As Anthony and the strange dread he'd experienced as he'd watched the jeep bump over the track. Something else had happened at that May Ball, he suddenly recalled; something awful.

It was too late. For thirteen years he had deliberately forgotten. But now, as a finger of sunlight poked him in the eye, he remembered the whole ghastly scene.

He was pissed, as usual. Staggering from the main marquee, he collapsed onto the college lawns, where, folding his arms behind his head, he gazed at the fading stars. He felt pleasingly numbed, the way he liked it. The ball had been hideous and he was glad that it was over; the night finally giving way to dawn, the littered grass already dewy. Bottles lay everywhere; a few metres behind his head, a couple were drunkenly shagging.

If only he had fallen asleep, he might have avoided what happened next, but it was getting too cold to lie on the grass. He sat up, shivering and looking around the misty courtyard. That's when, with an unpleasant lurch, he noticed As Good As, slumped on the cobblestones besides the door to his staircase, his head lolling sleepily on his chest. Rising hurriedly to his feet, Ed started to walk unsteadily in the opposite direction, towards the Porter's Lodge and the street outside. He couldn't face As Good As, not right now. He'd go to Giles' set in Trinity, he thought, anywhere but his own rooms.

'Eddy?'

Wincing, he slowly turned around. The reedy, beseeching tone of As Good As's voice made him cringe. He felt sorry for the guy: as usual Giles had gone too far with his taunts. But couldn't he see that hanging around the place was only going to make things worse?

'What is it?'

'I need your help . . .'

He had a bottle, Ed saw with a jolt of disquiet. And now, as Ed began to reluctantly move towards him, he was waving it around, as if about to toss it on to the cobblestones.

'I'm knackered,' Ed called. 'I've got to crash.'

Lifting his head, As Good As gazed at him. He looked appalling: his skin was grey, his hair plastered over his clammy face.

'Can we talk?'

'I don't think so, mate, not now . . .'

With a decisive jerk of his arm, As Good As smashed the bottle on the bricks behind him.

'Fucking hell! What are you doing?'

'I needed you, Ed,' he drawled as he jabbed the jagged shards at his chin. 'I thought you were my friend.' Swishing the glass towards his neck, he closed his eyes.

Ed didn't wait to see As Good As ram the glass into his throat. Even if he had, there would have been nothing he could have done. That was why he didn't remember the blood. But he heard the screams of the girl who was at that very moment, appearing from the stairs. He should have run to help, should have pulled off his shirt to staunch the flow or shouted for help, of course he should. But he was Eddy Salisbury, who'd had life handed to him on a plate and who deserved nothing: useless, layabout Eddy, who never did the right thing. So he ran in the opposite direction, through the Lodge and out of the college, into the sanctuary of the empty street, the cold air blowing around his face. When the ambulance passed, he was already at the other end of Broad Street.

Within ten minutes he was prostrate on Giles's sofa, pleading an almighty hangover. He didn't tell Giles what had happened; he knew he'd turn it into a sick joke. Instead, he did what he always did: he put the incident from his mind. It wasn't hard; by the time he returned to the college, the blood had been cleared away, the incident hushed up. The boy hadn't died, the porters said when he gathered up the courage to ask, just made a nasty mess.

Giving himself a little shake, Ed moved into the living room. It was, what, twelve or thirteen years ago? And even if Jameson and As Good As were the same person, he was gone.

Retrieving his briefcase from under the table, he pulled out his notebook.

He had so many ideas that it was over an hour before he stopped writing. In London they could mobilize resources to set up a proper campaigning outfit to raise consciousness about the land evictions that were taking place all over the region, he wrote. He could hire people, get legal advice. He wouldn't just focus on Lalalpur but the whole of South Asia. And Sarah, with her gift of the gab and ability to connect to people, could help him run it. Within the time it took him to cover four pages of his exercise book the whole plan had crystallized in his mind. OK, he was being impetuous, but he'd never liked to hang around.

He'd include his plans with the letter, he decided, ripping out a fresh sheet of paper. After pausing for a second, he started to write:

Darling Sarah
The first question I want to ask is whether you can forgive me for lying to you. The second is if you'd like to get married.

It was easier than he'd expected. He told her everything: about his booze-induced decline, about how he'd come to Bangladesh to live a monastic life in which he 'paid back' his debts to society, but how instead of absolution, what he'd found was her. When he was finished, he stuffed the letter, plus the pages he had titled 'Ed's Plans, May 2003' into an envelope which he folded into the pouch he wore around his neck. He would give her the letter later that morning, he decided. After that, everything was going to change.

From the bedroom, he could hear Sarah yawn and shuffle over the wooden floor. After breakfast, he would go to the bazaar and arrange their transport back to Dhaka. Then he'd give her the letter and tell her that, so long as she agreed, they were leaving for Chittagong later that day. He peered at the clouds building in the sky. They'd wait until the rain had blown over then they'd be on their way.

The storm approached more quickly than he'd anticipated. By the time he reached the bazaar the traders were pulling down their shutters, the tarpaulin shades of the shops flapping like boat sails. Litter blew everywhere, great gusts of it that danced in his face. The trip had been a waste of time: the lines were down, no one's mobile was working.

'Tornado coming, Mister Edward! Big danger!' the man who ran the telephone booth had shouted above the roar. 'We have to go!'

With every second that passed the sky was slipping into a darker shade of blue, like nightfall speeded up. Eyeing the blooming clouds, Ed turned back towards the track, pushing his weight against the wind. He had enjoyed the short lived drama of previous storms, but sensed that the threat had shifted to a different level: not so much a squabble with an old mate as a fight with a psychopathic stranger. When the betel nut tree he had just passed was torn from its roots and hurled into the air, he swallowed down his fear.

A short distance away a man was running towards him. At first he assumed he must be hurrying towards the cyclone shelter, but he was waving his arms and shouting in a way that implied he wanted to attract Ed's attention. With the bellow of the wind he couldn't make out the words but after a moment he recognised him as Dan Jameson's driver.

'Come quick!' the man yelled. 'Your wife is in the sea!'

*   *   *

After that, he hardly registered what was happening, far less stop to wonder what Jameson's driver was doing on the road when, if what he said was true, he should have been approaching from the beach. At one point a palm frond struck him in the face, and later on, he slipped and twisted his knee in the soft mud, but if either caused him pain, he didn't notice. His only sensation was hot, pulsating panic. The driver was cutting directly through the fields, picking a route across the earth terraces. Following him, Ed ploughed through the mire.

'Where is she?' he gasped, as they approached the beach.

The man pointed towards the rearing waves. 'There.'

He couldn't see a thing. There was too much spray and sand whirling around. Shouting Sarah's name, he sprinted across the shore. The sea was wild, the waves bucking. Scanning the horizon, he tried to make out a figure in the water, but there was too much commotion. For one blinding moment he thought he saw her, but it was only a plank of wood bobbing in the churning froth.

'Sarah!'

He ran on, still desperately searching. He had assumed that the driver would follow him, but when he glanced back he saw that he had disappeared. He was so agitated by now that he was starting to hyperventilate. As he reached the place where the fisherman tethered their boats, he stopped, peering through the haze at the devastation. A jeep was waiting at the junction of the road, he realized, its headlights on full beam.

It was his only hope. Turning away from the sea, he started to clamber over the sand dunes to where the jeep was parked. Perhaps the occupant had seen something; perhaps Sarah was already rescued. Although he didn't believe in God, he had started to chant a prayer. *Please God, please God, please God.* When a coil of seaweed blew into his face he tossed it furiously aside, ignoring the hail which hammered into his back. As he reached the top of the dune he saw the door of the vehicle open, and a man step out.

It was As Good As. For some reason he'd returned.

'Dan!' he screamed over the clamour. 'Thank God you're here!'

As Good As was grinning and waving. 'It's OK!' he cried. 'I know where she is!'

Stumbling a little, Ed moved towards the light.

THIRTY-EIGHT

Postscript, 2007

E d's gone for good. The trust fund is closed, his passport lies unused. There are no emails sent to confuse us, no mysterious sightings; no bogus lawyers and no more lies. He's dead, just like he always was.

At the very beginning, I knew the truth. It filled my belly and lungs, pouring through my veins until every nerve of my body buzzed. I stood on the beach and I knew I would never see Ed again. He loved me; he would never run away. I watched the tumultuous waves and the knowledge hardened within me, like molten metal cooling down. It was only in the moments that followed that the doubts set in. How can somebody disappear, just like that? Trying to understand a sudden death is like smacking into a wall: a sudden, slamming certainty; no second takes, no hope of appeal and no going back. So it wasn't merely Dan Jameson who had me fooled, it was my own denial.

After the diggers unearthed his body, the villagers buried him by the mosque. In Islam, the dead are dispatched without delay: by the time Jamil sent his text, the funeral was over. Rosewater, prayers and, instead of a coffin, a simple white shroud; burial village style, Ed would have liked it. I visited his grave with Syeda, kneeling besides the freshly dug earth as I finally said goodbye. Syeda waited a short distance away, dabbing at her eyes with the ends of her sari. Later she would give me the pouch they had found around his neck.

In the end, it was Oxan that helped us find Ed for without their diggers his body would never have been unearthed. Nor, indeed, would Jameson have been forced to return to Lalalpur. Like me, he received a message from Lalalpur, but sent by his driver rather than Syeda. Panicking, he returned to Bangladesh in an aborted attempt to cover things up. What he hadn't expected to encounter was me, or indeed, Syeda. Now it's his decaying remains that are hidden by mud and leaves. If he's ever found few questions will be asked; after what happened at Jhomgram, few locals trust the police. The stranger was killed in the storm, people will say; his head bashed by a falling tree.

The weather grows hotter and finally the monsoon arrives, the rain battering the thick weeds and saplings that cover Jameson's grave. These days, no one comes near. There are no fishermen on the beach, no labourers planting paddy and no children playing in the fields. The construction workers have gone, and so have the few lingering villagers, their shanties long abandoned. All that remains of Lalalpur is the drill.

If Syeda saved me from Jameson, Ed's letter saved me from myself. Syeda kept it for me, and like his ring and his briefcase, I guard it jealously, a fragment of what I had and what I could have been. I've trained myself to avoid the whirlpool, though the twisting regret is always there. *If* Ed had given me his letter at breakfast, perhaps he'd still be here. *If* I'd asked what he meant when he said that everything would change. *If* I'd told him I loved him no matter who he was . . . I'd like to edit all those *ifs* away; for too long they've been dominating my life.

Since I can't, I've learned to focus on the facts: Anthony Wilson was a manipulative sociopath, the police said; a loner with no friends. Ed had known him for a while at Oxford and Wilson had developed a weird fixation on him. He'd hunted us down in cyberspace, discovering our address on Ed's website and come all the way to Bangladesh in the hope of getting something out of Ed: money probably, for at Oxford Ed had been famous both for his vast wealth and his generosity. When I mistakenly assumed that he was Dan Jameson, he never corrected me. He liked playing weird games, Giles Montgomery told me after Ed's memorial. He was a faker, someone more comfortable with lies than the truth. And for some reason he murdered Ed, enticing him onto the beach by passing on the message that I was drowning. There, the police think Wilson strangled Ed, dragged his body into the undergrowth and then drove to Noton Bazaar to shelter from the storm before returning to the village to 'help'. That dreadful night, when I was sitting in shock by the bungalow, he was burying Ed in the churned-up fields. When, a week later, Oxan started work, Wilson's driver called him in London. The man told the British police through an interpreter that Wilson had promised him a thousand dollars in cash if he informed him of anyone digging in the area where he'd left Ed's body. The driver claimed to have no idea there had been a murder; he was just a poor man, he said, trying to earn some foreign currency. They'll get Anthony Wilson in the end, the police concluded, even if he's currently disappeared from the face of the earth. I didn't say anything. I've never told anyone how Syeda and I buried his corpse in the jungle that day. I must have toughened up, for I don't feel guilty about what we did. What was that catchphrase Ed mentioned? *Local conditions call for local strategies.*

Ed's gone and for a while I thought my life was over, too. After I returned from Bangladesh, I returned to my parents' place where, for a few months, I could barely function. They did their best. They let me lie in bed all day with the curtains closed, or, if I needed, to talk for hours. Occasionally an old friend came to call, but I didn't have much energy for chat. Nick had a new girlfriend, I heard, and had moved to London; someone else had got hitched. I nodded and smiled but wasn't really listening, for the person I had once been was gone.

And then, one soft September afternoon, there was a call.

'Sarah?' It was a man, Scottish sounding, on a line that crackled with static. 'It's Dan Jameson, calling from the Department of International Development in Dhaka. Your friend – Alexandria, is it? – gave me your number.'

I gripped the phone, barely able to breathe. 'Dan Jameson?'

'You left a message on my phone in May?'

'Oh my God . . .'

'Look, I'm sorry I've not got back to you sooner . . . or sent my condolences about Ed. It's been a terrible business.'

He'd been tied up all summer with work in Bangkok, he said; his office should have directed Ed to a colleague who was temporarily handling his Bangladeshi work. Now he was back he'd had a look at what was happening with BNRC in the Noton Bazaar area and was planning to bring it up at what he called a 'Partnership Meeting' with the government.

'Hopefully some of Ed's persistence will pay off,' he concluded. 'We'll have to take things a bit more *diplomatically* than he might have liked, but I wanted you to know that his campaigning wasn't in vain.'

I listened politely, not sure how much he knew about what had happened to Ed or the activities of Anthony Wilson. It was kind of him to return my call, I eventually said. It was a shame we never got to meet.

After I'd put down the phone, I sat for a while by the window, staring at the road. For months I had been so deeply encased in despair that I had almost forgotten what had happened to Jhomgram and Lalalpur. But speaking to the real Dan Jameson had unblocked something. Now, as I gazed unseeingly at the shining saloons parked in the suburban street I remembered what Ed had written in his letter. He wanted to start up his own organization; he had more money than he knew what to do with, so the finances wouldn't be an issue. We wouldn't be involved in charity, handing things out; instead we'd be campaigning against the big corporations which ripped through poor people's lives in the name of profit.

Standing, I rushed across the room and picked up the phone. Since the memorial I'd kept in touch with Sylvia and I knew her number by heart.

'Sylvia?' I gasped, when she finally picked up. 'I've had an idea.'

So even though Ed is gone, I'm carrying on. The work helps. I've certainly got enough of it: the Dhaka offices to set up, press reports to prepare, lobbying the governments involved. I hope he'd be pleased with what we've done. Sylvia and I have stuck to the spirit of his plans, but diverged a little too, basing most of our operations in situ, rather than London, although we have a small office there too. If the journalists want to see our work – and increasingly they do – they'll have to come to Dhaka. It's not just about consciousness-raising and education, it's about enforcing the law. My legal team are fantastic, as are the caseworkers that we hired. Like me they live their life by one simple rule: don't let the bastards win.

Time ticks on. Anniversaries appear and I manage to survive. A year since I last saw Ed's face, then two. Three years since our first kiss, now almost four. In contrast to those first terrible weeks when I was deafened by white noise, what I hear is silence. He's not whistling or calling out my name;

he isn't laughing, or banging in the kitchen with his pots and pans. Instead, everything is quiet. He's gone, just like I always knew he was. I don't believe in God, or Heaven or ghosts. I know he's never coming back.

Yet when I'm alone and my mind's still, sometimes he returns and I feel his hand on my arm or the brush of bristles on my cheek. He speaks to me, too: a muffled whisper that increasingly I can't make out. Sometimes it's a fleeting visit. I might be in a meeting or working at the computer and for a moment or two I sense a movement behind me and know he's there. Mostly he comes at night, stretching out beside me beneath the whirring fan. We don't talk so much these days; we just lie under the net, our bodies almost touching. If for a moment my mind wanders, he disappears.

Reality pulls you back, that's what I've learnt. The weeks and months pass and slowly the longing is covered with a sediment of everyday concerns: the 'jam' my vehicle's in, a new policy directive from the donors, the Amnesty delegation arriving on the red eye from Heathrow. Four, five years on, and Ed is fading. I lie on the bed and he's beside me, just like he'll always be. For a second, I relax in his warmth. Then I open my eyes to the thick golden light of another Dhaka morning and hear the clatter and tring of rickshaws passing in the street below.

Sitting up, I swing my feet off the bed.